Civil War
Ghosts

Civil War Ghosts

Edited by

Martin H. Greenberg,
Frank D. McSherry, Jr.,
and Charles G. Waugh

August House Publishers
L I T T L E   R O C K

© 1991 by Martin H. Greenberg, Frank D. McSherry, Jr.,
and Charles G. Waugh
Published by August House, Inc.,
P.O. Box 3223, Little Rock, Arkansas 72203,
501/372-5450.

Printed in the United States of America

10 9 8 7 6 5 4

LIBRARY OF CONGRESS CATALOGING-IN-PUBLICATION DATA
Civil War Ghosts / edited by Martin H. Greenberg, Frank D. McSherry, Jr.,
Charles G. Waugh.— 1st ed.
p.   cm.
ISBN 0-87483-173-3 (tpb) : $9.95
1. United States—History—Civil War, 1861–1865—Fiction.
2. Ghost stories, American. 3. Supernatural—Fiction
I. Greenberg, Martin H. II. McSherry, Frank D. III.Waugh, Charles
PS648.C54C53   1991   91-11587
813'0873308358—dc20

Executive: Liz Parkhurst
Project Editor: Judith Faust
Cover design and illustration: Kitty Harvill
Typography: Lettergraphics, Little Rock

This book is printed on archival-quality paper which meets
the guidelines for performance and durability of the
Committee on Production Guidelines for Book Longevity of the
Council on Library Resources.

AUGUST HOUSE, INC.   PUBLISHERS   LITTLE ROCK

Acknowledgments

"The Army of the Dead" by John Bennett is reprinted by permission of Russell & Volkening, Inc.

"The Shot-Tower Ghost" by Mary Elizabeth Counselman, copyright by Mary Elizabeth Counselman, is reprinted by permission of the author.

"Iverson's Pits" by Dan Simmons, copyright 1988 by Dan Simmons, first appeared in *Night Visions 5*, published by Dark Harvest in 1988, and is reprinted by permission of the author.

"The Last Waltz" by Seabury Quinn is reprinted by permission of the Scott Meredith Literary Agency.

"Fearful Rock" by Manly Wade Wellman, copyright 1939 by Weird Tales, first appeared in *Weird Tales* in February, March, and April 1939, and is reprinted by permission of Karl Edward Wagner, Literary Executor for the Estate of Manly Wade Wellman.

Contents

Introduction

"Thou canst not say I did it," the king shrieked. "Never shake thy gory locks at me!"

Shrieked—for Macbeth, king of Scotland, had just seen the ghost of Banquo, the general and friend he had had killed, appear out of thin air—invisible to everyone else in the crowded banquet hall.

"Gentlemen," a courtier said, "His Highness is not well..."

Or was he?

Ghosts—eerie beings insubstantial as mist in moonlight, but able to kill—and ghost stories have disturbed and enthralled people long before and after Shakespeare wrote *Macbeth*. Ghost stories have been whispered around the night fires of primitive tribes and have appeared in ancient literature (Homer, the blind poet of Greece, sang of Ulysses meeting ghosts in the cold, fog-shrouded land of the dead)—and in tales of America's Civil War.

No wonder. War stories too (such as Homer's *Iliad*) are among the world's most suspenseful and long-lasting literature; and if ghosts are a part of the personality, dispatched at death to carry out some urgent unfinished task, then it should not be surprising that the Civil War is the center of ghost stories that grip and chill like frost on the back of the neck. In 1861, passions arising out of the debate over slavery and other differences led the states of the American South to secede from the Union. When Confederate shells rose redly through the night sky over Charleston Harbor toward Fort Sumter, the South ignited four long years of total war that touched almost every American family and turned father against son, brother against brother. The Civil War, noted historian Bruce Catton, was "our costliest, deadliest war.... More than 500,000 soldiers lost their lives, in a country whose total population, North and South together, numbered hardly more than 30 millions." Passions like that do not die easily, and some of them live with us yet.

The stories in this volume are chosen for their drama, entertainment, and power to chill. Civil War students will find a bonus; the historical background is accurate and interesting.

They include "Miranda," by John Jakes, author of the Civil War novel (and television mini-series) *North and South.* Here, Union Captain Coburn of the Tenth New York, feverish and left behind on Sherman's march to the sea, learns from a young woman in a Southern mansion that the dead can seek vengeance.

A Civil War veteran himself, brevet Major Ambrose Bierce gives us a classic American short story of terror and pity.

A ghostly cavalry squadron of Quantrill's guerrillas, sabers swinging in the white moonlight, rides again in "Fearful Rock," a novella by Manly Wade Wellman, winner of the World Fantasy Lifetime Award. Here, two Yankee soldiers must fight, with pistol and Bible, not only for a girl's life but for her soul.

"Iverson's Pits," by another World Fantasy Award winner, Dan Simmons, tells how Colonel Iverson sent the Tenth North Carolina into a Federal trap at Gettysburg that left most of them dead on the field, while staying safely behind himself. And now, at the 1913 reunion, the veterans of the Tenth want to discuss that with the colonel—the veterans, not just the survivors...

And there are more, stories by such authors as Southerner Mary Elizabeth Counselman, Northerner John William DeForrest, and others.

Stories—for there is no such thing as the supernatural. Is there? Surely not—and yet...

In March of 1865, President Abraham Lincoln told an audience that included his wife and his bodyguard Marshall Lamon of a strange dream he had had the night before. "A sound of sobbing in the White House seemed to waken me," he said. "I wandered through the deserted halls, finding in the East Room a corpse with a covered face, lying on a catafalque while a throng of people around it wept pitifully.

"'Who is dead in the White House?' I asked a soldier.

"'The president,' he replied. 'He was killed by an assassin.'"

An outburst of grief awoke the president. The dream, Lincoln confessed, "has gotten possession of me, and, like Banquo's ghost, will not down." Three weeks later, Lincoln lay dead in the White House, in the East Room, struck down by an assassin's bullet.

There is much we do not know, and perhaps these stories may not be *entirely* fiction. Who knows?

Frank D. McSherry, Jr.

Miranda

JOHN JAKES

In those grim days, men became much less than men, and only something more than animals. This was because we had only the most primitive of objectives: to eat when we could; to sleep if we might; to slaughter, pillage, burn as much as we had strength and endurance to do.

We rode and marched by day and by night. We lived in a daze of dirt, screams, fatigue, disease, death. On every night horizon, red stains seemed to signal that the whole state of Georgia was afire. Rumors ran that the General, who was called Cump behind his back, after his middle name, Tecumseh, intended to bring the Reb government to its knees by devastating the land.

On the road some days after Atlanta, fatigue and illness caught up with me. I blanked out for short periods of time as I rode, though I managed to remain with my unit. Then a more violent spell of fever seized me. I fell out of column to rest. The upshot was, I woke the next dawn to discover I had been left behind. Although I rode half the next night to find the 10th New York Horse, I failed.

I was lost. I was alone in a rural land full of trees and cabins where the Johnny Rebs might look out at me and snipe me from the saddle.

After I realized I was lost, I rode for another day and part of the next night, still without success. I was armed—my pistol, my saber, and what they called a Texas toothpick, a big wicked fighting knife which a sergeant had swapped me, and which I had put away in my boot. I had no food.

After a period of fever from which I remember nothing, I suddenly found myself on a corduroy road at the entrance to a dark avenue between gigantic water oaks. I weaved in the saddle. The stars blurred, then sharpened. Otherwise the sky was black. The land smelled of dampness and the smoke of pillage. But I was so far out into the back country, I saw no signs of fires burning.

At the head of the avenue a white glimmering revealed a plantation house. I nudged my weary horse toward it, for I thought I'd seen a lantern gleam. Half way up the avenue between the rustling trees, my horse's hoofs rattled suddenly on boards.

We were crossing a flat bridge, unseen in the dark. It spanned a bubbling creek. My horse's left forehoof came down on rotted board. Planks creaked, snapped. The whole decayed center of the bridge gave way beneath us.

I fell, twisting free of the screaming, frantic animal. I struck the water. It was not deep, but my head cracked a rock. A fresh lance of pain added to that already racking my bones.

The chill creek water plucked at my elbows. I saw my horse scramble up and blow noisily, unhurt in the fall. If she wandered off, I would have no way to catch up to my unit. I tried to rise. I fell back, and all went dark.

When I opened my eyes again, the aching and chill had grown worse. My teeth rattled. Judging by the silence of the birds and the slight pall in the sky, the time was near false dawn. I dragged myself upright and clambered up the creek bank.

A whinny near one of the water oaks showed that my horse had not wandered off. I lurched toward her, through a clammy ground mist which swirled and eddied around my boots.

This mistiness hid the great house at the head of the avenue, except where a solitary yellow square seemed to glisten, as though a lamp were lit. I walked toward my horse, reached out to stroke her muzzle. Suddenly the back of my neck crawled.

A man peered at me from the mist, a scarecrow-thin figure in sodden clothes so befouled with dirt, it was impossible to recognize what sort they were. His face was stubbled. His mouth hung open in a kind of wrenched grin. His eyes were without pupils, white as milk.

"Give me a hand," I said. "Where can I find some food and a bed?"

The apparition let out a low sound, like a moan. The mist drifted higher. I thought the figure had turned and fled. I stumbled after it.

"Wait! Come back here! I'm a Union officer, I order you to—"

The words floated eerily in the mist. There was no one there.

Through my fever, I realized that the spectre of the pasty-faced man must be an hallucination, the result of weeks of weariness, hunger, illness, of seeing dead men left behind at the roadside while Cump Sherman's juggernaut moved across Georgia. But I did need help. So I cupped my hands to my mouth and began to shout.

In the echoing silence after my shout, I heard a door creak and slam.

The exertion of calling for help began a new, racking pain in my chest. My boot slipped on a moisture-slimed rock along the creek's bank. I caught a clump of shrub for balance. But I tumbled over, sprawling in the water again.

A sibilant whisper of wind drifted between the water oaks on the avenue. Somehow, as I crouched on hands and knees in the bubbling creek, I knew that a person was coming toward me along that avenue.

I swung my head. The mere exertion started my forehead buzzing and thudding again. I felt that I might blank out. As I made an effort to scrabble toward the bank, my left hand brushed against my holster.

It was empty.

Had my pistol dropped out into the water? I tried to peer under the surface of the black, swirling stuff. I did not see the weapon. Then, as fresh waves of dizziness washed over me, two sensations struck me almost together, one visual, the other aural.

The first was the sight of wavering orange firedots burning through the mist at the tips of a many-branched candlestick.

Someone was carrying the candlestick down the avenue through the mist.

The noise, far out on the road, was the unmistakable clatter of hoofs and wheels. I turned toward it.

A caisson whipped by, rumbling. A squad of cavalrymen in blue rode behind. They wore blue uniforms. I was not totally cut off from Cump Sherman's army after all!

I reared up in the water to shout. The cry never left my mouth. I felt new rushes of dizziness, felt my hands slipping beneath me. My face plunged back in the water, an instant after I had a macabre impression of a beautiful young woman, the many-branched candlestick held in her pale right hand, gazing at me through the mist from the creek bank. The candlelights danced and went out—

I woke with a thick, feverish feeling in my head and a smell of dust in my nostrils. I was staring into the burning candlestick set upon a low table. Beyond it, where darkness clotted in the corner of what once must have been a genteel parlor, a fat spider crawled lazily up a cobwebbing near the ceiling.

These impressions, and others, filtered through a haze of fever, made me uneasy. So did the great, grotesque shadows thrown by the sheeted furnishings, and the thick patina of dirt upon the windows. In the sky outside I saw the last, brooding smear of a sunset, indicating that I had been unconscious most of the day.

My hands rested on the arms of a high-backed chair. My booted feet were propped on a low stool in front of me. I became conscious of both my pistol and saber being missing. Just then the saber's blade flashed across my vision and hung there like a glittering metal bar.

I turned my head.

"I thought you'd never come round, Yank."

Her voice was musical but edged with mockery. The wine-velvet gown she wore had seen more prosperous days, like the house and the land. But her body was young and firm, and her chin was tilted up.

She had a pretty mouth, sharp gray eyes and a long, shiny-gold tress of hair tied at the nape of her neck with common string. To see a Southern girl in such a state of disarray, holding a cavalry saber at my throat to boot, would have been an unnerving sight even for a man not plagued by fever.

"How did I get here?"

"Walked. I helped you some."

"I don't remember."

"You going to make a fuss?" she said.

"No," I said. "I guess you could put that through my gullet if I did."

She nodded, almost primly. "Yes, 'twouldn't take much."

"This your place?" I asked.

"Twelveoaks belonged to my husband."

"I don't know where I am, exactly," I said, eyeing that shining strip of iron in her hand, a hand which did not shake by a fraction. "I think I picked up some kind of fever, and I got separated from my unit."

She continued to watch me steadily. "Do you have a name?"

"Coburn," I said. "Captain Joshua Coburn, 10th New York Horse."

"Riding with that devil Sherman?" she said, though tonelessly.

Again I nodded. "Does that earn me the saber through the neck?"

Slowly she raised the blade, examined its shining surface. Then, with a shrug, she laid it on one of the sheet-draped pieces of furniture.

"It should, right enough. Except I haven't quite turned to acting like an animal, even though the Yankees who've been riding through this part of the country have set a fine example. My name is Miranda Saxby."

She walked a step closer, displayed a gold ring on her left hand. "Mrs. Saxby. Or the widow Saxby, you could say."

I must make clear that all that happened between us happened as though I saw, heard, took part in it while staring through layers of gauze. I was light-headed, inclined to talk foolishly because of the fever, and unable to summon up

15

much energy to stir from the high-backed chair, even though the sternness of her gaze warned me that, because I was a Union officer, alone and sick, she knew she enjoyed an advantage not many of her fellow-Georgians had enjoyed of late—a chance for revenge.

As if to reinforce this idea, she turned and walked off a ways. She paused by another table where several dusty goblets and a cut glass decanter full of some berry wine had been laid out.

"I've good reason to hate your kind, Captain, don't think I have not," she said, back turned.

The term 'widow' had struck home a moment before. "Your husband, ma'am?"

"Yes." Her skirts rustled as she swung. "Shiloh Church. He was one of the first to die. The slaves have all run off, thanks to that monster who runs your guv'mint. Down here we call him Linkum the Ape."

She laughed, a sound like bells. But there was little humor in her eyes as she continued, "We heard General Sherman was marching in this district. Most of the owners pulled out, but I stayed. I didn't have a place in the world to go. I came from the sort of place where—well, it was in New Orleans, Captain. Some try to prettify the type of place by calling it a boarding school for young ladies. I saw men killed there. Gamblers, riffraff." She nodded at the saber. "So I'm not exactly unfamiliar with how it's done."

Chill sweat began to bead up on the palms of my hands, and upon my face as well. She unstoppered the decanter. She poured out two goblets of the wine, sipped a bit of hers, then carried the other to me.

"Cherry wine," she said. "Might warm you."

"I could use some food if there's any," I said.

"For a damnyank, you're mighty high-handed in your wants."

For the first and only time during the encounter, I laughed aloud. It came out as more of a dry croak. "Ma'am, you've got no reason to like Union soldiers, as you say, and probably plenty of reason for disliking them. So I figure you'll either make things easy for me or kill me, with no inbetween."

Miranda smiled. "That's a fact."

"So which is it? Food or the sword through my neck?" Standing there a foot or so in front of me, the wine goblet catching the lights of the candlestick and reflecting them in odd little sparkles in her eyes, she grew tense. She extended the goblet, yet did not offer it fully. A door creaked somewhere. I had a wild, foolish pang of fright.

I wished just then, for no clear reason, that the clattering caisson I'd seen on the corduroy road had wheeled in.

It is not right to say I felt afraid of the Reb widow, yet I did. Consider it this way. I was not afraid of what I saw, namely, a beautiful, hungry, defeated woman who had me at her mercy because I was feverish and weak; I was afraid of something about her I could not see, but only sensed.

"There's plenty of reason for me to hate Yankees," she repeated softly.

"I'm sure there is."

"Don't pretend you hate all this burnin' and killin'."

"Believe whatever you want, but I don't enjoy it."

"Three of them, a sergeant and two corporals—they rode in here a week ago."

"Ours?"

"What else?"

"What did you give them?" I asked. "Wine or the sword?"

I'd spoken rashly, trying to humor her. The wine goblet glittered as she threw it against my face with great violence. The impact of the glass didn't matter much. But the droplets running down through my beard had a nauseatingly sweet stink, and seemed to sting and burn. I rubbed them away and the back of my hand seemed to sting for a time afterward, too.

"They used me," Miranda said in a whisper. "They hurt and used me."

Silent, I watched her. I wondered why she was taking on so.

"The word for it in New Orleans," she said low, "is rape."

Again I was unsure about the proper reaction. Certainly an inmate of a 'boarding school for young ladies' could not have been all that repelled by such an act. It must have been the fact that she and they were partisans of different causes that produced all the pent-up hate I heard seething in her voice. In any case, her quickly-formed fists decided me against commenting on that aspect of it.

"There are scum in all armies," I said. "In any army, there are scum."

She appeared to compose herself a little. She shook off a light shudder and retrieved the goblet, which somehow had not broken when it fell to the floor. As she poured more wine, she said over her shoulder, "That's bound to be the way you Yanks will explain it. Well, there have been enough others stopping by since."

While I was still wondering about that odd remark, she brought me the glass.

"Here."

"I'll ride out as soon as I'm able," I told her.

"Frankly, Captain, you don't look very damn able."

She almost smiled again. And somehow, in the merry cast of her mouth, I thought I saw one of those little miracles which give the lie to the warmongers who say the Rebs are monsters to a man, or that we are, for that matter. Ill-used by some of Sherman's scavengers, she was still human enough not to kill me outright. I had some dim, pretentious hope or other that, after the bloody conflict was done, people like Miranda Saxby—people even like myself—might bind up the wounds.

I sipped some of the wine. She did also. Then I said:

"Yes, I'm worn out. I could enjoy a night's rest."

"Won't Butcher Sherman miss one of his officers?"

"I've been gone a night already. One more hardly matters."

"Well," she said thoughtfully, "I can give you a bed. But first some food. Wait."

She vanished through a curtain. The house creaked in silence. Outside, full dark had fallen.

An owl hooted in the distance. A whisper of chill air brushed against my cheek. I swung my head. I felt, rather than saw, someone at the edge of the parlor, there in the dark.

I knew I must pull myself up out of the chair. I did, staggering. The saber lay a great distance away. Almost against my own will, I looked around.

The same ghastly white-eyed creature I had glimpsed down by the creek stood in the wide doorway which led from the hall. Behind him, other hideous figures stirred, unseen except for glimmers of empty white eyes.

The right shoulder of the bescummed, pale white apparition in the doorway displayed a tattering of dirty gold. What was it? I pounded my brains, but they were too thick with fever for me to quite grasp at the answer I wanted.

But I was filled with a terror beyond anything I had ever experienced.

The thing there in the parlor's entrance had bloated, paste-white cheeks. Down those cheeks ran crooked blackish lines which some inward sense told me were tracks of blood, long dried.

The figure lifted its grimed hands, as though reaching for me. It made a sound with its yellow-toothed mouth, a sound which could only be transcribed as a guttural groan something like, "Urrrrghhh-uh."

The other horrors behind it, three or four of them, it was impossible to tell, took up the plaint until the ghastly moaning, though not excessively loud, seemed to press on my ears with actual pain.

As I stared, the mewlings of the things standing there intensified. I almost had a feeling that, rather than menace, they represented some kind of warning. The spectre nearest me reached out toward me, and all reason slipped away. With a terrified curse I blundered after the saber, picked it up, whirled around and drove it as hard as I could, straight into the befouled jacket of the creature approaching.

Candlelight seemed to flare up white. I felt an impact through the blade. Blinded, I reeled away a step.

When the dazzle faded, I saw my saber impaled in the woodwork of the great door, vibrating faintly. It had passed through—nothing at all.

The apparitions were gone.

Cold sweat rivered down my cheeks as I dug my knuckles into my eyes and strove to keep from falling. Was I mad? Was I so sick that I saw phantoms?

I started back to the high-backed chair, accidentally knocking against the table bearing the decanter. As I made a vain effort to prevent it, the decanter tipped, crashed to the floor.

The stopper flew out. The cherry wine leaked onto the pegged planking. I watched a tiny wisp of smoke curl up, then another. The wine seeped down through the cracks between the planking, leaving a wide, ugly scar upon the wood.

"Did you see something, Yankee?"

Her muted voice spun me around. She watched from the curtain, where she had appeared suddenly and silently. She carried a small tray on which rested a butt of gray, mold-tinged bread. I swallowed the bile taste of fear and said:

"I'm not certain. There was a man—several men, so it looked like."

"Fever dreams?" she asked, amused.

"They were too real for that. One had a patch of gold at his shoulder."

Miranda's golden hair gleamed when she nodded. She set the tray aside as if it were no longer necessary, as if pretense were at an end. Her gray eyes pierced mine.

"Yes, Captain Coburn, he was a full Colonel."

Then I knew:

"His uniform—all fouled with filth. It was a blue uniform."

"That's right, Captain. He was a Yank. Since a week ago, since those first three men came by late one night—" The softness in her face vanished, to be replaced by an angular, blinding fury, as her voice dropped and came buzzing through the fever: "—since then, others have stopped, hunting food, or rest, or an available woman for their brute appetites. Four of them have come, Captain, two together, two separately. And I served them each a bit of wine. Here, come to the window. Your bed is ready."

I tottered halfway across that shadow-thick chamber before the awful pain began to twist my belly. I doubled over, tumbling across the high-backed chair.

Cramped in that awkward position, I saw her lift a moldering yellow curtain. Outside, near the window of the plantation house, moonlight gleamed on a patch of black dew-slimed sward. Four small piles of rocks glistened, each at the head of a hump of earth. Yawning beside the mound on the right was a fifth freshly-dug open grave.

Somehow I got my hand down to my boot where the hideout knife was stashed. I drew it though it felt lead-heavy. Miranda Saxby laughed and let the curtain fall.

"'Twon't do a bit of good on me, Captain, the same as it didn't on them when they came in a while ago."

God help me, somehow I knew she was right.

The motions she made were all the more evil because she attempted to mock the provocative as she turned her back toward me while her hands worked at the sash of her gown.

"I want you to rest well in your bed, Captain. I want you to be warm and comfortable in your bed, so that's why I mean to come into your bed to warm it. At least for a while, anyway, till you settle in for a long rest. Don't fret, it won't be so bad."

Abruptly, she dropped her gown so that, as she stood with her back toward me, she was bare to the waist, except for where the soft skin was hidden by the gold banner of her hair hanging down. Over her shoulder she looked at me with the eyes of hell itself.

"Most men, even Yankees, think I'm pretty, Captain. Don't you?"

The flesh of her back showed three round, crusted, black bullet holes.

For what I did then there can be no apology, no moral justification, save that I knew I faced evil beyond comprehension. I lurched forward and stabbed the knife into her back, up to the hilt.

No blood appeared, not a droplet, not a stain. Over her shoulder, like some ghastly coquette, Miranda Saxby looked at me with the toothpick sticking from between her shoulder blades, just above the bullet wounds, and she laughed merrily.

If not exactly a brave man, I had never fled from weapons fired in anger. But I fled then, summoning the last vestiges of my fever-sapped strength. I turned and fled with a cry, past the table with the candlestick which I knocked over.

I staggered through the haunted hallway, beating on the outer door until I sprung it open. I stumbled from the porch, smashed my jaw in the dirt as I fell, but somehow managed to get up and continue running, down the avenue between the water oaks. My stomach wrenched and I was sick, my system ridding itself of the poison by violent spasms.

At last I stumbled again and sprawled out, wondering if the wine would still kill me or only drug me, wondering, wondering if I would die this night. The ground on which I fell crawled with eerie radiance.

Lying in the avenue, I twisted over. The candlestick had fired the place. Flames leaped behind the dusk-thick windows. I heard a single, awful, piercing shriek. Then my mind received the blackness again with a full welcome.

A Union corporal from Ohio, scavenging the neighborhood for provisions in company with a small, tuft-whiskered turncoat Georgian named Hanno, discovered me.

I learned later that they had been loading grain into a wagon at a cabin roughly a mile up the corduroy road when the flames in the sky drew their notice. I wakened with my back propped against one of the water oaks as dawn was breaking. The few timbers of Twelveoaks still standing were black, smoking fingers poked upward to a leaden sky. It had burned to the foundations.

Shaken, uncertain of what I had seen or experienced the night before, I said little to my rescuers at first, drinking from a canteen and gnawing on a hunk of jerky until the Ohio corporal pressed me for details. I laid aside the canteen, still feeling feverish. There was a fierce ache in my belly. But I felt a peculiar certainty that I would recover because what had transpired in that house last night was worse than any illness ever conceived by man, save perhaps war.

I carefully falsified a story in a cracked voice:

"I rode into this avenue late last evening. When that bridge yonder gave in beneath me, I think I crawled to the creek bank."

"You was a-lyin' right in the middle of the avenue when we come on you, sir," said the corporal.

"Then I must have crawled there. I was in a daze, I don't remember. Except—" This much I had to ask, the man Hanno being a resident of the neighborhood. "—I thought that once a woman looked out of the window of that house. A young, yellow-haired woman. Perhaps the owner's wife. I can't explain how the fire started, but—did you see anything of the woman this morning?"

Hanno tugged at his whisker-tufts. "Just dreams, sir."

"What?"

"Mrs. Saxby, bless her soul—she was killed last week. Now I'm not criticizing you Yankees, sir. No, sir, you've treated me mighty fine, mighty fine indeed. 170—the Ohio corporal snorted in contempt, turning his head as Hanno went on. "—but some elements in the soldiery, well—it was three enlisted men, sir. Union enlisted men, I regret to say. They reined in at Twelveoaks late one night, asking for provender. I gather they took a shine to Mrs. Saxby because—well, sir, one of the slaves lived long enough afterward to tell the tale. First the Union enlisted men—ah—forced their wills upon Mrs. Saxby, a poor widow lady. Then, because they'd been drinking, these particular soldiers, well—they lined Mrs. Saxby and the four slaves still faithful an' staying with her up against a wall of the house and shot them all in the back. Then they rode about the neighborhood boasting of it, until they moved on. Some of us citizens in the district, we buried them all. Yes, all five, a week ago."

So the crux of it then became, who occupied those graves? In truth, I did not especially want to learn.

The Army of the Dead

John Bennett

At the time of the Confederate war, Trumbo's Court was a
dead-end street. But Trapman ran from Broad to Queen; and
as that section of the city was beyond the range of the Federal
siege guns, a constant traffic, both by night and by day,
flowed up and down the little street.

After the war was over the traffic left the little street, and
the dust and sand lay deep and still till midnight.

Then, at the stroke of twelve, the quiet street awoke to
the sound of wheels rolling by...and the sound of wheels
passing by in the night is a curious and intriguing sound.

A moment before, except for the rustle of the palmettos
and the light pattering of the dew upon the roof, there was
no sound whatever. But on the twelfth stroke, everywhere
came the sound of heavily burdened wheels far too heavy
for common wagon wheels; not even the night-soil wagon
wheels could bring such a rumble from the earth, like far-off
thunder out at sea; and, every now and then, the sonorous
sound of metal heavily smitten.

Every now and then the iron lid of the manhole of the
sewer at the corner lifted with the force of the air beneath it
compressed by the rising tide...the lid lifted...pff-ff-ff! a gust
of air blew out like the blast from a gun, and with a loud
clang of metal the manhole lid fell back again upon its iron
ring.

But the sound in the street was another sound, utterly different...a rumble and a clang, heavy and deep. Every night the laundress who lodged on the upper floor was wakened by that sound. Night after night, weary after the hard day, her sleep was broken. At last, spent by broken rest, she said to her husband: "Can't you do something to stop that noise in the night? It breaks my sleep, and I get no rest."

Her husband answered angrily: "Jesus! Woman, don't ask me that. It is no business of mine, or yours. Don't speak of it."

"Why should I not speak of it?"

"Because it is their affair and God's. I advise you to let it alone."

So she did, for a time. But still it troubled her...who and what was it went by in the night, night after night, endlessly faring, whither and whence? It troubled her the more since she was quite often alone.

One night when, at the stroke of twelve, the noise began, she got up from the bed and went to the window to open the shutter and look out into the street. She had taken but two steps when her husband overtook her, and snatched her from the window, angry and trembling: "Use what little sense God gave you, woman," he said, "and let what you do not know alone!"

So that night also she let it alone. But next day she said to the woman at the next tub: "What is it goes by in the night?"

The woman looked at her gravely, then said: "I take it that your heart is sincere in asking, and that you truly desire to know. For that reason, and that reason only, I speak: it is the Army of the Dead going by."

"Where on earth are they going?"

"To reinforce Lee in Virginia. They are the dead who died in the hospital here before the war came to an end.

"At the end of the war came peace for the living. But no one could sign a peace for the dead. So they, not knowing that peace has come, rise from their graves at midnight and march off, forever, until Judgment Day, to reinforce Lee in Virginia.

"While all still went well for the South, they slept and rested from battle. But when the armies of the North came crowding down and the army of the South began to bend, they who lay dead in the hospital yard pushed off their coffin lids, rose from their graves, and marched to strengthen the bending battle line.

"They do not know that peace has come, and so, until the last trump sounds, they rise and march to Virginia forever."

That was what the woman at the next tub said.

I am not bold. Nor have I looked out my window to see that army marching by; only fools meddle with things like that. But a woman in Trumbo's Court looked out one night when the Army of the Dead went by. All she saw at first was the gray fog drifting in from the river, and the mist lying cold and low in the hollow street among the gray tenements, the trees overhead only bunches of shadow in the fog, and the shredded fog drifting and trailing like smoke over the fence tops...nothing more. There was no sound anywhere but the rustle of the palmettos and the dripping of the dew on the roof.

But at the stroke of twelve came the sound of heavy wheels rolling, and a smell in the fog of horses and wet leather. The sound was a rumble heavy and deep: there is no other sound like it...it is the sound of cannon rolling along uneven ground.

She could hear the horses grunt as they heaved their burden through the heavy sand and over the obstructing roots of the trees; she could hear the horses panting; and the fog grew thick with the hot steam rising from their lathered flanks...and with the panting of the horses there was a sound of rough human voices distinctly audible. She could hear the saddle leathers squeak and the trace chains rattle, and the crack of the drivers' whips.

For hours the rumble and the rattle kept on, with the stamping of the horses, the shouts of the teamsters, the chink of metal bits, and the jingle of chains. Team after team came snorting by, the horses straining against the breast leathers, tugging at their rumbling burden, the gray steam rising like fog from their flanks.

And, behind the sound of horses and cannon, and through it, the tramp of marching feet...rr-r-r-r-r-rup, rr-r-r-r-r-r-rup, rr-r-r-r-r-r-rup!

Hosts of horsemen went riding by, with flags and banners trailing like fog, and rank after rank of foot soldiers in gray, their long, uncut hair and beards dripping with the gathered mist.

All night they marched, horse, foot, wagons, ambulances, cannon...and at the last a belated wagon driving at a gallop to overtake the rest, whips crick-cracking and horses snorting for wind.

Then, far away, and thin, and faint, somewhere beyond Gadsden's Green, shrill, but muffled by the fog, came the notes of a bugle blowing...then a cock crew...and all suddenly was still.

Dazed and bewildered she went back to her bed. When she woke in the morning one arm was paralyzed, so that she never again could do a good day's wash.

That is the legend of the Army of the Dead. Their names were not written in the book of peace. They ride as they rode, unrested ghosts, through the gray mist, with banners as gray as the gray sea fog.

They ride as they rode, and stride as they strode, with the tireless swing of veteran soldiery. Through the night they pass like the wind through a bystreet, marching to reinforce Lee in Virginia until the Judgment Day.

These were men who were hard to stop, who would not stay dead when slain, still hoping to wring desperate victory from the jaws of defeat. An unnumbered host, rising like the mist from their scattered graves to the sound of far-off trumpets calling, the muffled beat of ghostly drums setting their step, the long, distance-destroying step of veteran soldiers. Horse, foot and artillery, with sabers and carbines clattering, with muskets over their thin shoulders, and bayonets slapping their thighs, clad in coats as gray as the mist of the night. Death clapped them into medlied graves, after their victories and defeats; their bloody battles and weary marches unfinished behind them, and all unfinished before, they still march to reinforce Lee in Virginia.

The Army of the Dead.

As told by Mary Simmons.

The Shot-Tower Ghost

MARY ELIZABETH COUNSELMAN

Most of us have nostalgic, so-dear-to-my-heart memories tucked into the back of our minds, our subconscious minds, to be coaxed out briefly now and then by some particular sound, some odor, some half-familiar sight...

As for me, I can not hear a whippoorwill crying at night but I go flying back through time and space to our old family "Homeplace" in Wythe County, Virginia. The ferry is no longer there—replaced by a coldly efficient steel bridge that the state built. Cars and wagons, herds of sheep and leisurely riders on horseback no longer pause at the brink of New River to call across: *"Hello-o-o!"* for the stocky, smiling ferryman to raft them over to where the road to Wytheville begins again. But on the east bank, the tall square fieldstone shot-tower still broods over the green-velvet countryside—a grim reminder of a day when Virginia was wracked with civil war, and brother turned against brother.

Yes; the shot-tower is still there, a historical landmark which my family at last turned over to the United Daughters of the Confederacy, for the edification of the passing tourist. The spiral staircase that winds up and up inside the tower is new—not rotten and precarious as it was when I was there, one of the scattered cousins who came "Back Home" every summer for a visit. The sturdy beamed floor of the single room, high up against the ceiling, used to be spattered with little hardened splashes of lead, spilled eighty-five years ago by determined Rebels and loyal sweating negroes frantically making ammunition for Lee's troops. The leaden souvenirs are probably gone by now; and the square hole in the floor is fenced in by chicken wire, lest the unwary tourist fall through it into that dark matching hole in the tower's dirt floor below. This leads, well-like, into the river. I am not sure about the huge iron cauldron which caught the shot. (Molten lead formed round rifle balls when it fell, hissing, into cold water.) The pot may yet be hanging down there into the river. Once, on a dare from another visiting cousin, I climbed halfway down the slimy ladder into that chill murmuring darkness. But something slithered against my arm, and I never finished the adventure...especially as it was almost nightfall, and time for the Shot-Tower Ghost to appear.

Let me say here, to your probable disappointment, that there never was a "shot-tower ghost." This gruesome family-spectre was nothing more than a product of my Great-uncle Robert's imagination. He is dead now, a white-bearded irascible old bachelor of the "hoss-racin' and cyard game" school. Dead, too, is Shadrach, his stooped and gray-haired "body-servant," last of the family slaves who accepted their "freedom" with a bored sniff as the impractical notion of "a passel o' po-white Yankees." To the last day of their lives— about two weeks apart—Uncle Robert and Shadrach, respectively, remained unreconstructed and unfreed. And the fact that one of my aunts married a Northerner, bore him a fine son, got rich, and came back to buy and remodel another old countryplace adjoining the Homeplace, was a great shock to both of them. I think they were convinced that "Yankees" were a roving tribe of gipsy marauders, and incapable of fathering offspring.

That son was my Cousin Mark, who had none of the gracious charm of his mother's side of the family and all of the butt-headed stubbornness of his Connecticut father. But in those days just after World War I—"the war in Europe" as Uncle Robert verbally shrugged off any of our conflicts but the one between the States—I was a very young fluttery miss with a terrible crush on Francis X. Bushman, thence my Cousin Mark because he slightly resembled him.

This particular summer, however, another cousin of mine from the Georgia branch was also visiting the Homeplace, a red-headed minx named Adelia—she is fat and has five children now, may I add with vicious satisfaction. But she was two years older than I, and just entering the Seminary, so Cousin Mark's eyes were all for her, not for a gawky high school sophomore from Birmingham, Alabama.

Adelia was also popular with the younger set of Wytheville. Almost every night a squealing, laughing carful of young people would bear down on the ferryman, who had orders to ferry Miss Adelia's friends across free of charge. Uncle Robert and Shadrach would roll their eyes at each other and moan faintly, but a short while later my uncle would be grinning from ear to ear, seated in his favorite chair on the wide columned veranda with a bouquet of pretty girls clustered around him, begging for "ghost stories." Shadrach, his eyeballs and teeth the only white thing about his grinning ebony face, would circulate around, offering syllabub and tiny beaten-biscuits with baked ham between them, or calling "rounds" for an old-fashioned reel in the big living room where the Victrola played incessantly.

Cousin Mark was a member of this coterie more often than anyone else, and Uncle Robert always made him welcome in a formally polite manner that Adelia, giggling beside me later in our big featherbed upstairs, would mock outrageously. Mark and Uncle Robert seemed to clash as naturally as a hound and a fox, for Mark had a rather rude way of finding holes in Uncle Robert's tall tales, mostly about the supernatural.

"Did you ever actually *see* a ghost, sir?" Mark demanded once, sitting at ease on the front steps against a backdrop of gray dusk and twinkling fireflies...and the distant plaintive crying of whippoorwills.

"I have, suh!" my uncle lashed back at him stiffly. "With mah own two eyes...and if Ah may say so, Ah could pick off a Yankee sniper right now at fifty yards with a good rifle!"

"Unless he picked you off first," my cousin pointed out blandly. Then, with stubborn logic that seemed to infuriate my uncle: "*When* did you ever see a ghost, sir, may I ask?" he pursued. "And where? And how do you know it wasn't just an...an optical illusion?"

31

"Suh...!" Uncle Robert drew himself up, sputtering slightly like an old firecracker. "Suh, the Shot-Tower Ghost is no optical illusion. He is, and Ah give you mah word on it, a true case of psychic phenomena. You understand," Uncle slipped into his act—a very convincing one, in spite of Adelia's covert giggling, "you understand that, after some very dramatic or tragic incident in which a person dies suddenly, there may be left what is called...ah...I believe the American Society for Psychic Research calls it 'psychic residue.' An emanation, an...an ectoplasmic replica of the person involved. This replica is sometimes left behind after death occurs—the death of the body, that is. For the circumstances under which the person died may have been so...so impossible to leave hanging, the ectoplasmic replica of that person lives on, repeating and repeating his last act or trying to finish some task that he strongly wishes to finish...."

"Poppycock!" my cousin interrupted flatly. "I don't believe there's any such thing as an...'ectoplasmic replica'! What a term!" he laughed lightly. "Where'd you dig that one up, sir? At some table-tapping seance—price ten bucks a spook?"

"No, suh, I did not." Uncle Robert was bristling now; Adelia punched me and giggled. We could all see how very much he wanted to take this young Yankee-born whippersnapper down a peg or two. "I find the term used often," Uncle drawled, "in Madame Blavatsky's four-volume work on the metaphysical. She was considered the foremost authority on the supernatural during the last century, the Nineteenth Century, when such notables as Arthur Conan Doyle were seriously studying the possibility of life after death...."

"Blavatsky...Blavatsky," Mark murmured, then grinned and snapped his fingers. "Oh yes. I remember reading about her, something in *The Golden Bough*. Sir James Frazer says she's either the greatest authority...*or* the biggest fraud in the history of metaphysical study! I read that once in the library at Tech, just browsing around...."

Uncle Robert choked. Most young people listened in wide-eyed awe to his erudite-sounding explanations of his "tower ghost" and certain other spook-yarns that he cooked up for our naive pleasure. But Mark was tossing his high-sounding phrases right back at him with great relish, and a covert wink at Adelia who was perched on the arm of Uncle's chair. His smug air seemed to annoy her, though, for:

"Oh, the shot-tower ghost isn't any fraud!" Adelia proclaimed tauntingly, with an affectionate pat for Uncle's gnarled old hand—at the moment gripping his cane as if he intended breaking it over Mark's head. "I've seen it, myself," she announced. "Lib has, too—haven't you, Lib?" she demanded, and I nodded solemnly.

"Now *you've* seen it!" Mark jeered, flipping a coin in the air and watching it glint softly in the mellow glow that slanted through the fan-light over the door. "Anybody else? Hmm? I've been hearing about this spook of Uncle Robert's ever since we moved here from Connecticut—but I've yet to catch a glimpse of him myself! A Confederate soldier with his legs cut off—how touching! Making shot for his comrades up to the day of Lee's surrender at Appomattox. And when the sad news comes, he throws himself off the tower into the river...Haha!" Mark chuckled suddenly, fastening a cold matter-of-fact young eye on Uncle Robert's face. "Come on, Unk. Didn't you make that one up out of whole cloth? It sounds like something out of one of those old paper-back dime novels I found in the attic. *Capitola, the Madcap, Or: Love Conquers All....*"

"Young man!" Uncle Robert stood up abruptly, quivering. "Ah must ask you to mend yoah Yankee manners to yo' elders, suh! Are you havin' the...the temerity to dispute my word, you young...?"

At that moment Shadrach took over, gently but firmly. Throwing a light shawl around his master's shoulders, he maneuvered around beside him, preparing to help him to his feet.

"Marse Robert, hit's yo' bedtime," the old darkey pronounced. "Come along, now, Marse Robert. Tell de young folks good night, cause Ah'm fixin' to help you up to yo' room."

"Shadrach—damme, Ah'll take a hosswhip to yo' black hide!" My uncle roared petulantly, shrugging off the shawl and banging on the porch with his cane. "Quit babyin' me, confound it! Ah'll go to bed when Ah please! Get! Get away from me! Ah'll bend this cane over yoah nappy head! Ah'll..."

"Yassuh," said Shadrach imperturbably. "Hit's leb'm-thirty. Time you was asleep. Come on, now, Marse Robert...." He tugged gently at my uncle's arm, finally wielding his heaviest weapon, the mention of my great-grandmother. "Miss Beth wouldn't like you settin' up so late, catchin' yo' death o' dampness...."

"Oh, the devil!" Uncle snapped at him peevishly. "Ah'm comin', Ah'm comin'! Soon as Ah tell these pretty young ladies good night...and take a cane to this young smartalec!" He glared at Cousin Mark, who grinned back at him lazily. "It's not a wise thing," Uncle Robert intoned ominously, "to joke about the supernatural or regard it as a...parlor-game! And one of these days, young suh, you're going to find that out in a way you'll never forget!"

With that, and followed by a chorus of subdued giggles, he stamped into the house, leaving Adelia and me to bid our guests farewell. At the gate, after the carful of others had rolled away toward the ferry, Cousin Mark lingered, trying to persuade Adelia to kiss him good night. I would gladly have obliged, but my red-headed Georgia cousin switched away from him coolly, tossing her long auburn mop of curls.

"No, I won't!" she said shortly. "The idea, poking fun at Uncle Robert right to his face! You ought to be ashamed of yourself, Mark...and besides, you're such a smartalec, like Uncle said! How do *you* know there's no such thing as a ghost, just because you happen never to have seen one?"

Mark laughed softly, derisively. "And neither have you and Lib," he added. "I saw you wink at each other. Did you really think I'd swallow that silly yarn about the Confederate soldier?"

Adelia nudged me all at once, a signal to stand by and back up whatever mischief she had in mind.

"I've just remembered," she said quietly, "what tomorrow is! Lib...it was a year ago that...that *we* saw the soldier throw himself off that lookout porch at the top of the tower...Remember? You and I were riding horseback up the hill, just at sundown. And you heard that awful scream, and we glanced up just in time to...to see that shadow falling from the tower into the river! On July 9, the date of Lee's surrender at Appomattox!"

"It was *April* 9!" I hissed in her ear. "You'll ruin every-thing....!"

"Sh-h!" Adelia hissed back, giggling. "A damyankee wouldn't know *what* day it was, hardly the *year!*....Oh, I'll never forget that sight," she whispered, shuddering. "Not as long as I live! The look of despair on that man's face, the glimpse I got of it as he fell down, down...."

"Bah!" Mark cut her off with a snort. "You're as big a liar as your Uncle Robert! He and his ridiculous...ectoplasmic replica!"

"But it's true!" I chimed in solemnly. "When we told about it, they dragged the river. But no body was ever found, and none turned up at the Falls downstream. He was wearing a...a shabby gray uniform. And...and a gray forage cap." I elaborated, warming to our little hoax. "And he wasn't more than four feet tall—his legs, you know; they'd been shot off by cannon fire...."

Adelia punched me again sharply. "Don't overdo it!" she hissed, then, with a grave frightened look turned on our cousin from Connecticut: "Oh, Mark, you mustn't scoff at such things! Tomorrow is the date of the surrender. Maybe if...if you watch for him on the hill at sundown, you'll...you'll see him, too!"

Mark snorted again, and strode toward the tethered horse he had ridden across the fields to Uncle's house earlier. In tan riding pants and sports shirt open at the neck, he was the handsomest thing I had ever seen—barring, of course, Fran-cis X. himself. I sighed faintly as Adelia and I, arms about each other's waist, watched him mount and start to ride away, then wheel his spirited little bay back to face us.

"So tomorrow's the witching hour, huh?" he laughed. "Okay, I'll be here—with bells on! But let's make this worth while, cuz!" he drawled tormentingly. "How about a little bet of...say, five bucks? You pay me if our ghost doesn't show up. If I see him, I'll pay you...and gladly!" he jeered.

Adelia stiffened. I saw her pretty chin set and her brown eyes flash, taking up the challenge Mark's cool blue eyes had thrown her.

"All right, Mr. Smartalec!" she snapped back. "It's a bet! Just be mighty sure you bring that five dollars!"

35

"Just you have yours in your hand!" Mark taunted, "Want to make a little side bet, huh? A kiss, maybe? That kiss you won't give me tonight?"

"That's a bet, too!" Adelia answered briskly. "That's how *sure* I am that there *is* a tower ghost, and that you'll see him tomorrow!"

"Okay, carrot-top!" our cousin laughed. "Remember, you're no Southern gentleman if you don't pay up!"

He galloped away with that, and we strolled back toward the house together, Adelia and I, listening to his lusty voice singing, out of sheer perversity, Sherman's "Marching through Georgia." Adelia stamped her foot.

"I *hate* that...that...!" she burst out, unconvincingly. "Lib, we've just got to fix his wagon tomorrow!" Her eyes began to twinkle all at once, and she ran up the curving staircase to burst into Uncle's room, where Shadrach was trying to make him drink his hot milk instead of another whiskey.

Quickly she related the bet to Uncle Robert, whose mild old eyes lighted up also with mischief. He slapped his knee, chuckling.

"We'll fix him!" he promised. "Shadrach, get me young Saunders on the phone, Bill Saunders's boy in Wytheville. He's short enough to look...Hmm." He tugged at his white beard, grinning. "Where's that old ratty Confederate uniform that belonged to your Great-uncle Claud, Lib? In the attic, is it? Well, get it out.... That Saunders boy won the highdive contest at VMI last year, didn't he? Yes. Then, jumping off that lookout porch on the tower and landing in the river won't be much of a feat for him. Yes, hmm. Then he can swim underwater, and come up inside the shot well. Hide under the cauldron until young Mark stops looking for him to come up....!"

"Uncle Robert, you old faker—I *knew* you'd think of something!" Adelia burst out laughing, and hugged him, then went dancing around the high-ceiled bedroom where four generations of our kin had been born, made love, had babies, and died. "I can't wait to see that smarty's face!" she exulted. "I just can't wait!"

Shadrach, with his glass of hot milk, had been fidgeting around in the background, his wide negro-eyes flitting from one of our faces to the other. Suddenly he blurted:

"Marse Robert...s'posin' dey *is* a shot-tower ha'nt up yonder? Seem lak I reecollect dey *was* a little runty soldier what got one leg shot off at Murfreesboro. Name o' Jackson...and he *did* make shot up yonder in de tower. And he *did* jump off and git drownded!"

"Ah know that," Uncle Robert cut him short irritably. "Knew him personally; he was in my platoon. But he didn't jump. He..."

"Yassuh. Got drunk and *fell* off'n de lookout porch," the old darkey recalled uncomfortably. "But dat wouldn't stop his sperrit from comin' back, if'n he took a notion...."

"Oh, balderdash!" Uncle Robert roared at him. "There's no such thing as...as a spirit! Ghost, haunt, call it whatever you like! You know very well Ah...Ah simply make up these yarns to amuse the young folks."

"Yassuh." Shadrach subsided meekly, but his eyes were large and troubled in his wrinkled black face.

Adelia and I giggled and whispered half the night about our practical joke on Cousin Mark. We gobbled our waffles and wild honey as early as Aunt Cornelia would cook them, and spent the rest of the morning on the phone. Everyone in our little crowd had to be told about Uncle Robert's hoax, and since most of them rather disliked Cousin Mark for his abrupt and opinionated manner, all were looking forward to seeing him "taken down a peg."

At noon Bill Saunders turned up, a small freckled youth. He made two or three "practice dives" off the tower porch, disappearing from sight each time mysteriously and reappearing through the shot well, slime-covered and draped with cobwebs.

"Splendid, splendid!" Uncle Robert applauded, chuckling. "You're an excellent swimmer, my boy....Well, Adelia?" His old eyes twinkled as my cousin stood with her arm about his waist, watching the performance from the point below the tower where she and I were supposed to have seen the ghost a year ago.

"It's perfect!" she laughed. "Mark doesn't know you can swim underwater and come up inside the shot well. He'll be skeptical, of course, until our spook disappears into the river! Oh, when he goes back to Connecticut to visit his father's people, he'll certainly have a tale that will curl their hair!"

The day passed slowly under the weight of our young impatience. After dinner our friends began to turn up, by twos and fours, laughing and whispering together, and winking at Uncle Robert, who was enjoying his little jest immensely. As the long Virginia twilight began to fall, Adelia and I, in fluffy organdy, proposed an innocent-looking game of croquet under the big leafy maples on the lawn. Fireflies were beginning to wink and dart among the hedges. The sun had gone down below the distant blue-gray mountains, but a queer flat light lingered in the sky, giving everything the look of a stereopticon picture.

"Don't anybody dare to snicker and give us away," Adelia ordered. "I want Mark to think this is just another evening of fun and dancing. Unrehearsed....Oh, I can't wait another minute!" she giggled, consulting the tiny wristwatch Uncle Robert had given her as a graduation present. "He's late! It'll be too dark in another half-hour for him to see Bill. But I've painted him all over with luminous paint....You don't suppose Mark's got cold feet and backed out on his bet?"

"Not that hard-headed stubborn Yankee!" I scoffed. "An earthquake wouldn't keep him from...See?" I broke off, triumphant. "Here he comes now over the north hill!"

A solitary rider in white sport shirt and brown jodhpurs was indeed coming, hell-for-leather, over the far hill that separated the Homeplace from my aunt's remodeled home. The little bay mare Mark always rode took the hill at a hard gallop and plunged down the other side without slackening speed. A narrow creek with a fence rambling along its farther bank divided the "bottom land" where the cows and horses grazed. As we watched, holding our breath, my cousin spurred his mount recklessly to take this precarious jump, ignoring the wide-open gate further down.

"Young idiot!" Uncle Robert muttered. "Rides like a damyankee. No consideration for the hoss....Hah! He'll break his fool...."

Even as he spoke the words, the little bay, sailing over creek and fence, caught a hoof on the top rail and fell head over heels. Her rider went sprawling, and did not rise, even after the mare scrambled to her feet and went galloping back home through the open gate.

Adelia and I gasped, and started to run in that direction. But as we reached the orchard gate, we saw Cousin Mark striding toward us along the narrow path past the springhouse. We waved, he waved back, and Adelia sniffed.

"He's okay," she said, almost resentfully. "Nothing could make a dent in that rhinoceros hide!"

But as he approached us, I saw that he looked very pale and dazed. There was a great dark gash across his forehead at the temple, and he limped slightly. With a twinge of remorse we beckoned, ready to call off our little joke. But Mark shook his head mockingly, and pointed to the shot-tower, turning his steps in that direction before he reached the orchard. He shouted something, but wind must have blown the sound away from us, for we could hear nothing but the faint quavering cry of a whippoorwill somewhere along the river.

Adelia stamped her foot. "See?" she exploded. "He's so smug, so sure of himself! Going to show us up for a bunch of superstitious nitwits! Just you wait...!"

We ran back through the orchard to join the others, lined up along the fence to watch Mark. Through the gathering dusk we could see his lone figure toiling up the hill toward the shot-tower, its bleak silhouette picked out sharply against the pale pink-and-gold of the western sky. White sheep dotted the green hillside, but as Mark picked his way among them, they did not start and run, but went on grazing, undisturbed.

We began to laugh and chatter excitedly as my cousin reached the point where the ghost could best be seen. Uncle Robert signaled surreptitiously with a flashlight, and instantly a foreshortened figure, glowing with an eerie green radiance, appeared on the lookout porch. Laughing, we saw Mark stop short, staring up at the apparition.

Uncle Robert signaled again. Promptly a harsh quavering cry broke the evening stillness, heart-rending in its despair. The figure on the lookout porch, in gray Confederate uniform and forage cap, suddenly flung itself out into space. Screaming, it fell down, down, to disappear in the swirling river far below. We saw Mark standing on the riverbank, watching intently for the swimmer to bob up. When he did not, my cousin turned uncertainly, looking up-

and downstream, while we watched, bent double with mirth at his obvious bewilderment. He turned at last and entered the door of the shot-tower, evidently preparing to climb the spiral staircase and examine the lookout porch from which the spectre had jumped. We fell upon one another, rocked with laughter.

But abruptly my cousin's figure reappeared and started limping down the hill. He reached the front gate and stood there, swaying slightly, very pale and disheveled, but smiling in mocking triumph. As Adelia opened the iron gate for him, questioningly, trying to keep her face straight and solemn, Mark began to laugh silently—and held out his hand, palm up.

At that instant a second dripping figure, in soggy gray uniform and minus the forage cap, was seen slogging down the hill. Bill Saunders reached us and leaned on the fence, grinning disgustedly and coughing a bit as if strangled. Most of the phosphorescent paint had washed off, and he glowed ludicrously only in spots on Uncle Claud's faded uniform.

"Bill!" Adelia wailed, half-laughing. "Oh, shoot! What went wrong? How did Mark find out...?"

"Aw-w!" Saunders ducked his head sheepishly. "I did it perfectly twice before! But *this* time I had to swim up under the wrong side of the shot cauldron! Got strangled and darn near drowned! Would have, if Mark hadn't heard me splashing around and caught me by the collar...."

All eyes turned on my cousin Mark then, standing there quietly in the gathering dusk, looking oddly weak and pale but smiling with sardonic satisfaction. His hand was still held out mockingly, and Adelia flounced over to him, disgruntled.

"All right, General Grant!" she lashed out peevishly as Mark still did not speak. "Start rubbing it in, why don't you? You outflanked us! You won the bet...and I'm no welsher!" Her brown eyes twinkled suddenly. "But...I didn't say *where* you could kiss me—just on the cheek!" She turned her pretty face up to him, at the same time thrusting a crumpled bill into his hand; I gasped as I saw that it was a worthless piece of 1864 currency we had found in the attic, along with Uncle Claud's uniform. "And here's your five," Adelia jeered. "I didn't promise I wouldn't pay off...in Confederate money!"

Mark smiled at her, a one-sided ironic little smile of reluctant admiration. He shrugged and bent to kiss her on the cheek. But abruptly he swayed, an expression of pain and confusion crossing his handsome face, now only a white blur against the darkness. One hand groped for the money Adelia held out, the other went to the dark gash in his forehead. And I saw my pretty cousin's face soften with tenderness.

"Oh, Mark!" she cried out. "You *were* hurt when your horse threw you! Why didn't you tell us, instead of going on with this silly bet we...?"

Someone screamed—a rasping high-pitched sound of utter terror. We all whirled toward the sound, startled. Shadrach, coming across the lawn gravely to find Uncle Robert, had halted abruptly. His darkey eyes were distended with horror, one black hand pointing shakily in our direction. We laughed, thinking he had seen Bill Saunders's glowing figure, and followed him into the house as he ran from us, still shrieking. But he locked himself in his room and no amount of coaxing would bring him out.

In the hallway we noticed the phone, off the hook. Uncle Robert picked it up, and was startled by the sound of sobbing coming over the wire.

It was my aunt, a rather hysterical woman. Mark's horse, she said, had returned, riderless, to the stable. She was sure something had happened to him. Was he alright? Was he there with us?

Uncle Robert soothed her, assured her that Mark was with us, quite uninjured, then called him to the phone to convince his mother.

There was no answer, other than the eerie cry of a distant whippoorwill. Mark had vanished, left abruptly—after collecting, Adelia remarked in a covert tone of disappointment, only the money-half of their little bet. We'd phone and tease him about that when he reached home, she laughingly said....

But an hour later, my aunt called back. Mark had not arrived. When she called again frantically around midnight, a search was instituted. Toward morning they found his body.

41

He was lying, all crumpled up, where his little bay mare had thrown him when she fell. A quick examination showed that his right leg had been broken in two places; but mercifully, he had not had to lie there suffering all night. A blow on the temple, when his head struck a rock, had killed him—instantly, the coroner said.

Mark had been dead all that time. The coroner jeered at the fantastic account we told of his saving Bill Saunders's life, then collecting that bet from Adelia. A case of mass-hypnotism, he called it, induced by the fact that we were all so anxious for Mark's presence to complete our little hoax about the shot-tower ghost. He quoted the illusion of the Indian rope-trick as an example: how a group of people in broad daylight can be made to "see" a small boy climb a rope rising in midair, and disappear before their very eyes. "Psychic residue" and "ectoplasmic replica" were terms he had never heard...nor did anyone ever hear of them again from Uncle Robert's lips. He and Shadrach were thereafter conspicuously silent, exchanging a long look, whenever the supernatural was mentioned. And as for me, the cry of a whippoorwill at dusk still makes me shiver uncontrollably....

For, there was one little item that the coroner could not explain. There was a crumpled five-dollar bill in my Cousin Mark's dead hand when they found him—a worthless piece of currency, printed by the Southern Confederacy in 1864.

Iverson's Pits

DAN SIMMONS

As a young boy, I was not afraid of the dark. As an old man, I am wiser. But it was as a boy of ten in that distant summer of 1913 that I was forced to partake of communion with that darkness which now looms so close. I remember the taste of it. Even now, three-quarters of a century later, I am unable to turn over black soil in the garden or to stand alone in the grassy silence of my grandson's backyard after the sun has set without a hint of cold fingers on the back of my neck.

The past is, as they say, dead and buried. But even the most buried things have their connections to the present, gnarled old roots rising to the surface, and I am one of these. Yet there is no one to connect to, no one to tell. My daughter is grown and gone, dead of cancer in 1953. My middle-aged grandson is a product of those Eisenhower years, that period of endless gestation when all the world seemed fat and confident and looking to the future. Paul has taught science at the local high school for twenty-three years and were I to tell him now about the events of that hot first day and night of July, 1913, he would think me mad. Or senile.

My great-grandchildren, a boy and a girl in an age that finds little reason to pay attention to such petty distinctions as gender, could not conceive of a past as ancient and irretrievable as my own childhood before the Great War, much less the blood-and-leather reality of the Civil War era from which I carry my dark message. My great-grandchildren are as colorful and mindless as the guppies Paul keeps in his expensive aquarium, free from the terrors and tides of the ocean of history, smug in their almost total ignorance of everything that came before themselves, Big Macs, and MTV.

So I sit alone on the patio in Paul's backyard (why was it, I try to recall, that we turned our focus away from the front porch attention to the communal streets and sidewalks into the fenced isolation of our own backyards?) and I study the old photograph of a serious ten-year-old in his Boy Scout uniform.

The boy is dressed far too warmly for such a hot summer day—his small form is almost lost under the heavy, woolen Boy Scout tunic, broad-brimmed campaign hat, baggy wool trousers, and awkward puttees laced almost to the knees. He is not smiling—a solemn, miniature doughboy four years before the term doughboy had passed into the common vocabulary. The boy is me, of course, standing in front of Mr. Everett's ice wagon on that day in June when I was about to leave on a trip much longer in time and to places much more unimaginably distant than any of us might have dreamed.

I look at the photograph knowing that ice wagons exist now only as fading memories in aging skulls, that the house in the background has long since been torn down to be replaced by an apartment building which in turn was replaced by a shopping mall, that the wool and leather and cotton of the Boy Scout uniform have rotted away, leaving only the brass buttons and the boy himself to be lost somewhere, and that—as Paul would explain—every cell in that unsmiling ten-year-old's body has been replaced several times. For the worse, I suspect. Paul would say that the DNA is the same, and then give an explanation which makes it sound as if the only continuity between me *now* and me *then* is some little parasite-architect, blindly sitting and smirking in each otherwise unrelated cell of the then-me and the now-me.

Cow manure.

I look at that thin face, those thin lips, the eyes narrowed and squinting in the light of a sun seventy-five years younger (and hotter, I *know*, despite the assurances of reason and the verities of Paul's high school science) and I feel the thread of sameness which unites that unsuspecting boy of ten—so confident for one so young, so unafraid—with the old man who has learned to be afraid of the dark.

I wish I could warn him.

The past is dead and buried. But I know now that buried things have a way of rising to the surface when one least expects them to.

&ᴀ &ᴀ &ᴀ

In the summer of 1913 the Commonwealth of Pennsylvania made ready for the largest invasion of military veterans the nation had ever seen. Invitations had been sent out from the War Department for a Great Reunion of Civil War veterans to commemorate the fiftieth anniversary of the three-day battle at Gettysburg.

All that spring our Philadelphia newspapers were filled with details of the anticipated event. Up to 40,000 veterans were expected. By mid-May, the figure had risen to 54,000 and the General Assembly had to vote additional monies to supplement the Army's budget. My mother's cousin Celia wrote from Atlanta to say that the Daughters of the Confederacy and other groups affiliated with the United Confederate Veterans were doing everything in their power to send their old men North for a final invasion.

My father was not a veteran. Before I was born, he had called the trouble with Spain "Mr. Hearst's War" and five years after the Gettysburg Reunion he would call the trouble in Europe "Mr. Wilson's War." By then I would be in high school, with my classmates chafing to enlist and show the Hun a thing or two, but by then I shared my father's sentiments; I had seen enough of war's legacy.

But in the late spring and early summer of 1913 I would have given anything to join those veterans in Gettysburg, to hear the speeches and see the battle flags and crouch in the Devil's Den and watch those old men reenact Pickett's Charge one last time.

And then the opportunity arrived.

Since my birthday in February I had been a Boy Scout. The Scouts were a relatively new idea then—the first groups in the United States had been formed only three years

45

earlier—but in the spring of 1913 every boy I knew was either a Boy Scout or waiting to become one.

The Reverend Hodges had formed the first Troop in Chestnut Hill, our little town outside of Philadelphia, now a suburb. The Reverend allowed only boys of good character and strong moral fiber to join: Presbyterian boys. I had sung in the Fourth Avenue Presbyterian Boys' Choir for three years and, in spite of my frailness and total inability to tie a knot, I was allowed to become a Boy Scout three days after my tenth birthday.

My father was not totally pleased. Our Scout uniforms might have been castoffs from the returning Roughriders' army. From hobnailed boots to puttees to campaign hats we were little troopers, drowning in yards of khaki and great draughts of military virtue. The Reverend Hodges had us on the high school football field each Tuesday and Thursday afternoon from four to six and every Saturday morning from seven until ten, practicing close-order drill and applying field dressings to one another until our Troop resembled nothing so much as a band of mummies with swatches of khaki showing through our bandages. On Wednesday evening we met in the church basement to learn Morse Code—what the Reverend called General Service Code—and to practice our semaphore signals.

My father asked me if we were training to fight the Boer War over again. I ignored his irony, sweated into my khaki woolens through those warming weeks of May, and loved every minute of it.

When the Reverend Hodges came by our house in early June to inform my parents that the Commonwealth had requested all Boy Scout Troops in Pennsylvania to send representatives to Gettysburg to help with the Great Reunion, I knew that it had been Divine Intervention which would allow me to join the Reverend, thirteen-year-old Billy Stargill (who would later die in the Argonne), and a pimply-faced overweight boy whose name I cannot recall on the five-day visit to Gettysburg.

My father was noncommittal but my mother agreed at once that it was a unique honor, so on the morning of June 30 I posed in front of Mr. Everett's ice wagon for a photograph taken by Dr. Lowell, Chestnut Hill's undertaker and official photographer, and at a little after two P.M. on that same day I joined the Reverend and my two comrades-in-arms for the three-hour train ride to Gettysburg.

ﾞ冊 ﾞ冊 ﾞ冊

As a part of the official celebration, we paid the veterans' travel rate of one cent a mile. The train ride cost me $1.21. I had never been to Gettysburg. I had never been away from home overnight.

We arrived late in the afternoon; I was tired, hot, thirsty, and desperately needing to relieve myself since I had been too shy to use the lavatory aboard the train. The small town of Gettysburg was a mass of crowds, confusion, noise, horses, automobiles, and old men whose heavy uniforms smelled of camphor. We stumbled after Reverend Hodges through muddy lanes between buildings draped in flags and bunting. Men outnumbered women ten to one and most of the main streets were a sea of straw boaters and khaki caps. As the Reverend checked in the lobby of the Eagle Hotel for word from his Scouting superiors, I slipped down a side hall and found a public restroom.

Half an hour later we dragged our duffel bags into the back of a small motor carriage for the ride out southwest of town to the Reunion tent city. A dozen boys and their Scoutmasters were crowded into the three benches as the vehicle labored its way through heavy traffic down Franklin Street, past a temporary Red Cross Hospital on the east side of the street and a score of Ambulance Corps wagons parked on the west side, and then right onto a road marked Long Lane and into a sea of tents which seemed to stretch on forever.

It was past seven o'clock and the rich evening light illuminated thousands of canvas pyramids covering hundreds of acres of open farmland. I craned to make out which of the distant hills was Cemetery Ridge, which heap of rocks the Little Round Top. We passed State Policemen on horseback, Army wagons pulled by Army mules, huge heaps of firewood, and clusters of portable field bakeries where the aroma of fresh-baked bread still lingered.

Reverend Hodges turned in his seat. "Afraid we missed the evening chow lines, boys," he said. "But we weren't hungry, were we?"

I shook my head despite the fact my stomach was cramping with hunger. My mother had packed me a dinner of fried chicken and biscuits for the train, but the Reverend had eaten the drumstick and the fat boy had begged the rest. I had been too excited to eat.

We turned right onto East Avenue, a broad dirt road between neat rows of tents. I looked in vain for the Great Tent I had read about—a huge bigtop with room for 13,000 chairs where President Wilson was scheduled to speak in four days, on Friday, the Fourth of July. Now the sun was low and red in the haze to the west, the air thick with dust and the scent of trampled grass and sun-warmed canvas. I was starving and I had dirt in my hair and grit between my teeth. I do not ever remember being happier.

Our Boy Scout Station was at the west end of East Avenue, a hundred yards past a row of portable kitchens set in the middle of the Pennsylvania veterans' tent area. Reverend Hodges showed us to our tents and commanded us to hurry back to the station for our next day's assignments.

I set my duffel on a cot in a tent not far from the latrines. I was slow setting out my bedroll and belongings and when I looked up the fat boy was asleep on another cot and Billy was gone. A train roared by on the Gettysburg and Harrisburg tracks not fifty feet away. Suddenly breathless with the panic of being left behind, I ran back to the Scoutmasters' tent to receive my orders.

Reverend Hodges and Billy were nowhere to be seen but a fat man with a blond mustache, thick spectacles, and an ill-fitting Scoutmaster's uniform snapped, "You there, Scout!"

"Yessir?"

"Have you received your assignment?"

"No, sir."

The fat man grunted and pawed through a stack of yellow cardboard tags lying on a board he was using as a desk. He pulled one from the stack, glanced at it, and tied it to the brass button on my left breast pocket. I craned my neck to read it. Faint blue, type-written letters said: MONTGOMERY, P.D., Capt., 20th N.C. Reg., SECT. 27, SITE 3424, North Carolina Veterans.

"Well, *go,* boy!" snapped the Scoutmaster.

"Yessir," I said and ran toward the entrance. I paused. "Sir?"

"What is it?" The Scoutmaster was already tying another ticket on another Scout's blouse.

"Where am I to go, sir?"

The fat man flicked his fingers as if brushing an insect away. "To find the veteran you are assigned to, of course."

I squinted at the ticket. "Captain Montgomery?"

"Yes, yes. If that is what it says."

I took a breath. "Where do I find him, sir?"

The fat man scowled, took four angry steps toward me, and glared at the ticket through his thick glasses. "20th North Carolina...Section 27...up *there.*" He swept his arm in a gesture that took in the railroad tracks, a distant stream lined with trees, the setting sun, and another tent city on a hill where hundreds of pyramid tents glowed redly in the twilight.

"Pardon me, sir, but what do I do when I find Captain Montgomery?" I asked the scoutmaster's retreating back.

The man stopped and glowered at me over his shoulder with a thinly veiled disgust that I had never guessed an adult would show toward someone my age. "You do whatever he *wants,* you young fool," snapped the man. "Now *go.*"

I turned and ran toward the distant camp of the Confederates.

છે. છે. છે.

Lanterns were being lighted as I made my way through long rows of tents. Old men by the hundreds, many in heavy gray uniforms and long whiskers, sat on campstools and cots, benches and wooden stumps, smoking and talking and spitting into the early evening gloom. Twice I lost my way and twice I was given directions in slow, Southern drawls that might as well have been German for all I understood them.

Finally I found the North Carolina contingent sandwiched in between the Alabama and Missouri camps, just a short walk from the West Virginians. In the years since I have found myself wondering why they put the Union-loyal West Virginian veterans in the midst of the rebel encampment.

Section 27 was the last row on the east side of the North Carolina camp and Site 3424 was the last tent in the row. The tent was dark.

"Captain Montgomery?" My voice was little more than a whisper. Hearing no answer from the darkened tent, I ducked my head inside to confirm that the veteran was not home. It was not my fault, I reasoned, that the old gentleman was not here when I called. I would find him in the morning, escort him to the breakfast tent, run the necessary errands for him, help him to find the latrine or his old comrades-in-arms, or whatever. *In the morning.* Right now I thought I would run all the way back to the Boy Scout Station, find Billy and Reverend Hodges, and see if anyone had any cookies in their duffel bags.

"I been waitin' for you, Boy."

I froze. The voice had come from the darkness in the depths of the tent. It was a voice from the South but sharp as cinders and brittle with age. It was a voice that I imagined the Dead might use to command those still beyond the grave.

"Come in here, Johnny. Step lively!"

I moved into the hot, canvas-scented interior and blinked. For a second my breath would not come.

The old man who lay on the cot was propped on his elbows so that his shoulders looked like sharp wings in the dim light, predatory pinions rising above an otherwise indistinct bundle of gray cloth, gray skin, staring eyes, and faded braid. He was wearing a shapeless hat which had once boasted a brim and crown but which now served only to cast his face into deeper shadow. A beak of a nose jutted into the dim light above wisps of white beard, thin purplish lips, and a few sharp teeth gleaming in a black hole of a mouth. For the first time in my life I realized that a human mouth was really an opening into a skull. The old man's eye sockets were darker pits of shadow beneath brows still black, the cheeks hollowed and knife-edged. Huge, liver-spotted hands, misshapen with age and arthritis, glowed with a preternatural whiteness in the gloom and I saw that while one leg ended in the black gleam of a high boot, the other terminated abruptly below the knee. I could see the rolled trouser leg pulled above pale, scarred skin wrapped tautly around the bone of the stump.

"Goddamnit, boy, did you bring the wagon?"

"Pardon me, sir?" My voice was a cicada's frightened chirp.

"The wagon, goddamnit, Johnny. We need a wagon. You should be knowin' that, boy." The old man sat up, swung his leg and his stump over the edge of the cot, and began fumbling in his loose coat.

"I'm sorry, Captain Montgomery...uh...you *are* Captain Montgomery, aren't you, sir?"

The old man grunted.

"Well, Captain Montgomery, sir, my name's not Johnny, it's..."

"*Goddamnit,* boy!" bellowed the old man. "Would you quit makin' noise and go get the goddamned wagon! We need to get up there to the Pits before that bastard Iverson beats us to it."

I started to reply and then found myself with no wind with which to speak as Captain Montgomery removed a pistol from the folds of his coat. The gun was huge and gray and smelled of oil and I was certain that the crazy old man was going to kill me with it in that instant. I stood there with the wind knocked out of me as certainly as if the old Confederate had struck me in the solar plexus with the barrel of that formidable weapon.

The old man laid the revolver on the cot and reached into the shadows beneath it, pulling out an awkward arrangement of straps, buckles, and mahogany which I recognized as a crude wooden leg. "Come on now, Johnny," he mumbled, bending over to strap the cruel thing in place, "I've waited long enough for you. Go get the wagon, that's a good lad. I'll be ready and waitin' when you get back."

"Yessir," I managed, and turned, and escaped.

ఇ ఇ ఇ

I have no rational explanation for my next actions. All I had to do was the natural thing, the thing that every fiber of my frightened body urged me to do—run back to the Boy Scout Station, find Reverend Hodges, inform him that my veteran was a raving madman armed with a pistol, and get a good night's sleep while the grownups sorted things out. But I was not a totally rational creature at this point. (How many ten-year-old boys are, I wonder?) I was tired, hungry, and already homesick after less than seven hours away from home, disoriented in space and time, and—perhaps most pertinent—not used to disobeying orders. And yet I am sure to this day that I would have run the entire way back to the Boy Scout Station and not thought twice about it if my parting glance at the old man had not been of him painfully strapping on that terrible wooden leg. The thought of him standing in the deepening twilight on that awful pegleg, trustingly awaiting a wagon which would never arrive was more than I could bear.

As fate arranged it, there was a wagon and untended team less than a hundred yards from Captain Montgomery's tent. The back of the slat-sided thing was half-filled with blankets, but the driver and deliverers were nowhere in sight. The team was a matched set of grays, aged and swaybacked but docile enough as I grabbed their bridles and clumsily turned them around and tugged them back up the hill with me.

I had never ridden a horse or driven a team. Even in 1913, I was used to riding in automobiles. Chestnut Hill still saw buggies and wagons on the street occasionally, but already they were considered quaint. Mr. Everett, our iceman, did not allow boys to ride on his wagon and his horse had the habit of biting any child who came in range.

Gingerly, trying to keep my knuckles away from the grays' teeth, I led the team up the hill. The thought that I was stealing the wagon never crossed my mind. Captain Montgomery needed a wagon. It was my job to deliver it.

"Good boy, Johnny. Well done." Outside, in the light, the old man was only slightly less formidable. The long gray coat hung in folds and wrinkles and although there was no sight of the pistol, I was sure that it was tucked somewhere close to hand. A heavy canvas bag hung from a strap over his right shoulder. For the first time I noticed a faded insignia on the front of his hat and three small medals on his coat. The ribbons were faded so that I could not make out their colors. The Captain's bare neck reminded me of the thick tangle of ropes dangling into the dark maw of the old well behind our house.

"Come on, Boy. We have to move smartly if we're to beat that son-of-a-bitch Iverson." The old man heaved himself up to the seat with a wide swing of his wooden leg and seized the reins in fists that looked like clusters of gnarled roots. With no hesitation I ran to the left side of the wagon and jumped to the seat beside him.

ॐ ॐ ॐ

Gettysburg was filled with lights and activity that last, late evening in June, but the night seemed especially dark and empty as we passed through town on our way north. The house and hotel lights felt so distant to our purpose—whatever that purpose was—that the lights appeared pale and cold to me, the fading glow of fireflies dying in a jar.

In a few minutes we were beyond the last buildings on the north end of town and turning northwest on what I later learned was Mummasburg Road. Just before we passed behind a dark curtain of trees, I swiveled in my seat and caught a last glimpse of Gettysburg and the Great Reunion Camp beyond it. Where the lights of the city seemed pale and paltry, the flames of the hundreds of campfires and bonfires in the Tent City blazed in the night. I looked at the constellations of fires and realized that there were more old veterans huddling around them that night than there were young men in many nations' armies. I wondered if this is what Cemetery Ridge and Culp's Hill had looked like to the arriving Confederate armies fifty years earlier.

Suddenly I had the chilling thought that fifty years ago Death had given a grand party and 140,000 revelers had arrived in their burial clothes. My father had told me that the soldiers going into battle had often pinned small scraps of paper to their uniforms so that their bodies could be identified after the killing was finished. I glanced to my right as if half-expecting to see a yellowed scrap of paper pinned to the old man's chest, his name, rank, and home town scrawled on it. Then I realized with a start that *I* was wearing the tag.

I looked back at the lights and marveled that fifty years after Death's dark festival, 50,000 of the survivors had returned for a second celebration.

We passed deeper into the forest and I could see no more of the fires of the Reunion Camp. The only light came from the fading glow of the summer sky through limbs above us and the sporadic winking of fireflies along the road.

"You don't remember Iverson, do you, Boy?"

53

"No, sir."

"Here." He thrust something into my hands. Leaning closer, squinting, I understood that it was an old tintype, cracked at the edges. I was able to make out a pale square of face, shadows which might have been mustaches. Captain Montgomery grabbed it back. "He's not registered at the goddamn reunion," he muttered. "Spent the goddamn day lookin'. Never arrived. Didn't expect him to. Newspaper in Atlanta two years ago said he died. Goddamn lie."

"Oh," I said. The horse's hooves made soft sounds in the dirt of the road. The fields we were passing were as empty as my mind.

"Goddamn lie," said the Captain. "He's goin' be back here. No doubt about it, is there, Johnny?"

"No, sir." We came over the brow of a low hill and the old man slowed the wagon. His pegleg had been making a rhythmic sound as it rattled against the wooden slat where it was braced and as we slowed the tempo changed. We had passed out of the thickest part of the forest but dark farmfields opened out to the left and right between stands of trees and low stone walls. "Damn," he said. "Did you see Forney's house back there, boy?"

"I...no, sir. I don't think so." I had no idea if we had passed Forney's house. I had no idea who Forney was. I had no idea what I was doing wandering around the countryside at night with this strange old man. I was amazed to find myself suddenly on the verge of tears.

Captain Montgomery pulled the team to a stop under some trees set back off the right side of the road. He panted and wheezed, struggling to dismount from the driver's seat. "Help me down, Boy. It's time we bivouacked."

I ran around to offer my hand but he used my shoulder as a brace and dropped heavily to the ground. A strange, sour scent came from him and I was reminded of an old, urine-soaked mattress in a shed near the tracks behind our school where Billy said hoboes slept. It was fully dark now. I could make out the Big Dipper above a field across the road. All around us, crickets and tree toads were tuning up for their nightly symphony.

"Bring some of them blankets along, Boy." He had picked up a fallen limb to use as a walking stick as he moved clumsily into the trees. I grabbed some Army blankets from the back of the wagon and followed him.

We crossed a wheat field, passed a thin line of trees, and climbed through a meadow before stopping under a tree where broad leaves stirred to the night breeze. The Captain directed me to lay the blankets out into rough bedrolls and then he lowered himself until he was lying with his back propped against the tree and his wooden leg resting on his remaining ankle. "You hungry, Boy?"

I nodded in the dark. The old man rummaged in the canvas bag and handed me several strips of something I thought was meat but which tasted like heavily salted leather. I chewed on the first piece for almost five minutes before it was soft enough to swallow. Just as my lips and tongue were beginning to throb with thirst, Captain Montgomery handed me a wineskin of water and showed me how to squirt it into my open mouth.

"Good jerky, ain't it, Boy?" he asked.

"Delicious," I answered honestly and worked to bite off another chunk.

"That Iverson was a useless son-of-a-bitch," the Captain said around his own jawful of jerky. It was as if he were picking up the sentence he had begun half an hour earlier back at the wagon. "He would've been a harmless son-of-a-bitch if those dumb bastards in my own 20th North Carolina hadn't elected him camp commander back before the war begun. That made Iverson a colonel sort of automatic like, and by the time we'd fought our way up North, the stupid little bastard was in charge of one of Rodes's whole damn brigades."

The old man paused to work at the jerky with his few remaining teeth and I reflected on the fact that the only other person I had ever heard curse anything like the Captain was Mr. Bolton, the old fire chief who used to sit out in front of the firehouse on Third Street and tell stories to the new recruits, apparently oblivious to the uninvited presence of us younger members of the audience. Perhaps, I thought, it has something to do with wearing a uniform.

"His first name was Alfred," said the Captain. The old man's voice was soft, preoccupied, and his southern accent was so thick that the meaning of each word reached me some seconds after the sound of it. It was a bit like lying in bed, already dreaming, and hearing the soft voices of my mother and father coming upstairs through a curtain of sleep. Or like magically understanding a foreign language. I closed my eyes to hear better. "Alfred," said the Captain, "just like his daddy. His daddy'd been a Senator from Georgia, good friend of the President." I could feel the old man's gaze on me. "President Davis. It was Davis, back when he was a senator too, who give young Iverson his first commission. That was back durin' the trouble with Mexico. Then when the real war come up, Iverson and his daddy got 'em up a regiment. Them days, when a rich goddamn family like the Iversons wanted to play soldiers, they just bought themselves a regiment. Bought the goddamn uniforms and horses and such. Then they got to be officers. Goddamn grown men playin' at toy soldiers, Boy. Only once't the real war begun, *we* was the toy soldiers, Johnny."

I opened my eyes. I could not recall ever having seen so many stars. Above the slope of the meadow, constellations came all the way down to the horizon; others were visible between the dark masses of trees. The Milky Way crossed the sky like a bridge. Or like the pale tracks of an army long since passed by.

"Just goddamned bad luck we got Iverson," said the Captain, "because the brigade was good 'un and the 20th North Carolina was the best goddamn regiment in Ewell's corps." The old man shifted to look at me again. "You wasn't with us yet at Sharpsburg, was you, Johnny?"

I shook my head, feeling a chill go up my back as he again called me by some other boy's name. I wondered where that boy was now.

"No, of course not," said Captain Montgomery. "That was in '62. You was still in school. The regiment was still at Fredericksburg after the campaign. Somebody'd ordered up a dress parade and Nate's band played 'Dixie.' All of the sudden, from acrost the Rappahannock, the Yankee band starts playin' Dixie back at us. Goddamnest thing, Boy. You could hear that music so clear acrost the water it was like two parts of the same band playin'. So our band—all boys from the 20th—they commence to playin' 'Yankee Doodle.' All of us standin' there at parade rest in that cold sunlight, feelin' mighty queer by then, I don't mind tellin' you. Then, when our boys is done with 'Yankee Doodle,' just like they all rehearsed it together, both bands commence playin' 'Home Sweet Home.' Without even thinkin' about it, Perry and ol' Thomas and Jeffrey an' me and the whole line starts singin' along. So did Lieutenant Williams—young Mr. Oliver hisself—and before long the whole brigade's singin'—the damn Yankees too—their voices comin' acrost the Rappahannock and joinin' ours like we'd been one big choir that'd gotten busted up by mistake or accident or somethin'. I tell you, Boy, it was sorta like singin' with ghosts. And sorta like we was ghosts our own selves."

I closed my eyes to hear the deep voices singing that sad, sweet song, and I realized suddenly that even grownups— soldiers even—could feel as lonely and homesick as I had felt earlier that evening. Realizing that, I found that all of my own homesickness had fled. I felt that I was where I should be, part of the Captain's army, part of all armies, camping far from home and uncertain what the next day would bring but content to be with my friends. My comrades. The voices were as real and as sad as the soughing of wind through the mid-summer leaves.

The Captain cleared his throat and spat. "And then that bastard Iverson kilt us," he said. I heard the sound of buckles as the old man unstrapped his false leg.

I opened my eyes as he pulled his blanket over his shoulders and turned his face away. "Get some sleep, Boy," came his muffled voice. "We step off at first light come mornin'."

I pulled my own blanket up to my neck and laid my cheek against the dark soil. I listened for the singing but the voices were gone. I went to sleep to the sound of the wind in the leaves sounding like angry whispers in the night.

≈ ≈ ≈

I awoke once before sunrise when there was just enough false light to allow me to see Captain Montgomery's face a few inches from my own. The old man's hat had slipped off in the night and the top of his head was a relief map of reddened scalp scarred by liver spots, sores, and a few forlorn wisps of white hair. His brow was furrowed as if in fierce concentration, eyebrows two dark eruptions of hair, eyelids lowered but showing a line of white at the bottom. Soft snores whistled out of his broken gourd of a mouth and a thin line of drool moistened his whiskers. His breath was as dry and dead as a draft of air from a cave unsealed after centuries of being forgotten.

I stared at the time-scoured flesh of the old face inches from mine, at the swollen and distorted fingers clutching, childlike, at his blanket, and I realized, with a precise and prescient glimpse at the terrible fate of my own longevity, that age was a curse, a disease, and that all of us unlucky to survive our childhoods were doomed to suffer and perish from it. Perhaps, I thought, it is why young men go willingly to die in wars.

I pulled the blanket across my face.

When I awoke again, just after sunrise, the old man was standing ten paces from the tree and staring toward Gettysburg. Only a white cupola was visible above the trees, its dome and sides painted in gold from the sun. I disentangled myself from the blankets and rose to my feet, marveling at how stiff and clammy and strange I felt. I had never slept out of doors before. Reverend Hodges had promised us a campout but the Troop had been too busy learning close order drill and semaphore. I decided that I might skip the campout part of the agenda. Staggering upright on legs still half asleep, I wondered how Captain Montgomery had strapped on his wooden leg without awakening me.

"Mornin', Boy," he called as I returned from the edge of the woods where I had relieved myself. His gaze never left the cupola visible to the southeast.

We had breakfast while standing there under the tree—more beef jerky and water. I wondered what Billy, the Reverend, and the other Scouts were having down in the tents near the field kitchens. Pancakes, probably. Perhaps with bacon. Certainly with tall glasses of cold milk.

"I was there with Mr. Oliver when muster was called on the mornin' of the first," rasped the old man. "Fourteen hundred and seventy present for duty. One hundred and fourteen was officers. I wasn't among 'em. Still had my sergeant stripes then. Wasn't 'til the second Wilderness that they gave me the bar. Anyway, word had come the night before from A.P. Hill that the Federals was massin' to the south. Probably figurin' to cut us off. Our brigade was the first to turn south to Hill's call.

"We heard firin' as we come down the Heidlersburg Pike, so General Rodes took us through the woods 'til we got to Oak Hill." He turned east, smoothly pivoting on his wooden leg, shielding his eyes from the sun. "Bout there, I reckon, Johnny. Come on." The old man spun around and I rolled the blankets and scurried to follow him back down the hill toward the southeast. Toward the distant cupola.

"We come right down the west side of this ridge then, too, didn't we, Boy? Not so many trees then. Been marchin' since before sunup. Got here sometime after what should've been dinner time. One o'clock, maybe one-thirty. Had hardtack on the hoof. Seems to me that we stopped a while up the hill there so's Rodes could set out some guns. Perry an' me was glad to sit. He wanted to start another letter to our ma, but I told him there wasn't goin' to be time. There wasn't, either, but I wish to hell I'd let him write the damned thing.

"From where we was, you could see the Yanks comin' up the road from Gettysburg and we knew there'd be a fight that day. Goddamn it, boy, you can put them blankets down. We ain't goin' to need 'em today."

Startled, I dropped the blankets in the weeds. We had reached the lower end of the meadow and only a low, split rail fence separated us from what I guessed to be the road we had come up the night before. The Captain swung his pegleg over the fence and after we crossed we both paused a minute. I felt the growing heat of the day as a thickness in the air and a slight pounding in my temples. Suddenly there came the sound of band music and cheering from the south, dwindled by distance.

The Captain removed a stained red kerchief from his pocket and mopped at his neck and forehead. "Goddamn idiots," he said. "Celebratin' like it's a county fair. Damned nonsense."

"Yessir," I said automatically, but at that moment I was thrilled with the idea of the Reunion and with the reality of being with a veteran—*my* veteran—walking on the actual ground he had fought on. I realized that someone seeing us from a distance might have mistaken us for *two* soldiers. At that moment I would have traded my Boy Scout khaki for butternut brown or Confederate gray and would have joined the Captain in any cause. At that moment I would have marched against the Eskimoes if it meant being part of an army, setting off at sunrise with one's comrades, preparing for battle, and generally feeling as *alive* as I felt at that instant.

The Captain had heard my "yessir" but he must have noticed something else in my eyes because he leaned forward, rested his weight on the fence, and brought his face close to mine. "Goddamnit, Johnny, don't you fall for such nonsense twice. You think these dumb sons-of-bitches would've come back all this way if they was honest enough to admit they was celebratin' a slaughterhouse?"

I blinked.

The old man grabbed my tunic with his swollen fist. "That's all it is, Boy, don't you see? A goddamn *abattoir* that was built here to grind up *men* and now they're reminiscin' about it and tellin' funny stories about it and weepin' old man tears about what good times we had when we was fed to it." With his free hand he stabbed a finger in the direction of the cupola. "Can't you see it, Boy? The holdin' pens and the delivery chutes and the killin' rooms—only not everybody was so lucky as to have their skull busted open on the first pop, some of us got part of us fed to the grinder and got to lay around and watch the others swell up and bloat in the heat. Goddamn slaughterhouse, Boy, where they kill you and gut you down the middle...dump your insides out on the goddamn floor and kick 'em aside to get at the next fool...hack the meat off your bones, grind up the bones for fertilizer, then grind up everythin' else you got that ain't prime meat and wrap it in your own guts to sell it to the goddamn public as sausage. Parades. War stories. Reunions. *Sausage*, Boy." Panting slightly, he released me, spat, wiped his whiskers and stared a long minute at the sky. "And we was led into that slaughterhouse by a Judas goat named Iverson, Johnny," he said at last, his voice empty of all emotion. "Never forget that."

༄ ༄ ༄

The hill continued to slope gently downward as we crossed the empty road and entered a field just to the east of an abandoned farmhouse. Fire had gutted the upper stories years ago and the windows on the first floor were boarded up, but irises still grew tall around the foundation and along the overgrown lane leading to sagging outbuildings. "John Forney's old place," said Captain Montgomery. "He was still here when I come back in '98. Told me then that none of his farmhands'd stay around here after night begun to settle. Because of the Pits."

"Because of what, sir?" I was blinking in the early heat and glare of a day in which the temperatures certainly would reach the mid-nineties. Grasshoppers hopped mindlessly in the dusty grass.

The old man did not seem to hear my question. The cupola was no longer visible because we were too close to the trees, but the Captain's attention was centered on the field which ran downhill less than a quarter of a mile to a thicker line of trees to the southeast. He withdrew the pistol from his coat and my heart pounded as he drew back the hammer until it clicked. "This is a double-action, Boy," he said. "Don't forget that."

We forced our way through a short hedge and began crossing the field at a slow walk. The old man's wooden leg made soft sounds in the soil. Grass and thistles brushed at our legs. "That son-of-a-bitch Iverson never got this far," said the Captain. "Ollie Williams said he heard him give the order up the hill there near where Rodes put his guns out. 'Give 'em hell,' Iverson says, then goes back up to his tree there to sit in the shade an' eat his lunch. Had him some wine too. Had wine every meal when the rest of us was drinkin' water out of the ditch. Nope, Iverson never come down here 'til it was all over and then it was just to say we'd tried to surrender and order a bunch of dead men to stand up and salute the general. Come on, Boy."

We moved slowly across the field. I could make out a stone fence near the treeline now, half-hidden in the dapple of leaf shadow. There seemed to be a jumble of tall grass or vines just this side of the wall.

"They put Daniels' brigade on our right." The Captain's pistol gestured toward the south, the barrel just missing the brim of my hat. "But they didn't come down till we was shot all to pieces. Then Daniels' boys run right into the fire of Stone's 149th Pennsylvania...them damn sharpshooters what were called the Bogus Bucktails for some damn reason I don't recall now. But we was all alone when we come down this way before Daniels and Ramseur and O'Neal and the

61

rest come along. Iverson sent us off too soon. Ramseur wasn't ready for another half hour and O'Neal's brigade turned back even before they got to the Mummasburg Road back there."

We were halfway across the field by then. A thin screen of trees to our left blocked most of the road from sight. The stone wall was less than three hundred yards ahead. I glanced nervously at the cocked pistol. The Captain seemed to have forgotten he was carrying it.

"We come down like this at an angle," he said. "Brigade stretched about halfway acrost the field, sorta slantin' northeast to southwest. The 5th North Carolina was on our left. The 20th was right about here, couple of hundred of us in the first line, and the 23rd and 12th was off to our right there and sorta trailin' back, the right flank of the 12th about halfway to that damned railroad cut down there."

I looked toward the south but could see no railroad tracks. There was only the hot, wide expanse of field which may have once borne crops but which had now gone back to brambles and sawgrass.

The Captain stopped, panting slightly, and rested his weight on his good leg. "What we didn't know, Johnny, was that the Yanks was all set behind that wall there. Thousands of them. Not showin' a goddamn cap or battle flag or rifle barrel. Just hunkerin' down there and waitin'. Waitin' for the animals to come in the door so the slaughter could begin. And Colonel Iverson never even ordered skirmishers out in front of us. I never even *seen* an advance without skirmishers, and there we was walkin' across this field while Iverson sat up on Oak Hill eatin' lunch and havin' another glass of wine."

The Captain raised his pistol and pointed at the treeline. I stepped back, expecting him to fire, but the only noise was the rasp of his voice. "Remember? We got to that point...'bout there where them damn vines is growing...and the Yanks rise up along that whole quarter mile of wall there and fire right into us. Like they're comin' up out of the ground. No noise at all except the swish of our feet 'n legs in the wheat and grass and then they let loose a volley like to sound like the end of the world. Whole goddamn world disappears in smoke and fire. Even a Yank couldn't miss at that range. More of 'em come out of the trees back up there..." The Captain gestured toward our left where the wall angled northwest to meet the road. "That puts us in an enfilade fire that just sweeps through the 5th North Carolina. Like a scythe, boy. There was wheat in these fields then. But it was just stubble. No place to go. No place to hide. We could've run back the way we come but us North Carolina boys wasn't goin' to start learnin' ourselves how to run this late in the day. So the scythe just come sweepin' into us. Couldn't move forward. That goddamn wall was just a wall of smoke with fire comin' through it there fifty yards away. I seen Lieutenant Colonel Davis of the 5th—Old Bill his boys called him—get his regiment down into that low area there to the south. See about where that line of scrub brush is? Not nearly so big as a ditch, but it give 'em some cover, not much. But us in the 20th and Cap'n Turner's boys in the 23rd didn't have no choice but to lie down here in the open and take it."

The old man advanced slowly for a dozen yards and stopped where the grass grew thicker and greener, joining with tangles of what I realized were grapevines to create a low, green thicket between us and the wall. Suddenly he sat down heavily, thrusting his wooden leg out in front of him and cradling the pistol in his lap. I dropped to my knees in the grass near him, removed my hat, and unbuttoned my tunic. The yellow tag hung loosely from my breast pocket button. It was very hot.

"The Yanks kept pourin' the fire into us," he said. His voice was a hoarse whisper. Sweat ran down his cheeks and neck. "More Federals come out of the woods down there...by the railroad gradin'...and started enfiladin' Old Bill's boys and our right flank. We couldn't fire back worth horseshit. Lift your head outta the dirt to aim and you caught a Minié ball in the brain. My brother Perry was layin' next to me and I heard the ball that took him in the left eye. Made a sound like someone hammerin' a side of beef with a four-pound hammer. He sort of rose up and flopped back next to me. I was yellin' and cryin', my face all covered with snot and dirt and tears, when all of a sudden I feel Perry tryin' to rise up again. Sort of jerkin', like somebody was pullin' him up with strings. Then again. And again. I'd got a glimpse of the hole in his face where his eye'd been and his brains and bits of the back of his head was still smeared on my right leg, but I could *feel* him jerkin' and pullin', like he was tuggin' at me to go with him somewhere. Later, I seen why. More bullets had been hittin' him in the head and each time it'd snap him back some. When we come back to bury him later, his head looked like a mushmelon someone'd kicked apart. It wasn't unusual, neither. Lot of the boys layin' on the field that day got just torn apart by that Yankee fire. Like a scythe, Boy. Or a meatgrinder."

I sat back in the grass and breathed through my mouth. The vines and black soil gave off a thick, sweet smell that made me feel lightheaded and a little ill. The heat pressed down like thick, wet blankets.

"Some of the boys stood up to run then," said Captain Montgomery, his voice still a hoarse monotone, his eyes focused on nothing. He was holding the cocked pistol in both hands with the barrel pointed in my direction, but I was sure that he had forgotten I was there. "Everybody who stood up got hit. The sound was...you could hear the balls hittin' home even over the firin'. The wind was blowin' the smoke back into the woods so there wasn't even any cover you usually got once't the smoke got heavy. I seen Lieutenant Ollie Williams stand up to yell at the boys of the 20th to stay low and he was hit twice while I watched.

"The rest of us was tryin' to form a firin' line in the grass and wheat, but we hadn't got off a full volley before the Yanks come runnin' out, some still firin', some usin' their bayonets. And that's when I seen you and the other two little drummers get kilt, Johnny. When they used them bayonets..." The old man paused and looked at me for the first time in several minutes. A cloud of confusion seemed to pass over him. He slowly lowered the pistol, gently released the cocked hammer, and raised a shaking hand to his brow.

Still feeling dizzy and a little sick myself, I asked, "Is that when you lost your...uh...when you hurt your leg, sir?"

The Captain removed his hat. His few white hairs were stringy with sweat. "What? My leg?" He stared at the wooden peg below his knee as if he had never noticed it before. "My leg. No, Boy, that was later. The Battle of the Crater. The Yankees tunneled under us and blowed us up while we was sleepin'. When I didn't die right away, they shipped me home to Raleigh and made me an honorary Cap'n three days before the war ended. No, that day...*here*...I got hit at least three times but nothin' serious. A ball took the heel of my right boot off. Another'n knocked my rifle stock all to hell and gave me some splinters in my cheek. A third'n took off a chunk of my left ear, but hell, I could still hear all right. It wasn't 'til I sat down to try to go to sleep that night that I come to find out that another ball'd hit me in the back of the leg, right below the ass, but it'd been goin' so slow it just give me a big bruise there."

We sat there for several minutes in silence. I could hear insects rustling in the grass. Finally the Captain said, "And that son-of-a-bitch Iverson never even come down here until Ramseur's boys finally got around to clearin' the Yankees out. That was later. I was layin' right around here somewhere, squeezed in between Perry and Nate's corpses, covered with so much of their blood an' brains that the goddamn Yanks just stepped over all three of us when they ran out to stick bayonets in our people or drive 'em back to their line as prisoners. I opened my eyes long enough to see ol' Cade Tarleton bein' clubbed along by a bunch of laughin' Yankees. They had our regimental flag, too, goddamnit. There was no one left alive around it to put up a fight.

"Ramseur, him who the Richmond papers was always callin' the Chevalier Bayard, whatever the hell that meant, was comin' down the hill into the same ambush when Lieutenant Crowder and Lieutenant Dugger run up and warned him. Ramseur was an officer but he wasn't nobody's fool. He crossed the road further east and turned the Yankees' right flank, just swept down the backside of that wall, drivin' 'em back towards the seminary.

"Meanwhile, while the few of us who'd stayed alive was busy crawlin' back toward Forney's house or layin' there bleedin' from our wounds, that son-of-a-bitch Iverson was tellin' General Rodes that he'd seen our regiment put up a white flag and go over to the Yanks. Goddamn lie, Boy. Them who got captured was mostly wounded who got drove off at the point of a bayonet. There wasn't any white flags to be seen that day. Leastways not here. Just bits of white skull and other stuff layin' around.

"Later, while I was still on the field lookin' for a rifle that'd work, Rodes brings Iverson down here to show him where the men had surrendered, and while their horses is pickin' their way over the corpses that used to be the 20th

North Carolina, that bastard Iverson..." Here the old man's voice broke. He paused a long minute, hawked, spat, and continued. "That *bastard* Iverson sees our rows of dead up here, seven hundred men from the finest brigade the South ever fielded, layin' shot dead in lines as straight as a dress parade, and Iverson thinks they're still duckin' from fire even though Ramseur had driven the Yanks off, and he stands up in his stirrups, his goddamn sorrel horse almost steppin' on Perry, and he screams, 'Stand up and salute when the general passes, you men! Stand up this instant!' It was Rodes who realized that they was lookin' at dead men."

Captain Montgomery was panting, barely able to get the words out between wracking gasps for breath. I was having trouble breathing myself. The sickeningly sweet stench from the weeds and vines and dark soil seemed to use up all of the air. I found myself staring at a cluster of grapes on a nearby vine; the swollen fruit looked like bruised flesh streaked with ruptured veins.

"If I'd had my rifle," said the Captain, "I would have shot the bastard right then." He let out a ragged breath. "Him and Rodes went back up the hill together and I never seen Iverson again. Captain Halsey took command of what was left of the regiment. When the brigade reassembled the next mornin', three hundred and sixty-two men stood muster where fourteen hundred and seventy had answered the call the day before. They called Iverson back to Georgia and put him in charge of a home guard unit or somethin'. Word was, President Davis saved him from bein' court-martialed or reprimanded. It was clear none of us would've served under the miserable son-of-a-bitch again. You know how the last page of our 20th North Carolina regimental record reads, Boy?"

"No, sir," I said softly.

The old man closed his eyes. "Initiated at Seven Pines, sacrificed at Gettysburg, and surrendered at Appomattox. Help me get to my feet, boy. We got to find a place to hide."

"To hide, sir?"

"Goddamn right," said the Captain as I acted as a crutch for him. "We've got to be ready when Iverson comes here today." He raised the heavy pistol as if it explained everything. "We've got to be ready when he comes."

ᨈ ᨈ ᨈ

It was mid-morning before we found an adequate place to hide. I trailed along behind the limping old man and while part of my mind was desperate with panic to find a way out of such an insane situation, another part—a larger part—had no trouble accepting the logic of everything. Colonel Alfred Iverson, Jr., would have to return to his field of dishonor this day and we had to hide in order to kill him.

"See where the ground's lower here, Boy? Right about where these damn vines is growin'?"

"Yessir."

"Them's Iverson's Pits. That's what the locals call 'em according to John Forney when I come to visit in '98. You know what they are?"

"No, sir," I lied. Part of me knew very well what they were.

"Night after the battle...battle, hell, *slaughter*...the few of us left from the regiment and some of Lee's pioneers come up and dug big shallow pits and just rolled our boys in where they lay. Laid 'em in together, still in their battle lines. Nate 'n Perry's shoulders was touchin'. Right where I'd been layin'. You can see where the Pits start here. The ground's lower an' the grass is higher, ain't it?"

"Yessir."

"Forney said the grass was always higher here, crops too, when they growed them. Forney didn't farm this field much. Said the hands didn't like to work here. He told his niggers that there weren't nothing to worry about, that the U.C.V.'d come up and dug up everythin' after the war to take our boys back to Richmond, but that ain't really true."

"Why not, sir?" We were wading slowly through the tangle of undergrowth. Vines wrapped around my ankle and I had to tug to free myself.

"They didn't do much diggin' here," said the Captain. "Bones was so thick and scattered that they jes' took a few of 'em and called it quits. Didn't like diggin' here any more than Forney's niggers liked workin' here. Even in the daytime. Place that's got this much shame and anger in it...well, people *feel* it, don't they, Boy?"

"Yessir," I said automatically, although all I felt at that moment was sick and sleepy.

The Captain stopped. "Goddamnit, that house wasn't here before."

67

Through a break in the stone wall I could see a small house—more of a large shack, actually—made of wood so dark as to be almost black and set back in the shade of the trees. No driveway or wagon lane led to it, but I could see a faint trampling in Forney's field and the forest grass where horses might have passed through the break in the wall to gain access. The old man seemed deeply offended that someone had built a home so close to the field where his beloved 20th North Carolina had fallen. But the house was dark and silent and we moved away from that section of the wall.

The closer we came to the stone fence, the harder it was to walk. The grass grew twice as high as in the fields beyond and the wild grapevines marked a tangled area about the size of the football field where our Troop practiced its close order drill.

In addition to the tangled grass and thick vines there to hamper our progress, there were the holes. Dozens of them, scores of them, pockmarking the field and lying in wait under the matted foliage.

"Goddamn gophers," said Captain Montgomery, but the holes were twice as wide across the opening as any burrow I had seen made by mole or gopher or ground squirrel. There were no heaps of dirt at the opening. Twice the old man stepped into them, the second time ramming his wooden leg in so deeply that we both had to work to dislodge it. Tugging hard at his wool-covered leg, I suddenly had the nightmarish sense that someone or something was pulling at the other end, refusing to let go, trying to suck the old man underground.

The incident must have disconcerted Captain Montgomery as well, because as soon as his leg popped free of the hole he staggered back a few steps and sat down heavily with his back against the stone wall. "This is good enough, Boy," he panted. "We'll wait here."

It was a good place for an ambush. The vines and grass grew waist high there, allowing us glimpses of the field beyond but concealing us as effectively as a duck blind. The wall sheltered our backs.

Captain Montgomery removed his topcoat and canvas bag and commenced to unload, clean, and reload his pistol. I lay on the grass nearby, at first thinking about what was going on back at the Reunion, then wondering about how to get the Captain back there, then wondering what Iverson had looked like, then thinking about home, and finally thinking about nothing at all as I moved in and out of a strange, dream-filled doze.

Not three feet from where I lay was another of the ubiquitous holes, and as I fell into a light slumber I remained faintly aware of the odor rising from that opening: the same sickening sweetness I had smelled earlier, but thicker now, heavier, almost erotic with its undertones of corruption and decay, of dead sea creatures drying in the sun. Many years later, visiting an abandoned meat processing plant in Chicago with a real estate agent acquaintance, I was to encounter a similar smell; it was the stench of a charnel house, disused for years but permeated with the memory of blood.

The day passed in a haze of heat, thick air, and insect noises. I dozed and awoke to watch with the Captain, dozed again. Once I seem to remember eating hard biscuits from his bag and washing them down with the last water from his wineskin, but even that fades into my dreams of that afternoon, for I remember others seated around us, chewing on similar fare and talking in low tones so that the words were indistinguishable but the southern dialect came through clearly. It did not sound strange to me. Once I remember awakening, even though I was sitting up and staring and had thought I was already awake, as the sound of an automobile along the Mummasburg Road shocked me into full consciousness. But the trees at the edge of the field shielded any traffic from view, the sounds faded, and I returned to the drugged doze I had known before.

Sometime late that afternoon I dreamed the one dream I remember clearly.

I was lying in the field, hurt and helpless, the left side of my face in the dirt and my right eye staring unblinkingly at a blue summer sky. An ant walked across my cheek, then another, until a stream of them crossed my cheek and eye, others moving into my nostrils and open mouth. I could not move. I did not blink. I felt them in my mouth, between my teeth, removing bits of morning bacon from between two molars, moving across the soft flesh of my palate, exploring

69

the dark tunnel of my throat. The sensations were not unpleasant.

I was vaguely aware of other things going deeper, of slow movement in the swelling folds of my guts and belly. Small things laid their eggs in the drying corners of my eye.

I could see clearly as a raven circled overhead, spiralling lower, landed nearby, paced to and fro in a wing-folding strut, and hopped closer. It took my eye with a single stab of a beak made huge by proximity. In the darkness which followed I could still sense the light as my body expanded in the heat, a hatchery to thousands now, the loose cloth of my shirt pulled tight as my flesh expanded. I sensed my own internal bacteria, deprived of other foods, digesting my body's decaying fats and rancid pools of blood in a vain effort to survive a few more hours.

I felt my lips wither and dry in the heat, pulling back from my teeth, felt my jaws open wider and wider in a mirthless, silent laugh as ligaments decayed or were chewed away by small predators. I felt lighter as the eggs hatched, the maggots began their frenzied cleansing, my body turning toward the dark soil as the process accelerated. My mouth opened wide to swallow the waiting Earth. I tasted the dark communion of dirt. Stalks of grass grew where my tongue had been. A flower found rich soil in the humid sepulcher of my skull and sent its shoot curling upward through the gap which had once held my eye.

Settling, relaxing, returning to the acid-taste of the blackness around me, I sensed the others there. Random, shifting currents of soil sent decaying bits of wool or flesh or bone in touch with bits of them, fragments intermingling with the timid eagerness of a lover's first touch. When all else was lost, mingling with the darkness and anger, my bones remained, brittle bits of memory, forgotten, sharp-edged fragments of pain resisting the inevitable relaxation into painlessness, into nothingness.

And deep in that rotting marrow, lost in the loam-black acid of forgetfulness, I remembered. And waited.

ও⹁ ও⹁ ও⹁

"Wake up, Boy! It's him. It's Iverson!"

The urgent whisper shocked me up out of sleep. I looked around groggily, still tasting the dirt from where I had lain with my lips against the ground.

"Goddamnit, I *knew* he'd come!" whispered the Captain, pointing to our left where a man in a dark coat had come out of the woods through the gap in the stone wall.

I shook my head. My dream would not release me and I knuckled my eyes, trying to shake the dimness from them. Then I realized that the dimness was real. The daylight had faded into evening while I slept. I wondered where in God's name the day had gone. The man in the black coat moved through a twilight grayness which seemed to echo the eerie blindness of my dreams. I could make out the man's white shirt and pale face glowing slightly in the gloom as he turned our direction and came closer, clearing a path for himself with short, sharp chops with a cane or walking stick.

"By God, it *is* him," hissed the Captain and raised his pistol with shaking hands. He thumbed the hammer back as I watched in horror.

The man was closer now, no more than twenty-five feet away, and I could see the dark mustaches, black hair, and deepset eyes. It did indeed look like the man whose visage I had glimpsed by starlight in the old tintype.

Captain Montgomery steadied his pistol on his left arm and squinted over the sights. I could hear hisses of breath from the man in the dark suit as he walked closer, whistling an almost inaudible tune. The Captain squeezed the trigger.

"No!" I cried and grabbed the revolver, jerking it down, the hammer falling cruelly on the web of flesh between my thumb and forefinger. It did not fire.

The Captain shoved me away with a violent blow of his left forearm and struggled to raise the weapon again even as I clung to his wrist. "No!" I shouted again. "He's too young! *Look*. He's too young!"

The old man paused then, his arms still straining, but squinting now at the stranger who stood less than a dozen feet away.

It was true. The man was far too young to be Colonel Iverson. The pale, surprised face belonged to a man in his early thirties at most. Captain Montgomery lowered the pistol and raised trembling fingers to his temples. "My God," he whispered. "My God."

"Who's there?" The man's voice was sharp and assured, despite his surprise. "Show yourself."

I helped the Captain up, sure that the mustached stranger had sensed our movement behind the tall grass and vines but had not witnessed our struggles nor seen the gun. The Captain squinted at the younger man even as he straightened his hat and dropped the pistol in the deep pocket of his coat. I could feel the old man trembling as I steadied him upright.

"Oh, a veteran!" called the man and stepped forward with his hand extended, batting away the grasping vines with easy flicks of his walking stick.

&▲ &▲ &▲

We walked the perimeter of the Pits in the fading light, our new guide moving slowly to accommodate the Captain's painful hobble. The man's walking stick served as a pointer while he spoke. "This was the site of a skirmish before the major battles began," he said. "Not many visitors come out here...most of the attention is given to more famous areas south and west of here...but those of us who live or spend summers around here are aware of some of these lesser-known spots. It's quite interesting how the field is sunken here, isn't it?"

"Yes," whispered the Captain. He watched the ground, never raising his eyes to the young man's face.

The man had introduced himself as Jessup Sheads and said that he lived in the small house we had noticed set back in the trees. The Captain had been lost in his confused reverie so I had introduced both of us to Mr. Sheads. Neither man paid notice of my name. The Captain now glanced up at Sheads as if he still could not believe that this was not the man whose name had tormented him for half a century.

Sheads cleared his throat and pointed again at the tangle of thick growth. "As a matter of fact, this area right along here was the site of a minor skirmish before the serious fighting began. The forces of the Confederacy advanced along a broad line here, were slowed briefly by Federal resistance at this wall, but quickly gained the advantage. It was a small Southern victory before the bitter stalemates of the next few days." Sheads paused and smiled at the Captain.

"But perhaps you know all this, sir. What unit did you say you have had the honor of serving with?"

The old man's mouth moved feebly before the words could come. "20th North Carolina," he managed at last.

"Of course!" cried Sheads and clapped the Captain on the shoulder. "Part of the glorious brigade whose victory this site commemorates. I would be honored, sir, if you and your young friend would join me in my home to toast the 20th North Carolina regiment before you return to the Reunion camp. Would this be possible, sir?"

I tugged at the Captain's coat, suddenly desperate to be away from there, lightheaded from hunger and a sudden surge of unreasoning fear, but the old man straightened his back, found his voice, and said clearly, "The boy and me would be honored, sir."

ža ža ža

The cottage had been built of tar-black wood. An expensive-looking black horse, still saddled, was tied to the railing of the small porch on the east side of the house. Behind the house, a thicket of trees and a tumble of boulders made access from that direction seem extremely difficult if not impossible.

The house was small inside and showed few signs of being lived in. A tiny entrance foyer led to a parlor where sheets covered two or three pieces of furniture or to the dining room where Sheads led us, a narrow room with a single window, a tall hoosier cluttered with bottles, cans, and a few dirty plates, and a narrow plank table on which burned an old-style kerosene lamp. Behind dusty curtains there was a second, smaller room, in which I caught a glimpse of a mattress on the floor and stacks of books. A steep staircase on the south side of the dining room led up through a hole in the ceiling to what must have been a small attic room, although all I could see when I glanced upward was a square of blackness.

Jessup Sheads propped his heavy walking stick against the table and busied himself at the hoosier, returning with a decanter and three crystal glasses. The lamp hissed and tossed our shadows high on the roughly plastered wall. I glanced toward the window but the twilight had given way to true night and only darkness pressed against the panes.

"Shall we include the boy in our toast?" asked Sheads, pausing, the decanter hovering above the third wineglass. I had never been allowed to taste wine or any other spirits.

"Yes," said the Captain, staring fixedly at Sheads. The lamplight shone upward into the Captain's face, emphasizing his sharp cheekbones and turning his bushy, old-man's eyebrows into two great wings of hair above his falcon's beak of a nose. His shadow on the wall was a silhouette from another era.

Sheads finished pouring and we raised our glasses. I stared dubiously at the wine; the red fluid was dull and thick, streaked through with tendrils of black which may or may not have been a trick of the flickering lamp.

"To the 20th North Carolina Regiment," said Sheads and raised his glass. The gesture reminded me of Reverend Hodges lifting the communion cup. The Captain and I raised our glasses and drank.

The taste was a mixture of fruit and copper. It reminded me of the day, months earlier, when a friend of Billy Stargill had split my lip during a schoolyard fight. The inside of my lip had bled for hours. The taste was not dissimilar.

Captain Montgomery lowered his glass and scowled at it. Droplets of wine clotted his white whiskers.

"The wine is a local variety," said Sheads with a cold smile which showed red-stained teeth. "Very local. The arbors are those which we just visited."

I stared at the thickening liquid in my glass. Wine made from grapes grown from the rich soil of Iverson's Pits.

Sheads' loud voice startled me. "Another toast!" He raised his glass. "To the honorable and valiant gentleman who led the 20th North Carolina into battle. To Colonel Alfred Iverson."

Sheads raised the glass to his lips. I stood frozen and staring. Captain Montgomery slammed his glass on the table. The old man's face had gone as blood red as the spilled wine. "I'll be goddamned to hell if I..." he spluttered. "I'll...*never!*"

The man who had introduced himself as Jessup Sheads drained the last of his wine and smiled. His skin was as white as his shirt front, his hair and long mustaches as black as his coat. "Very well," he said and then raised his voice. "Uncle Alfred?"

Even as Sheads had been drinking, part of my mind had registered the soft sound of footsteps on the stairs behind us. I turned only my head, my hand still frozen with the glass of wine half-raised.

The small figure standing on the lowest step was a man in his mid-eighties, at least, but rather than wearing the wrinkles of age like Captain Montgomery, this old man's skin had become smoother and pinker, almost translucent. I was reminded of a nest of newborn rats I had come across in a neighbor's barn the previous spring—a mass of pale-pink, writhing flesh which I had made the mistake of touching. I did not want to touch Iverson.

The Colonel wore a white beard very much like the one I had seen in portraits of Robert E. Lee, but there was no real resemblance. Where Lee's eyes had been sad and shielded under a brow weighted with sorrow, Iverson glared at us with wide, staring eyes shot through with yellow flecks. He was almost bald and the taut, pink scalp reinforced the effect of something almost infantile about the little man.

Captain Montgomery stared, his mouth open, his breath rasping out in short, labored gasps. He clutched at his own collar as if unable to pull in enough air.

Iverson's voice was soft, almost feminine, and edged with the whine of a petulant child. "You all come back sooner or later," he said with a hint of a slight lisp. He sighed deeply. "Is there no end to it?"

"You..." managed the Captain. He lifted a long finger to point at Iverson.

"Spare me your outrage," snapped Iverson. "Do you think you are the first to seek me out, the first to try to explain away your own cowardice by slandering me? Samuel and I have grown quite adept at handling trash like you. I only hope that you are the last."

The Captain's hand dropped, disappeared in the folds of his coat. "You goddamned, sonofabitching..."

"Silence!" commanded Iverson. The Colonel's wide-eyed gaze darted around the room, passing over me as if I weren't there. The muscles at the corners of the man's mouth twitched and twisted. Again I was reminded of the nest of newborn rats. "Samuel," he shouted, "bring your stick. Show this man the penalty for insolence." Iverson's mad stare returned to Captain Montgomery. "You will salute me before we are finished here."

"I will see you in hell first," said the Captain and pulled the revolver from his coat pocket.

Iverson's nephew moved very fast, lifting the heavy walking stick and slamming it down on the Captain's wrist before the old man could pull back the hammer. I stood frozen, my wineglass still in my hand, as the pistol thudded to the floor. Captain Montgomery bent and reached for it—awkward and slow with his false leg—but Iverson's nephew grabbed him by the collar and flung him backward as effortlessly as an adult would handle a child. The Captain struck the wall, gasped, and slid down it, his false leg gouging splinters from the uneven floorboards as his legs straightened. His face was as gray as his uniform coat.

Iverson's nephew crouched to recover the pistol and set it on the table. Colonel Iverson himself smiled and nodded, his mouth still quivering toward a grin. I had eyes only for the Captain.

The old man lay huddled against the wall, clutching at his own throat, his body arching with spasms as he gasped in one great breath after another, each louder and more ragged than the last. It was obvious that no air was reaching his lungs; his color had gone from red to gray to a terrible dark purple bordering on black. His tongue protruded and saliva flecked his whiskers. The Captain's eyes grew wider and rounder as he realized what was happening to him, but his horrified gaze never left Iverson's face.

I could see the immeasurable frustration in the Captain's eyes as his body betrayed him in these last few seconds of a confrontation he had waited for through half a century of single-minded obsession. The old man drew in two more ragged, wracking breaths and then quit breathing. His chin collapsed onto his sunken chest, the gnarled hands relaxed into loose fists, and his eyes lost their fixed focus on Iverson's face.

As if suddenly released from my own paralysis, I let out a cry, dropped the wineglass to the floor, and ran to crouch next to Captain Montgomery. No breath came from his grotesquely opened mouth. The staring eyes already were beginning to glaze with an invisible film. I touched the gnarled old hands—the flesh already seeming to cool and stiffen in death—and felt a terrible constriction in my own chest. It was not grief. Not exactly. I had known the old man too briefly and in too strange a context to feel deep sorrow so soon. But I found it hard to draw a breath as a great emptiness opened in me, a knowledge that sometimes there is no justice, that life was not fair. *It wasn't fair.* I gripped the old man's dead hands and found myself weeping for myself as much as for him.

"Get out of the way." Iverson's nephew thrust me aside and crouched next to the Captain. He shook the old man by his shirt-front, roughly pinched the bruise-colored cheeks, and laid an ear to the veteran's chest.

"Is he dead, Samuel?" asked Iverson. There was no real interest in his voice.

"Yes, Uncle." The nephew stood and nervously tugged at his mustache.

"Yes, yes," said Iverson in his distracted, petulant voice. "It does not matter." He flicked his small, pink hand in a dismissive gesture. "Take him out to be with the others, Samuel."

Iverson's nephew hesitated and then went into the back room to emerge a moment later with a pickaxe, a long-handled shovel, and a lantern. He jerked me to my feet and thrust the shovel and lantern into my hands.

"What about the boy, Uncle?"

Iverson's yellow gaze seemed absorbed with the shadows near the foot of the stairs. He wrung his soft hands. "Whatever you decide, Samuel," he whined. "Whatever you decide."

The nephew lighted the lantern I was holding, grasped the Captain under one arm, and dragged his body toward the door. I noticed that some of the straps holding the old man's leg had come loose; I could not look away from where the wooden peg dangled loosely from the stump of dead flesh and bone.

The nephew dragged the old man's body through the foyer, out the door, and into the night. I stood there—a statue with shovel and hissing lantern—praying that I would be forgotten. Cool, thin fingers fell on the nape of my neck. A soft, insistent voice whispered, "Come along, young man. Do not keep Samuel and me waiting."

≈ ≈ ≈

Iverson's nephew dug the grave not ten yards from where the Captain and I had lain in hiding all day. Even if it had been daylight, the trees along the road and the grape arbors would have shielded us from view of anyone passing along the Mummasburg Road. No one passed. The night was brutally dark; low clouds occluded the stars and the only illumination was from my lantern and the faintest hint of light from Iverson's cabin a hundred yards behind us.

The black horse tied to the porch railing watched our strange procession leave the house. Captain Montgomery's hat had fallen off near the front step and I awkwardly bent to pick it up. Iverson's soft fingers never left my neck.

The soil in the field was loose and moist and easily excavated. Iverson's nephew was down three feet before twenty minutes had passed. Bits of root, rock, and other things glowed whitely in the heap of dirt illuminated by the lantern's glare.

"That is enough," ordered Iverson. "Get it over with, Samuel."

The nephew paused and looked up at the Colonel. The cold light turned the young man's face into a white mask, glistening with sweat, the whiskers and eyebrows broad strokes of charcoal, as black as the smudge of dirt on his left cheek. After a second to catch his breath, he nodded, set down his shovel, and reached out to roll Captain Montgomery's body into the grave. The old man landed on his back, eyes and mouth still open. His wooden leg had been dragging loosely and now remained behind on the brink of the hole. Iverson's nephew looked at me with hooded eyes, reached for the leg, and tossed it onto the Captain's chest. Without looking down, the nephew retrieved the shovel and quickly began scooping dirt onto the body. I watched. I watched the black soil land on my old veteran's cheek and forehead. I watched the dirt cover the staring eyes, first the left and then the right. I watched the open mouth fill with dirt and I felt the constriction in my own throat swell and break loose. Huge, silent sobs shook me.

In less than a minute, the Captain was gone, nothing more than an outline on the floor of the shallow grave.

"Samuel," lisped Iverson.

The nephew paused in his labors and looked at the Colonel.

"What is your advice about…the other thing?" Iverson's voice was so soft that it was almost lost beneath the hissing of the lantern and the pounding of pulse in my ears.

The nephew wiped his cheek with the back of his hand, broadening the dark smear there, and nodded slowly. "I think we have to, Uncle. We just cannot afford to…we cannot risk it. Not after the Florida thing…"

Iverson sighed. "Very well. Do what you must. I will abide by your decision."

The nephew nodded again, let out a breath, and reached for the pickaxe where it lay embedded in the heap of freshly excavated earth. Some part of my mind screamed at me to run, but I was capable only of standing there at the edge of that terrible pit, holding the lantern and breathing in the smell of Samuel's sweat and a deeper, more pervasive stench that seemed to rise out of the pit, the heap of dirt, the surrounding arbors.

"Put the light down, young man," Iverson whispered, inches from my ear. "Put it down carefully." His cool fingers closed more tightly on my neck. I set the lantern down, positioning it with care so that it would not tip over. Iverson's cold grip moved me forward to the very brink of the pit. His nephew stood waist-high in the hole, holding the pickaxe and fixing his dark gaze on me with a look conveying something between regret and anticipation. He shifted the pick handle in his large, white hands. I was about to say "It's all right" when his determined stare changed to wide-eyed surprise.

Samuel's body lurched, steadied, and then lurched again. It was as if he had been standing on a platform which had dropped a foot, then eighteen inches. Where the edges of the grave had come just to his waist, they now rose to his armpits.

Iverson's nephew threw aside the pickaxe and thrust his arms out onto solid ground. But the ground was no longer solid. Colonel Iverson and I stumbled backwards as the earth seemed to vibrate and then flow like a mudslide. The nephew's left hand seized my ankle, his right hand sought a firm grip on thick vines. Iverson's hand remained firm on my neck, choking me.

Suddenly there came the sound of collapsing, sliding dirt, as if the floor of the grave had given way, collapsing through the ceiling of some forgotten mine or cavern, and the nephew threw himself forward, half out of the grave, his chest pressed against the slippery edges of the pit, his fingers releasing my ankle to claw at loam and vines. He reminded me of a mountain climber on a rocky overhang, using only his fingers and the friction of his upper body to defy the pull of gravity.

"Help me." His voice was a whisper, contorted by effort and disbelief.

Colonel Iverson backed away another five steps and I was pulled along.

Samuel was winning the struggle with the collapsing grave. His left hand found the pickaxe where he had buried it in the mound of dirt and he used the handle for leverage, pulling himself upward until his right knee found purchase on the edge of the pit.

The edge collapsed.

Dirt from the three-foot-high mound flowed past the handle of the pick, over the nephew's straining arm and shoulder, back into the pit. The earth had been moist but solid where Samuel excavated it; now it flowed like frictionless mud, like water...like black wine.

Samuel slid back into the pit, now filled with viscous dirt, with only his face and upraised fingers rising out of the pool of black, shifting soil.

Suddenly there came a sound from all around us as if many large forms had shifted position under blankets of grass and vines. Leaves stirred. Vines snapped. There was no breeze.

Iverson's nephew opened his mouth to scream and a wave of blackness flowed in between his teeth. His eyes were not human. Without warning, the ground shifted again and the nephew was pulled violently out of sight. He disappeared as quickly and totally as a swimmer pulled down by a shark three times his size.

There came the sound of teeth.

Colonel Iverson whimpered then, making the sound of a small child being made to go to his room without a light. His grip loosened on my neck.

Samuel's face appeared one last time, protruding eyes filmed with dirt. Something had taken most of the flesh from his right cheek. I realized that the sound I now heard was a man trying to scream with his larynx and esophagus half-filled with dirt.

He was pulled under again. Colonel Iverson took another three steps back and released my neck. I grabbed up the lantern and ran.

≈ ≈ ≈

I heard a shout behind me and I looked over my shoulder just long enough to see Colonel Iverson coming through the break in the fence. He was out of the field, staggering, wheezing, but still coming on.

I ran with the speed of a terrified ten-year-old, the lantern swinging wildly from my right hand, throwing shifting patterns of light on leaves, branches, rocks. I had to have the light with me. There was a single thought in my mind: the Captain's pistol lying where Samuel had laid it on the table.

The saddled horse was pulling at its tether when I reached the house; its eyes were wild, alarmed at me, the swinging lantern, Iverson shouting far behind me, or the sudden terrible stench that drifted from the fields. I ignored the animal and slammed through the doorway, past the foyer, and into the dining room. I stopped, panting, grinning with terror and triumph.

The pistol was gone.

For seconds or minutes I stood in shock, not being able to think at all. Then, still holding the lantern, I looked under the table, in the hoosier, in the tiny back room. The pistol was not there. I started for the door, heard noises on the porch, headed up the stairs, and then paused in indecision.

"Is this...what you are after...young man?" Iverson stood panting at the entrance to the dining room, his left hand braced against the doorjamb, his right hand raised with the pistol leveled at me. "Slander, all slander," he said and squeezed the trigger.

The Captain had called the pistol a "double action." The hammer clicked back, locked into place, but did not fire. Iverson glanced at it and raised it toward me again. I threw the lantern at his face.

The Colonel batted it aside, breaking the glass. Flames ignited the ancient curtains and shot toward the ceiling, scorching Iverson's right side. He cursed and dropped the revolver. I vaulted over the stair railing, grabbed the kerosene lamp from the table, and threw it into the back room. Bedding and books burst into flame as the lamp oil spread. Dropping on all fours, I scrabbled toward the pistol but Iverson kicked at my head. He was old and slow and I easily rolled aside, but not before the burning curtain fell between me and the weapon. Iverson reached for it, pulled his hand back from the flames, and fled cursing out the front door.

I crouched there a second, panting. Flames shot along cracks in the floorboards, igniting pitch pine and the framework of the tinder-dry house itself. Outside the horse whinnied, either from the smell of smoke or the attempts of the Colonel to gain the saddle. I knew that nothing could stop Iverson from riding south or east, into the woods, toward the town, away from Iverson's Pits.

I reached into the circle of flame, screaming silently as part of my tunic sleeve charred away and blisters erupted on my palm, wrist, and lower arm. I dragged the pistol back, tossing the heated metal from hand to hand. Only later did I wonder why the gunpowder in the cartridges did not explode. Cradling the weapon in my burned hands, I stumbled outside.

Colonel Iverson had mounted but had only one boot in a stirrup. One rein dragged loosely while he tugged violently at the other, trying to turn the panicked horse back toward the forest. Toward the burning house. The mare had backed away from the flames and was intent on running toward the break in the wall. Toward the Pits. Iverson fought it. The result was that the mare spun in circles, the whites of its eyes showing at each revolution.

I stumbled off the porch of the burning cottage and lifted the heavy weapon just as Iverson managed to stop the horse's gyrations and leaned forward to grab the loose rein. With both reins in hand and the mare under control, he kicked hard to ride past me—or ride me down—on his way into the darkness of the trees. It took all of my strength to thumb the hammer back, blisters bursting on my thumb as I did so, and fire. I had not taken time to aim. The bullet ripped through branches ten feet above Iverson. The recoil almost made me drop the gun.

The mare spun back toward the darkness behind it. Iverson forced it around again, urged it forward with violent kicks of his small, black shoes.

My second shot went into the dirt five feet in front of me. Flesh peeled back from my burned thumb as I forced the hammer back the third time, aiming the impossibly heavy weapon between the mare's rolling eyes. I was sobbing so fiercely that I could not see Iverson clearly, but I could clearly hear him curse as his horse refused to approach the flames and source of noise a third time. I wiped at my eyes with my scorched sleeve just as Iverson wheeled the mare away from the light and gave it its head. My third shot went high again, but Iverson's horse galloped into the darkness, not staying on the faint path, jumping the stone wall in a leap which cleared the rocks by two feet.

I ran after them, still sobbing, tripping twice in the darkness but keeping possession of the pistol. By the time I reached the wall, the entire house was ablaze behind me, sparks drifting overhead and curtains of red light dancing across the forest and fields. I jumped to the top of the wall and stood there weaving, gasping for breath, and watching.

Iverson's mount had made it thirty yards or so beyond the wall before being forced to a halt. It was rearing now, both reins flying free as the white-bearded man on its back clung desperately with both hands in its mane.

The arbors were moving. Tall masses of vines rose as high as the horse's head, vague shapes seeming to move under a shifting surface of leaves. The earth itself was heaving into hummocks and ridges. And holes.

I saw them clearly in the bonfire light. Mole holes. Gopher holes. But as broad across the opening as the trunk of a man. And ribbed inside, lined with ridges of blood-red cartilage. It was like looking down the maw of a snake as its insides pulsed and throbbed expectantly.

Only worse.

If you have seen a lamprey preparing to feed you might know what I mean. The holes had teeth. Rows of teeth. They were ringed with teeth. The earth had opened to show its red-rimmed guts, ringed with sharp white teeth.

The holes moved. The mare danced in panic but the holes shifted like shadows in the broad circle of bare earth which had cleared itself of vines. Around the circumference, dark shapes rose beneath the arbors.

Iverson screamed then. A second later his horse let out a similar noise as a hole closed on its right front leg. I clearly heard the bone snap and sever. The horse went down with Iverson rolling free. There were more snapping noises and the horse lifted its neck to watch with mad, white eyes as the earth closed around its four stumps of legs, shredding the ligament and muscle from bone as easily as someone stripping strands of dark meat from a drumstick.

In twenty seconds there was only the thrashing trunk of the mare, rolling in the black dirt and black blood in a vain attempt to avoid the shifting lamprey teeth. Then the holes closed on the animal's neck.

Colonel Iverson rose to his knees, then to his feet. The only sounds were the crackling of flames behind me, the rustling of vines, and the high, hysterical panting of Iverson himself. The man was giggling.

In rows five hundred yards long, in lines as straight as a dress parade and as precise as battle lines, the earth trembled and furrowed, folding on itself, vines and grass and black soil rising and falling, rippling like rats moving under a thin blanket. Or like the furling of a flag.

Iverson screamed as the holes opened under him and around him. Somehow he managed to scream a second time as the upper half of his body rolled free across the waiting earth, one hand clawing for leverage in the undulating dirt while the other hand vainly attempted to tuck in the parts of himself which trailed behind.

The holes closed again. There was no screaming now as only the small, pink oval rolled in the dirt, but I will be certain to my dying day that I saw the white beard move as the jaws opened silently, saw the flicker of white and yellow as the eyes blinked.

The holes closed a third time.

I stumbled away from the wall, but not before I had thrown the revolver as far out into the field as I could manage. The burning house had collapsed into itself but the heat was tremendous, far too hot for me to sit so close. My eyebrows were quickly singed away and steam rose from my sweat-soaked clothes, but I stayed as close to the fire as I could for as long as I could.

Close to the light.

          ઢ ઢ ઢ

I have no memory of the fire brigade that found me or of the men who brought me back to town sometime before dawn.

Wednesday, July 2, was Military Day at the Great Reunion. It rained hard all afternoon but speeches were given in the Great Tent. Sons and grandsons of General Longstreet and General Pickett and General Meade were present on the speakers' platform.

I remember awakening briefly in the hospital tent to the sound of rain on canvas. Someone was explaining to someone that facilities were better there than in the old hospital in town. My arm and hands were swathed in bandages. My brow burned with fever. "Rest easy, lad," said Reverend Hodges, his face heavy with worry. "I've cabled your parents. Your father will be here before nightfall." I nodded and stifled the urge to scream in the interminable seconds before sleep claimed me again. The beating of rain on the tent had sounded like teeth scraping bone.

Thursday, July 3, was Civic Day at the Great Reunion. Survivors of Pickett's brigade and ex-Union troops from the Philadelphia Brigade Association formed two lines and walked fifty feet north and south to the wall on Cemetery Ridge which marked the so-called high water mark of the Confederacy. Both sides lowered battleflags until they crossed above the wall. Then a bearer symbolically lifted the Stars and Stripes above the crossed battle flags. Everyone cheered. Veterans embraced one another.

I remember fragments of the train ride home that morning. I remember my father's arm around me. I remember my mother's face when we arrived at the station in Chestnut Hill.

Friday, July 4, was National Day at the Great Reunion. President Wilson addressed all of the veterans in the Great Tent at 11 a.m. He spoke of healing wounds, forgetting past differences, of forgetting old quarrels. He spoke of valor and courage and glory which the ages would not diminish. When he was finished, they played the National Anthem and an honor guard fired a salute. Then all the old men went home.

I remember parts of my dreams that day. They were the same dreams I have now. Several times I awoke screaming. My mother tried to hold my hand but I wanted nothing to touch me. Nothing at all.

ὣ ὣ ὣ

Seventy-five years have passed since my first trip to Gettysburg. I have been back many times. The guides and rangers and librarians there know me by name. Some flatter me with the title historian.

Nine veterans died during the Great Reunion of 1913—five of heart problems, two of heatstroke, and one of pneumonia. The ninth veteran's death certificate lists the cause of death as "old age." One veteran simply disappeared sometime between his registration and the date he was expected back at a home for retired veterans in Raleigh, North Carolina. The name of Captain Powell D. Montgomery of Raleigh, North Carolina, veteran of the 20th North Carolina Regiment, was never added to the list of the nine veterans who died. He had no family and was not missed for some weeks after the Reunion ended.

Jessup Sheads had indeed built the small house southeast of the Forney farm, on the site where the 97th New York Regiment had silently waited behind a stone wall for the advance of Colonel Alfred Iverson's men. Sheads designed the small house as a summer home and erected it in the spring of 1893. He never stayed in it. Sheads was described as a short, stout, redheaded man, cleanshaven, with a weakness for wine. It was he who had planted the grape arbors shortly before his death from a heart attack in that same year of 1893. His widow rented the summer house out through agents for the years until the cottage burned in the summer of 1913. No records were kept of the renters.

Colonel Alfred Iverson, Jr., ended the war as a Brigadier General despite being relieved of his command after undisclosed difficulties during the opening skirmishes of the Battle of Gettysburg. After the war, Iverson was engaged in unlucky business ventures in Georgia and then in Florida, leaving both areas under unclear circumstances. In Florida, Iverson was involved in the citrus business with his grand-nephew, Samuel Strahl, an outspoken member of the KKK and a rabid defender of his grand-uncle's name and reputation. It was rumored that Stahl had killed at least two men in illegal duels and he was wanted for questioning in Broward County in relation to the disappearance of a seventy-eight-year-old man named Phelps Rawlins. Rawlins had been a veteran of the 20th North Carolina Regiment. Stahl's wife reported him missing during a month-long hunting trip in the summer of 1913. She lived on in Macon, Georgia, until her death in 1948.

Alfred Iverson, Jr., is listed in different sources as dying in 1911, 1913, or 1915. Historians frequently confused Iverson with his father, the Senator, and although both are supposed to be buried in the family crypt in Atlanta, records at the Oakland Cemetery show that there is only one coffin entombed there.

ია ია ია

Many times over the years have I dreamt the dream I remember from that hot afternoon in the grape arbors. Only my field of view in that dream changes—from blue sky and a stone wall under spreading branches to trenches and barbed wire, to rice paddies and monsoon clouds, to frozen mud along a frozen river, to thick, tropical vegetation which swallows light. Recently I have dreamed that I am lying in the ash of a city while snow falls from low clouds. But the fruit and copper taste of the soil remains the same. The silent communion among the casually sacrificed and the forgotten-buried also remains the same. Sometimes I think of the mass graves which have fertilized this century and I weep for my grandson and great-grandchildren.

I have not visited the battlefields in some years. The last time was twenty-five years ago in the quiet spring of 1963, three months before the insanity of that summer's centennial celebration of the battles. The Mummasburg Road had been paved and widened. John Forney's house had not been there for years but I did note a proliferation of iris where the foundation had once stood. The town of Gettysburg is much larger, of course, but zoning restrictions and the historical park have kept new houses from being built in the vicinity.

Many of the trees along the stone wall have died of Dutch elm disease and other blights. Only a few yards of the wall itself remain, the stones having been carried off for fireplaces and patios. The city is clearly visible across the open fields.

No sign of Iverson's Pits remains. No one I spoke to who lives in the area remembers them. The fields there are green when lying fallow and incredibly productive when tilled, but this is true of most of the surrounding Pennsylvania countryside.

Last winter a friend and fellow amateur historian wrote to tell me that a small archaeological team from Penn State University had done a trial dig in the Oak Hill area. He wrote that the dig had yielded a veritable gold mine of relics—bullets, brass buttons, bits of mess kits, canister fragments, five almost intact bayonets, bits of bone—all of the stubborn objects which decaying flesh leaves behind like minor footnotes in time.

And teeth, wrote my friend.

Many, many teeth.

The Drummer Ghost

JOHN WILLIAM DEFORREST

A bit of village,—we can hardly call it a street; at best, the mere fag-end of a street; six houses and a church spire in sight,—one of the houses, brick.

This is by no means the whole of Johnsonville, for the greater number of its dwellings lie in a neighboring hollow, clustered industriously beside the mill-dam over the Wampoosue, or loafing, as it were, at the two ends of the wooden bridge, or straggling, like picnickers, down the course of the black streamlet. But as these are all hidden from us by trees, and are, moreover, of not the least consequence to our story, we will not invade their sequestered insignificance. A young man, and also, of course, a young woman, demand our instant attention.

"Your uncle's appearance quite interests me," says Mr. Adrian Underhill. "Is n't there something,—I don't quite know how to express myself,—something rather remarkable about him?"

"I don't perceive that there is, except his appetite for wives; he is just finishing his third."

To think of a girl of nineteen, and a blond, blue-eyed girl at that, making such a speech! But in Miss Marian Turner's auburn there was a slightly disquieting dash of red, and about the corners of her rosy mouth there was a flexible twist which reminded one of the snapper of a whip-lash.

89

Furthermore, she carried herself upright, in a knightly manner, always ready for joust; she had a quick, positive step, as if she knew to the ends of her little bootees what she wanted; and there was a look in her eyes which declared, "I always mean more than I say." Clearly, if she had not seen life, she had guessed more than enough of it.

"Is that speaking light-mindedly of uncles?" she added. "I don't remember that it is anywhere commanded to be reverential towards them. Well, I must n't perplex you. Don't mention my queerness to anyone."

"Of course not," answered Mr. Underhill, meanwhile studying her with profound attention.

Just graduated from Winslow University, and from the quiet, bookish sociables of New Boston, he had fancied himself well read up in young ladies, and was almost awed at meeting one whom he could not understand. She said and did the most original things; that is, he considered them most original; and to him what was the difference? Moreover, she had a way of ordering him which was quite new in his experience, for he had been a bit of a Grandison among the female circles of New Boston, and at home he was an only son, the natural governor of his mother and sisters. What was still more curious, and what was even alarming, he had begun to perceive that he liked to be thus ordered.

"There he is," she resumed, nodding towards a tall, thin, haggard man of fifty-five, who just then appeared in the veranda of the brick house; "he looks as if he wanted to see one of us. It can't be me. You had better come in."

Underhill hesitated. Parents in New Boston had put it to him about his "intentions," and perhaps Mr. Joshua Turner was waiting to ask him what he meant to do for Marian. He was aware that he had paid the girl some undeniable courtship, and still he was perplexedly conscious that he did not as yet hanker for marriage. But he drifted along, as is the manner of his unwise sex, and so presently found himself in the veranda of the brick house.

While Marian walked haughtily into the dwelling, without speaking to or looking at her uncle, the latter arrested Underhill with a grim, skeleton-like shake of the hand. Although a landgoing citizen from his youth, Mr. Joshua Turner was as long and lean and brown as the Ancient

Mariner, and had moreover somewhat of his ghostly expression of enchantment. A shock of towzled, iron-gray hair; a high, narrow, wrinkled, tawny forehead; hollow black eyes, surrounded with circle on circle of brown and yellow; a lofty Roman nose, looking across a wide, thin-lipped mouth at a projecting chin; cheeks so sunken and pitted that they put you in mind of the epithets weather-beaten and worm-eaten; the whole face discolored by bile, indigestions, and lack of exercise, and corroded by care; the expression eager, anxious, and troubled, to the verge of lunacy;—such was the awful head of Joshua Turner.

"Mr. Underhill, come into the parlor," he said, in a deep, tremulous voice. "I have something private, strictly private, to tell you."

Leading the way into a sombre, curtained room, rendered additionally funereal by that musty smell which country parlors are apt to have, he turned the key in the door, and, without inviting his guest to sit, commenced striding from corner to corner.

"Mr. Underhill, I am almost crazy," he said. "I don't know but I am quite crazy. If I am, it is the drummer—the invisible, ghostly, fiendish, infernal drummer—who has made me so. Who would n't be crazy with that unearthly, horrible rubadub-dub?"

Here he began to beat upon his left hip, in the manner of one drumming, meanwhile repeating rapidly, "Rubadub-dub, rubadub-dub, rubadub-dub."

Underhill looked on in amazement and some slight alarm, suspecting that the man was really insane. He mustered up what anecdotes he had heard of lunatics, glanced at the door and windows, in order to settle upon his best method of escape, and finally took a chair by the fireplace, so as to have the poker within easy reach.

"Yes, that is his devilish tune," resumed Turner. "He began it only three days ago, and it has already driven me nearly mad. You are a college man; perhaps you can explain it all. I will tell you the whole story. I was sitting there, in that very chair where you are sitting now, when I first heard him. I was reading a paper,—reading about one of Sherman's battles,—when he came drumming down the street. I thought it was a pack of boys, or a company of furloughed soldiers. But it stopped, or he stopped, or she stopped,

91

whatever it may be, and drummed so long and loud that I laid down my candle and went to the window. I looked out; I could see the whole street by the bright moonlight; but there was no one there."

After two or three long sighs of profound depression, he resumed: "I thought that the boys or the soldiers had passed, and I went back to the fire. Then it began in the hall,—softly, very softly,—rubadub-dub. Thinking that some joker was playing pranks upon me, I rushed to the door and opened it. Nothing was there. I went through the hall; I ran upstairs and downstairs; I looked into every room;—nobody! But when I came back to the parlor, something quiet and cold, like a breath of winter wind, followed me. I slammed the door behind me, and I hoped that I had shut the thing out. Then I took up my paper and tried to read. But I was scarcely seated before I heard it again."

Here he stopped his march from corner to corner, and commenced circling a chair which stood in the centre of the room, his hands meanwhile beating gently on his breast.

"It started at the door," he continued, "and drummed straight up to me, rubadub-dub; then it drummed all around me, twice, in a circle, rubadub-dub, rubadub-dub; then it stood between me and the hearth, chilling me through, such a dub-dub, rubadub-dub, rubadub-dub. It had begun softly, but as it went on it beat louder and louder and louder, until at last it almost deafened me with its cursed uproar."

Once more he drummed violently on his hips, repeating in a hurried stammer, "Rubadub-dub, rubadub-dub, rubadub-dub."

Underhill, as may be supposed, was thinking fast without coming to any conclusion. He made a hasty muddle of the Stratford Mysteries, Rochester Knockings, Cock Lane Ghost, and Salem Witchcraft, and did not perceive that any light was thereby shed upon the case now brought under his consideration. Meanwhile he stared at Mr. Turner, and kept within arm's-length of the poker.

"Since then he has never left me for a day," resumed the "afflicted." "I have struck at him, and kicked at him, and thrown books at him, without touching anything, or hearing anything escape. But he has drummed; O, how he has drummed! Nothing will stop his drumming. He will drum me out of my senses; he will drum me out of my life. That is my story, Mr. Underhill. Can you make anything of it?"

It is not judicious to tell a man that he is a maniac, especially when there is a likelihood that he is one. Instead of venturing on this slightly perilous discourtesy, our young friend meekly replied, "No, Mr. Turner, I can't at once make anything of it. My college education does n't seem to come in play here," he added. "This sort of thing was n't lectured upon by the professors. If I had only been a medical student! It does strike me, Mr. Turner, that this is a matter of nerves. Have you consulted your doctor? Why not call him in?"

"My doctor is an old fool," exploded the haunted man. "He would give me a blue-pill or some morphine. What good would that do me? Do you suppose the drummer would care if I should take all the blue-pills in the universe? I won't have any medicine. I am a well man and a sane man, whatever you think to the contrary," he asseverated, loudly, his eyes glowing like fires within their deep, discolored hollows.

Although his expression was not reassuring, Underhill nodded assent to his declaration of sanity, being much guided at the moment by worldly wisdom.

"Come here to-night at ten o'clock, and you shall hear him for yourself," continued Turner. "Then judge whether drugs will stop him."

The *séance* was agreed upon, and the young man departed. As he went out, he gave the house a keener glance of investigation than he had hitherto bestowed upon it. The plan was obvious at first sight: a broad hall running from front to rear, with two rooms on each side; the second story an almost precise counterpart of the first; above, the usual pointed attics. The flooring was of considerable extent, while the stories were not more than eight feet in height, giving to the edifice a flattened, squat appearance.

The material was brick, originally soft, and now very old, so that the exterior had become strangely haggard and pitted, as if from a complex attack of architectural consumption and smallpox. It seemed as if the building were not only infirm with age, but infected, disfigured, and unwholesome with disease. A coat of glaring red paint, put on within the last three or four years, reminded one of rouge on the wrinkled visage of a dowager. In spite of the fresh coloring without, and the new papering within, the building had a mouldering look and a musty odor. Underhill could not help conceding that the nineteenth century, as it exists in the United States of America, rarely offers a more suitable haunting-place to a ghost.

At a quarter to ten in the evening, he returned to the house, and was received by Turner in the parlor.

"Excuse my wife for not seeing you," said the haunted man. "She has gone to bed. Her health is very feeble, and this mystery has nearly prostrated her. As for my niece, she has her own ways; I don't pretend to govern her. By the way, you may think it odd, Mr. Underhill, that I should make my niece earn her own living, in part, at least, as a school-teacher. I do it from principle, sir. Young people should learn how hard it is to get money; then they will know how to keep it. I understand that people talk about it; but what business is it of theirs? My conscience tells me that my course is the right one."

Underhill nodded; he rather thought that the young lady might make a better wife for a poor man because of this system of education; and he, just beginning the world, was a poor man, the very one that he was thinking of for her. Not finding it easy, however, to converse concerning Miss Marian, he asked: "Any more light as to the nature of your—your ghost?"

"Judge for yourself," replied Turner, with an anxious glance at the clock.

"Is he regular? Does he come at certain hours?"

"Not always. Morning and evening. He has been thrice at ten o'clock. There!"

Rubadub-dub! There was no doubt about it; a drum of some sort was being beaten upon by something; rubadub-dub, down the street, through the door-yard, and into the veranda; there it rattled furiously for a moment, and then stopped. Underhill was so startled by the sound,—it so surprised and convinced, or deluded, his hitherto in-credulous soul,—that he felt his skin writhe and the roots of his hair shudder. Perhaps he would not have been so moved had he not seen all the yellowish and brownish patches of Turner's complexion bleach to an ash-color at the first sound of the ghostly tattoo. For a full minute the two sat motion-less, staring at each other with an air of sentenced criminals. When the young man recovered himself, he sprang up, and stepped softly toward the door, his idea being to steal into the veranda, and surprise some practical joker. His companion arrested him with a wave of the hand, and a hoarse whisper, "It is coming in."

Did it come in? Underhill was not quite satisfied as to that point. The rattle of a drum entered, no doubt; it rolled through the parlor in a distressingly audible manner; but did the mysterious agency which produced it likewise find ingress? Turner evidently believed that the drummer, whoever or whatever it might be, was in the parlor; his ghastly glare said thus much, and he vehemently asserted it afterwards; but the younger man, healthy in body and soul, was even yet only half convinced.

Underhill's first impulse, however, was towards faith; he believed what he saw that his companion believed. For a minute it seemed to him that the drummer entered with a soft rat-tat-ta, the mere trembling of the sticks on the sheepskin; that within a few seconds thereafter he commenced beating a march at the door and continued it straight up to Turner; then came a circling around the haunted man, followed by a furious long roll between him and the fire. This was Underhill's first impression, and while it lasted it was a terrible one.

He had supposed that he was a radical unbeliever in spiritual manifestations; that, if phenomena purporting to be of that nature were presented to his attention, he would receive them with perfect coolness; that he would laugh the mystery to scorn and proceed to unravel it. But on the present occasion his soul did not work in this satisfactory fashion. He was almost paralyzed intellectually; he glared about the room wherever Turner glared; he was little less than thoroughly frightened.

Presently his mind swung back towards its normal rationality, and caught once more at the suspicion that the creator of the noise was in the hall. Rising softly and gliding to the door, he cautiously opened it. No one! nothing but the rolling of the drum; nothing but a clamor without a cause. Another remarkable fact was that the drumming did not seem quite so clear without as within. Unchecked by this observation, to which in fact he then hardly gave a thought, he walked to the lower end of the passage, severely shook a venerable overcoat which hung there upon a nail, returned as far as the foot of the stairway, and mounted to the upper hall.

It seemed to him now as if he were nearing the mystery; and finding another stairway, he pushed on to the garret, but there the uproar grew dull again. He had in his hand a candle which he had taken from the lower passage, and which answered in the Turner house the purpose of an entry lamp. By its light he glanced over the trunks, broken furniture, dismissed demijohns and bottles, fragments of carpets and other indescribable rubbish, which ordinarily encumber a garret, without discovering the smallest fraction of a band of music. Moreover the noise had ceased; it had died away as he set foot on the creaking garret floor; the house was as silent as a decrepit and sickly old mansion could be.

Now back to the second floor; and here he made a discovery. Marian Turner, dressed in her every-day guise and holding a lighted candle in her hand, met him with a mournful and stern countenance which put him in mind of Lady Macbeth.

"Tell my uncle," she whispered, "that my brother must be dead."

"Your brother?" he inquired. "I didn't know that you had a brother."

"I have none now," she answered, her voice shaking with unmistakable emotion. "You will learn yet that he is dead." After a brief hesitation she continued more firmly: "My uncle put him to a trade, and he hated it. Last year he ran away and joined the army as a drummer-boy. He would have been sixteen to-day, if he had lived."

Here her self-possession quite broke down, and she burst into a loud sobbing. Underhill tried to offer encouragement; he took her hand, and then he drew her towards him: indeed we have reason to suspect that she cried for a while upon his shoulder. At last she raised her head, and whispering, "Tell my uncle," slipped away to her own room.

Returning to the parlor, Underhill found Turner, his face buried in his hands, shivering in front of the fire. At the entry of the young man, the elder, without removing his bony fingers from his sunken eyes, inquired in a shuddering voice, "Did you find anything?"

"No. But perhaps I might, if you had gone with me. I did n't know the house and could n't get about it fast enough."

"No use. I have been about it at full speed, like a madman. No use."

"Have you seen nothing?" inquired Underhill, wondering why Turner covered his eyes.

"No," answered the haunted man, dropping his hands, "I tell you there is nothing to be seen." After a moment he added, "I was afraid I might see something."

"O, I met your niece upstairs," said Underhill. "She told me to tell you—well, it is very unaccountable and painful; but she has a strong impression that her brother—a drummer-boy, she called him—that he is dead."

"Ah!" exclaimed Turner, springing to his feet and staring at the young man with an expression of intense horror. "What did you tell me that for? O my God! What did you say it for? Do you want to drive me into the grave? Don't you see that I can't bear such things?"

After walking about the room for a moment, he partially recovered his self-possession, and broke out peevishly: "What does the fool mean by such nonsense! I won't have it in my house,—I won't have people under my roof talking such nonsense."

"I beg your pardon, Mr. Turner. I was in fault for telling you. Don't lay blame upon her. I assure you that she was quite beside herself with emotion."

As the only response to this was a groan, Underhill concluded that he could do little good by prolonging his stay, and, after a few words of useless sympathy, he took his departure.

During the next day, he learned something new about the Turners. It is time now to explain that he was a lawyer, and that he had set up his virgin shingle in Johnsonville, with the intention of removing to New Boston at the first flattering opportunity. Into his office strolled an elderly male gossip, one of those men who do the "heavy standing round" in villages, and who have discovered whispering galleries at certain sunny corners, where they can overhear all the marvels of the neighborhood.

"Curious goings-on at Josh Turner's, I understand," said this useful personage, dropping into one of Underhill's arm-chairs. "Sat up with 'em last night, I understand. Say he's troubled with a ghost. Pshaw! No ghosts nowadays; ain't legal tender; don't circulate. It's a bad conscience, that's what it is. Tell you, Josh Turner's got an awful sink-hole in one corner of his conscience. Ha'n't treated those children right,—brother's children, too,—only brother. Sam Turner came home, seven years ago, with fifty thousand dollars and two motherless children. Sam died,—left Josh executor,— gardeen of the boy and girl. Where'd the money go to? Josh Turner can't tell. Sam's estate settled up for nothing, an' Josh Turner turned out rich. Never made enough before to lay up anything, and here he is rich, retired from business, investing in railroads, painting his house. Looks kind o' ugly, don't it? Then he made the girl teach school, and 'prenticed the boy to a trade, and let him run off to the army. Can't say I'd take Josh Turner's conscience for all his money. Well, I must be going. Don't mention this, Mr. Underhill. A lawyer ought to know how to keep secrets. Good morning."

From other sources our young barrister learned further particulars. The four children who had been born to Joshua Turner by his first two wives were now all away from home, the two girls prosperously married, the boys in successful business. By his living wife he had another boy, at present five years old. In this youngster the whole affection of both father and mother seemed to have centred. They cared little for the other children; they cared nothing for the nephew and niece. It was currently reported in Johnsonville that little Jimmy Turner would inherit the whole, or nearly the whole, of the Josh Turner property.

"The old woman will bring that around certain," said Phineas Munson, the gossip above mentioned, during a second call on Underhill; "she won't let the old man catch his last breath till he makes out a will in favor of her Jimmy. Dunno why I call her old, though; ain't more'n forty. S'pose I call her so because she's such a poor, sickly, faded creetur. She's in a decline, and coughs to kill. But, sick as she is, she's got a temper like a wildcat, and she governs Josh Turner at the first yelp. By the way, heard any more about the ghost? Say it's a drummer, and drums like sixty. Wonder if Freddy Turner's dead? However, I don't believe in ghosts. All fiddle-faddle. Haw, haw, haw," he laughed just here. "I said, all fiddle-faddle. No drumming, don't ye see? *Fiddle*-faddle. Did n't mean to joke, though. Good morning."

While Underhill was thus studying the shadows of the Turner past, the village was going mad about the ghost. The Johnsonville drummings ought long since to have taken their place, in the history of "spiritual manifestations," by the side of the Stratford Mysteries and the Rochester Knockings. The house was invaded by so many people, and they were there at times in such incommodious crowds, that the Turners were nearly as much troubled by the living as by their spiritual visitant. What added to the excitement was the publication of a list of the casualties in one of Sherman's minor battles, wherein the name of Frederic Turner figured among the dead. Nothing could be more obvious than that the drummer was the ghost of Joshua Turner's ill-used nephew.

Of course, efforts were made to trace the disturbance to a human, or at least a physical origin. The village materialists, that is to say, the doctor, the apothecary, Phineas Munson, and two or three more, nosed about the house by day and watched it by night. One talked of a peculiar circulation in the chimney; another of a loose shingle on the roof which clattered in the wind; another suspected little Jimmy Turner, and wanted to tie him up. All these frantic hypotheses were laughed to scorn by the great majority of Johnsonvillians, who found it more rational to believe in a ghost, and far more amusing.

Curiously enough, Mrs. Turner was one of the most vehement of the unbelievers. This determined woman, feeble and ghastly under the prolonged gripe of consumption, searched the dwelling from garret to cellar, by day and by night, to discover the trick which she declared was being played upon her household. In this investigation she displayed a feverish eagerness which was attributed partly to her native fervor of character and partly to the nervous excitability of invalidism. Small, meagre, and narrow-shouldered, her clothes hanging straight along her skeleton figure, her puny and pointed face of a uniform waxen yellow, her large, prominent, lustreless eyes wandering hurriedly from object to object, her shrunken, glassy forefinger beckoning here and there in tremulous suspicion, she was woful and almost terrible to look upon. So anxious was she to dissipate the mystery, that, passionately as she loved her little boy, she threatened him and whipped him to make him avow that he did the drumming. Then, when convinced of his innocence, she cried and coughed over him until it seemed as if her flickering life would go out in the spasm.

Against the assumption that the noises were produced by Frederic Turner's ghost, she argued with praiseworthy energy though inexcusable logic. At first, she scouted the idea that the boy was dead, asserting that he would yet reappear to make trouble for his family. When further news demolished this supposition, she declared that the drummings had commenced a week after the decease, so that there could be no connection between the two facts. But popular credulity stepped in here to controvert her; people now remembered to have heard the mysterious uproar for some time back; one and another had been startled by it a week before Josh Turner complained of it; in short, the dates of the drumming and the death became identical. Even the cautious and intelligent were obliged to admit that the manifestations began several days before the news of the boy's decease reached the village, and to infer that this circumstance tended to disprove all supposition of trickery. Why should a person, who did not know that Fred Turner was dead, set out to counterfeit Fred Turner's ghost?

For the ear of her husband, Mrs. Turner had another theory which she did not care to make public. "It's that girl," she said. "It's your own niece, Marian Turner, that does it."

"But you've searched her room and found nothing," groaned the husband, as sick in soul as his wife in body. "You've searched the whole house."

"Yes, but I *shall* find something. She's precious sly and deep, but I shall find her out yet. I have my eye on her, every day, while I am talking about other things."

"But when the—the noises commenced, Marian did n't know about Freddy."

"Yes, she did. You believe me, Joshua Turner, she did. She had a letter or something. Then she knew that the news would get to us later, and she begun her tantrums. O, she's precious deep,—precious deep! I wish she 'd cleared out when her brother did."

"I wish he had n't gone," moaned the husband. "I wish I'd treated him better, and kept him by us."

"Joshua Turner, you have n't got the spirit of a man. If you had half my spunk, sick and dying as I am, you would n't whimper that way. Everything has gone right, except that you are a coward,—a poor, feeble, sick-headed creature,— afraid of your own shadow. If you only would pluck up a spirit and let this thing worry itself out, everything would be right."

"Pluck up a spirit? I tell you I can't. It 's killing me."

"Well," she gasped, laying her hand on her breast as if to aid the action of her withered lungs,—"well, it 's killing me, too. That is, you are killing me. But do I flinch? Just look at me and see how I bear it. I wish to Heavens," concluded this audacious woman, "that I could give you my courage."

"Sarah Turner, *you* have no conscience," he replied, in a tone which was not so much reproachful as horror-stricken.

"How dare you say that to me, Josh Turner? And you know who I am suffering for and slaving for! It is n't for myself that I care," she continued, coughing and crying. "It 's for Jimmy. I want Jimmy to be well off. And you want to rob him,—leave him a beggar!"

"O my God! my God!" groaned Turner, and walked from her without another word.

"See here," she called after him, suppressing her tears. "If I find that girl is doing it, will you turn her out of the house? Will you send her off?"

He hesitated, looking at her sternly, and at last sighed, "No; I have done harm enough to Sam's children."

She turned her back upon him and left him, with an ejaculation of anger and contempt.

Meanwhile the manifestations pursued their course, to the beatitude of the wonder-loving, and the perplexity of the philosophical. One noteworthy circumstance was that the drummer seemed to hate a crowd. He rarely vouchsafed his music to the swarms of curious who invaded the house, while he poured it forth without stint to enliven the solitude of the Turners. He drummed rarely on a Sunday, frequently on a Saturday, and almost always in the evening. His favorite place of recreation was the parlor, and the listener in whom he delighted was Joshua Turner. Nevertheless, he sometimes assailed little Jimmy with long rolls and tattoos which almost drove him out of his five-year-old senses. The poor child was hysterically afraid of the ghostly visitant, and, at the first murmur of spiritual sheepskin, would fly screaming to his mother.

"There! don't be scared at it," she was once heard to whisper, while looking in his face with the anxiety of ardent love. "If Jimmy won't mind it, he shall be very rich some day, and have all the pretty things he wants."

At last, Joshua Turner remarked, apropos of a clamor which had driven the boy into spasms, "Sarah, it is killing our child."

"I know it," she burst out with a despairing cry. "O, I wish you and I were both dead. Then it would stop."

"If justice were done it might stop," replied the man, solemnly.

"Joshua Turner, don't you do it!" she gasped, tottering up to him and putting her tallowy face close to his. "Don't you do what you're thinking of! If you do, I 'll haunt you. I will. I 'll haunt you to the grave, and beyond it."

Not long after this interview, Mrs. Turner began to hint to the neighbors that her husband's mind was failing. The charge seemed natural enough; it was countenanced by his extravagance of speech and violence of manner; at times, especially when he talked of the drummer, his conversation was little less than maniacal. For instance, he once broke out in the following fashion upon gossip Phineas Munson, meantime walking frantically round the rocking-chair in which that gentleman was blandly oscillating.

"What do you come here for? Rubadub-dub" (beating on his hip); "is that it? Like drumming? I 'll drum for you. Rubadub-dub, rubadub-dub. I 'll be your ghost, Mr. Munson, I 'll furnish you with the music of the spheres; send the whole band around to your house every evening; give you a diabolical drumming serenade; give you one now. Rubadub-dub, rubadub-dub, rubadub-dub. Had enough of it, Mr. Munson? Now go to every house in the village and report that you have seen the ghost. Do you want anybody to look more like a ghost than I do? I tell you I shall be one shortly; I am being killed by this thing and these people. Why can't they let me bear my torment alone? Why can't you go home, Mr. Munson? Yes, GO HOME!"

"Tell you I never was so insulted in my life," repeated Phineas to his fellow-citizens. "Begin to think the old woman's right. Turner must be cracked. Would n't 'a' pitched into me so, if he had n't been. Ought to have a conservator and a keeper. If he ain't watched, there'll be more ghosts of *his* manufacture."

What was the attitude of Marian Turner during this grotesque and yet horrible drama? Underhill watched her narrowly, not so much in a spirit of philosophical investigation, as because he was on the verge of being in love with her. The theory which he had constructed for the girl was, that she knew that she had been plundered by her uncle, and that she was now engaged in terrifying the plunderer into a restitution. Looking at her from this point of view, he was astonished at the determination, the hardness of spirit, with which she persecuted this family. She was killing her uncle and his wife; she was driving her childish cousin into chronic hysteria; yet she did not flinch. Perhaps she excused herself on the ground that the two elders had been in a manner the slayers of her brother, and that it was not in reality she, but their own evil consciences, which put them to the torture. Nevertheless, he would have been glad to discover in her more of feminine gentleness and even feminine weakness. It must be admitted that man does not easily adore a self-helpful woman.

Meanwhile the girl fascinated him. In the first place, she was the belle of the village, and the belles of other places were too far away to counteract her attraction. In the second place, she was bright and strange; she had entertaining oddities of thought and utterance; she had what he considered dazzling flashes of sarcasm. On the whole, she was the most interesting and original girl that he had ever seen, even putting aside her supposed connection with the so-called spiritual manifestations.

"Talking of ghosts," she one day said to Underhill, "I only know of Mrs. Turner. Did you ever see another person in this world, who so evidently belonged in the next? Why don't she follow her two predecessors? How it must provoke them to see her linger so, and the house new painted and papered!"

"You have very little pity for her," replied Underhill, gravely.

"I have n't a particle. Why should I pity a woman who would marry such an inveterate woman-killer as my uncle?

He reminds me of the returned missionaries who used to come to South Hadley School to pick out second and third wives. Why is it that missionaries have such a matrimonial hunger? I suppose it is living among cannibals that demoralizes them."

"I really don't like to hear you joke in this manner," Underhill ventured to protest, though in an imploring tone.

"People joke the most when they are most unhappy," she answered, coldly. "That is, some people. Do you suppose I am gay?" she continued, with energy. "Here I am, earning my own living, liable to be homeless any day, and wearing black for my only brother. Think of it. How do you suppose I can be soft-hearted towards people who—"

Here she stopped, as if she were saying more than was prudent; in another moment she pressed her hands to her face and began to sob. It is not difficult to believe that this interview might have ended in a very common and yet very efficacious sort of comforting; but just as Underhill had taken the girl's hand, a servant appeared in the veranda of the haunted house, and beckoned to them wildly.

They were soon at the door of Mrs. Turner's room; there was silence within, broken only by gurgling gasps for breath; the consumptive was stretched, pallid and quivering, on the bed; the husband was leaning over her, his face almost as cadaverous as hers. Marian Turner walked to the side of the dying woman, and looked at her steadily without speaking. Underhill hesitated, and then advanced, slowly, on tiptoe.

"Shall I call a doctor?" he whispered, while thinking, "It is too late."

"They have gone for him," replied Joshua Turner, without lifting his eyes from that incarnate spasm.

The invalid was struggling violently, not seemingly to live, but to speak. She rolled her glassy eyes frightfully; her dry, blue lips opened again and again, but only to gasp; her whole frame joined feebly in the wrestling for words. It was evident, from the dulness and the fixed direction of her eyes, that she did not see any one, and it is almost certain that she was not aware of the presence of Marian and Underhill. At last the utterance came; it was a kind of voiceless whispering; it merely breathed, "Don't do it, Joshua!"

"Here is Marian," replied the husband, doubtless fearing lest the ruling passion might avow too much. "Have you any word for her?"

A strange look crossed the dying face; it was an expression of many conflicting emotions; it hated, defied, implored, and wheedled. It said: "I detest you,—don't rob my child; I have been your enemy,—don't take advantage of my death."

But this look, and the emotion which writhed beneath it, exhausted her strength; she had not another word, or even another change of countenance, for any one on earth; the plannings, pleadings, and fightings of her feverish life were over. There was an air and almost a movement of sinking, and as it were flattening, into the calmness of dissolution. Expression slid from her lips; the waxen yellow of her skin turned ashy; the tremulous hands stiffened into peace;—she was gone.

The husband, already accustomed to such scenes, was the only one of the three spectators who instantly recognized the great change. He laid his ear upon the body, listened awhile for breathing, slowly raised his neglected head, shook it solemnly rather than sadly, and exhaled a profound sigh. The expression in his face, like that in the face of his wife, was mainly "long disquiet merged in rest." It seemed as if he were glad that the struggle was over, as if he were soothingly conscious of relief from oppression, as if he breathed freer because her breath had ceased.

Divining from his manner the presence of death, Marian Turner shuddered slightly and drew a pace backward. Then she stood like a statue, looking at the corpse askant and with slightly contracted eyes, as one sometimes watches an object of aversion while desiring to turn away from it. Her mien was that of distaste, and little less than disgust. Like her uncle, she did not utter a syllable.

Underhill was the only one who spoke; and his words were but a commonplace of announcement and surprise: "She is—she is dead—good heavens!" This was the only utterance of emotion over the body of one who had just gasped out a life of passionate hatred and love. The child for whom this mother had plotted and throbbed was not even in the village, having been sent the day before on a visit to one of his half-sisters. So far as concerned the presence of affection and mourning, she died alone.

Underhill retired from the scene with exceedingly painful impressions. What struck him most disagreeably was, not the fact of dissolution, but the coldness with which it had been regarded. Not that he wondered and groaned over the widower: it seemed natural that the decease of a third wife should be endured with equanimity; moreover, the departed had been a wretched invalid, and the survivor was a man; finally, what did Underhill care for Joshua Turner?

But that Marian should firmly carry her dislikes up to the verge of the grave was a circumstance which filled him with alarm and almost with horror. A woman, and not a relenting tear; almost a child, and not a start of pity! He called up, over and over again, the sidelong gaze of aversion which she had bent upon the helpless corpse, itself at peace with all the world. "What sort of a wife will she make?" was the selfish but natural question of the young man as he strolled alone at midnight by the sluggish stream of the Wampoosue, as black, silent, and funereal as if it were a gigantic grave. He walked there at that hour because he could not sleep; and he groaned aloud over his doubt, without being able to solve it.

Death, however, brought one relieving change in this drama; from the time that he entered the household, the drummer left it. Not another ghostly reveille or tattoo or long roll gladdened the ears of the gossips and wonder-lovers who had hitherto delighted in such uproars. During the funeral, the dwelling was filled and surrounded by a dense crowd, attracted by the belief that extraordinary manifestations would mingle with the burial rites, and so regardless of decorum in its curiosity that not a room was left unvisited by stealthy feet and peering faces. At times the whisper and buzz of discussion rose so loudly as to drown the voice of the clergyman. At other moments a suspense of expectation seemed to settle upon every one, producing a sudden, universal, profound silence which was inexpressibly sombre. But amid all the debate, and through all the agony of listening, not a note came from the mysterious visitant whose advent was so desired. Probably the prevailing feeling at the funeral of Mrs. Turner was extreme disappointment.

During the following week Underhill did not see any of the Turners. He was afraid to meet Marian, lest he should be fascinated by her presence, and should offer himself as her husband, only to repent of it for life. While he admitted that the girl had had great provocations, and was still suffering under grievous injustice, he could not clear her of a suspicion of cruelty. If she were really the author of the mysterious noises, she might be charged with having hastened the death of her aunt, and that with the full knowledge of what she was doing. No one could have watched the wild excitement of the consumptive during the last three weeks, without perceiving that it was lessening her hold on life. On the other hand, the drumming had ceased with her death. That looked like compunction; in that there was some mercy of womanliness, and from it he drew a hope.

In the midst of his indecisions he received a message requesting him to call upon Mr. Turner. He found the widower much changed,—no longer wild in manner and language, as during the whole course of the "manifestations"; with something, indeed, of his native excitability in the tones of his voice, but, on the whole, languid, melancholy, and meek.

"Mr. Underhill," he said, pointing to writing materials on the table, "I wish to make a new will. Can you do it here?"

The young man sat down, and prepared to write.

"Begin it thus," said the widower, bending his shaggy head low, as if in humiliation: "The last will and testament of Joshua Turner, the chief of sinners."

"Let us avoid expressions which may lead to doubts of sanity," remarked the lawyer. "There have been singular circumstances of late in your life. If your will is to be anywise unusual—"

"Leave it out then," interrupted Turner, with the abrupt pettishness of a sickly man. "So I must not even confess?"

After a moment, during which he bent his head almost to his lean knees, he resumed: "Here it is. Ten thousand dollars to my son, James Pettengill Turner. All the rest of my estate, real and personal, to my niece, Marian Turner, to her and to her heirs and assigns. That is all."

It was written; two neighbors were called in as witnesses; the testator affixed his signature. As soon as he was once more alone with Underhill, he walked feebly to the door, and called in a hoarse voice for his niece. Presently the girl entered, bowed gravely to the lawyer, and seated herself at a distance from her uncle, not even looking at him.

"Marian," said Turner, rising, and handing her the will, "read this through, and speak to me."

She read it, gradually flushing with emotion, and when it was finished, she raised her eyes to his face, but still without uttering a word. Evidently she was oppressed by surprise, and hampered by the presence of Underhill.

"The whole estate is sixty thousand dollars. Are you willing that James should have ten thousand?" asked the uncle, with an affecting humility. "If not, I will cross him out."

"I am willing," she replied.

"If you wish it," he continued, "I will give up the property at once, though I am dying."

"I do not wish it."

"And you can't say more?" he implored. "You can't forgive?"

Some hard barrier in the girl's heart gave way at once, and she threw herself into her uncle's arms, crying upon his neck. The outburst astonished the man who had called it forth; never before, probably, had any adult member of his family met him with tears and kisses; it was not thus that the Turners expressed themselves. His words were, "Marian, I thank you; Marian, you are a very strange girl"; and then he let her leave him. Underhill, differently educated in the language of emotion, was unspeakably delighted with the sight of this gush of tenderness, and stole away from the room with a haze of moisture across his eyelashes.

The very next day he heard that Joshua Turner was ill. He offered his services as a nurse, and for a fortnight was almost hourly in the house, watching the progress of an evidently hopeless malady. Through the clouds of a brain fever the invalid heard, and at times beheld, his old tormentor. He continually complained of the drummer; through the windows and down the chimney came the drummer; the street rang and the house trembled with the infernal music of the drummer; at the judgment-seat, ready to bear witness against him, stood the drummer.

The bemoanings and adjurations of the haunted man were horrible. "Has the demon come again?" he shouted, in a high, hard scream. "See him there, stepping through the wall. My nephew? Have I devils for nephews? How is that? Ah! I belong to him; I must go to him. O, *hear* him! Can nobody stop his beating? Is there no mercy for me?"

During a lucid interval, Underhill said to him, "You have been a little out of your head."

"I have been out of my head for months, for years," he returned, in the husky whisper which was now his only voice. "I have done only one sane thing in five years. Restitution! Restitution!"

"Do you still believe in the manifestations?" the young man ventured to add.

"Thank God that I *did* believe in them! That madness led me back to sanity."

When Underhill returned to the house on the following morning, Marian said to him, in a trembling whisper, "My poor uncle is dead."

He hailed the tone of sorrow and tenderness with such joy that he forgot the solemnity of the moment, and kissed her hand.

We must pass over six months; during their flight the hand was kissed many times again. Underhill and Marian Turner were engaged. She was greatly changed from what she was when he first knew her. Either prosperity, or penitence for some evil done, had divested her of her old bitterness, and even made her exceptionally gentle. She had taken her little cousin James to her heart, and was doing by him the part of a mother. In deep mourning for her brother, uncle, and aunt, she usually had a pensive gravity which befitted the garb, and she was handsomer than any one had ever before known her.

At last she was Mrs. Underhill. Among the many confessions which she doubtless made to her husband, did she admit a connection with the mystery of the drummings? No; not a word on that subject; not a response when it was mentioned. Nor did Underhill question her; he did not care to open old sorrows.

But one day he discovered, inside the lath and plaster casing of the parlor, a square tin pipe, four inches deep by seven or eight broad, the remnant of some ancient heating apparatus. The opening by which it had once communicated with the room was simply covered over with wall paper, while the upper extremity terminated in the closet of a chamber which, in the time of the manifestations, had been occupied by Marian Turner.

It struck him that a drum beaten in this closet might have sounded below as if in the parlor, and, beaten gently outside of a window, might have produced an illusion that it was coming down the street. A perturbed conscience, the imagination of a sickly man, and the epidemic power of popular credulity, might have completed the delusion. The mystery was as simple as a conundrum after you know it.

But he discovered no drum, and he put no queries concerning the drummer, so that we have a margin for charitable doubt as to Marian, and also a pleasing chance for faith in mysteries.

The Last Waltz

SEABURY QUINN

The Eighth Zouaves had stormed the ridge twice. It must have been five hundred feet up to the heights where the red flag with its blue St. Andrew's Cross and thirteen silver stars waved challengingly and the butternut-clad infantry lay waiting behind their rampart of boulders. Five hundred feet of steep up-grade with fallen trees and underbrush to clamber over, and veterans from Fredericksburg and Chancellorsville to meet them at the top. One out of every three men in the line had fallen, you could see the deep red of their baggy trousers and the deep blue of their jackets like bright flowers on the black soil underneath the bullet-riven trees.

"Attention!" Colonel Dutcher's foghorn voice smashed through the muted roar of cannonading on the left. "We're going up again, men—and this time we're staying. Charge bayonets—forward, double quick, march!"

Dwight Fairchild transferred his sword to his left hand, wrapping the hilt-knot about his wrist, and dragged his heavy Colt from its holster. Captain Schwing was down, so was Lieutenant Ditmas; he was company commander—just past twenty, and in command. Drusilla would be proud when he wrote her about this—"Guide right; dress the line!" he shouted as he glanced along the rank of leveled bayonets. "At the double—forward!"

They were halfway up the height, now. The whine of Minié balls was like the droning of a nest of angry hornets; sometimes they cut a branch above his head with a sharp *snick!* sometimes they struck a tree trunk with a dull *pung!* When they ricocheted from the stones underfoot they screamed like demons in frustration.

Twenty-five feet forward, thirty, maybe, a clump of boulders cropped waist-high from the loam. Funny they should stand like that—like a group of tombstones in a country churchyard—might be shelter for a Johnny behind them—

The face that rose behind the tallest stone was wreathed in a broad grin. It was a nice face, clean-shaved, boyish, and there was something almost friendly in the blue eyes underneath the battered broad-brimmed slouch hat. "Here y'are, Yank—tell Abe Lincoln I sent this!" the lad behind the rock called cheerfully, and then squeezed his trigger.

Fairchild felt the impact of the bullet like a fist-blow on his chest. It didn't hurt, not as much as he'd supposed it would, at any rate. Just knocked the wind from him, and made his left arm feel heavy and useless. "Right back at you, Reb—take this one to Jeff Davis!" He jerked his pistol up and fired.

It was comical, that look upon the other's face. A sort of shocked-surprised expression, as if to say, "You can't do this to me"—then the welling, gushing spate of blood that rushed out of the hole between the hatbrim and the smiling eyes; the opened gaping mouth. And then nothing. Like a jack-in-the-box the sharpshooter had dropped down behind the sheltering stone, a sliced second too late, and as the gray-clad boy fell Dwight stumbled, felt his left arm crumple under him, and lay against the leaf-mould with a spear of grass tickling his left ear and the sweet, clean smell of topsoil in his nostrils.

"Hully Gee, th' Loot's plugged!" he heard Sergeant Gilroy call, then, in his ear, but sounding far away, "Are ye hur-rt bad, sor?"

"Never mind me, Sergeant." Funny how he had to shout to make his voice sound even like a whisper. "Keep the men in line—"

Something bothered him. His mouth was full of sticky stuff. Salty. Nasty. And his left side hurt. It seemed as if a

112

hand were pressed against it, holding down his chest. He couldn't breathe, and when he tried it hurt so—hurt as if a bayonet bore into him just below the collar-bone.

As the gaitered legs swung past his face he reached out with his right hand, drawing himself nearer to the big pine tree. There, that was better. Lie here, take it easy, boy; you're going to be all right. They'll come back for you, soon as they have cleared the ridge. Mustn't ask 'em to stop now, though. This is a war we're having— Who cares about their old war? There's a flower—

It was a bloodroot, pale and pinkly-white, thrusting up through the dead black pine needles. He looked at it with his hand to his heart while the fresh, vigorous young blood trickled through his fingers and made an ugly stain on the precise blue tunic that he had always kept so carefully, brushing it each time he took it off, sponging it with a damp rag to remove dust and powder-stains. Who cares about the old coat? See that pretty flower—like the one Drusilla wore in her hair that night.

It was funny how the past reeled out before him, like one of those moving stereopticons they had in Hartley's Arcade, only run through in reverse. Somewhere near a bugle sounded—Retreat. Had they swept the Johnnies from the ridge? Why, no, it was no bugle, it was an orchestra, and it was playing a Strauss waltz. That flower was no humble country-blooming bloodroot, it was a pale pink rose, and it was in Drusilla's hair. "My waltz, Ma'am, I believe," he murmured to the little, nodding floret.

New York was in a winter mood. Since half past six the great white flakes had drifted through the breezeless air, the cobble stones of Broadway were cottoned by the thick snow-fall, and the carriage-horses' hooves were silenced as the long parade of family broughams and hired hacks streamed northward from the Fulton and Grand Street ferries or south and west from fashionable First Avenue to the Broadway Central where the military and civic ball was in progress for the benefit of the Women's Sanitary Ambulance Corps. Gas light blazed in every window of the hotel, the crystal chandeliers of the ballroom gleamed diamond-like with bright reflections as the orchestra struck up the music for the grand march:

De Camptown ladies sing dis song,
  Do-da, do-da;
De Camptown race-track ten miles long,
  Do-da, do-da, day!

Most of the men were uniformed, their gold braid and buttons and bright sashes vying with the costumes of the ladies. Everybody who aspired to be mentioned in the Social Columns was present.

Dwight Fairchild felt his fingers tremble as Drusilla laid her hand in his. "You're very beautiful tonight, dear," he whispered as he bent toward her, "and it was sweet of you to wear my flowers." He glanced down at the spray of pale pink roses at her waist, then at the single blossom nestled in her soft dark hair. "I should have called for you, but duty—"

"La!" she interrupted him with a pout. "Duty—always duty! Anyone would think that you were going to marry Mister Lincoln, 'stead of me." Then her brown eyes softened. "Why don't you resign from the army, Dwight? You know how Papa feels about this war, and," she added wistfully, "we could be married right away and have such fun together. The skating's lovely in the park these days, and all the roads are thick with snow. We could go sleighing out to Hempstead, or Freeport, and I know the sweetest little house in Williamsburg we can get for almost no rent—" The marchers separated as they reached the bandstand, and with a coaxing smile she turned away.

He kept time with the music as he followed the stout captain of hussars who marched before him, but though he still smiled he was troubled. It had not been easy to win Drusilla Willemese, for the dark-haired, pale-skinned heiress was conspicuous for her beauty even in the Brooklyn Eastern District, where pretty girls were by no means a rarity, and her suitors numbered scores. Afterwards, her parents' consent had been even harder to obtain, for the Willemese fortune was based upon the Southern cotton trade, and "Mr. Lincoln's war" had all but wrecked the cotton-factoring business. Only the insistent teasing of a pampered only daughter had secured a grudging assent to the engagement, with the understanding that no wedding should take place as long as young Fairchild continued in "King Lincoln's livery."

Now Drusilla urged him to resign, to quit his country in its time of peril. What if her father forced her to return his ring? There was Harold Martense, rich and handsome and outspoken in his Southern sympathies. Suppose the old man made her accept his suit?

The lines of marchers were together once more; her hand was in his again, her eyes were turned on him in entreaty. "Please, Dwight? They don't need you to fight their old war; there are plenty without you. Resign your commission and Papa will let us marry right away."

He danced a polka with her, then a rollicking mazurka; after that young Martense claimed her for the schottische. Now the orchestra struck up the *Blue Danube,* and he bowed before her. "My waltz, Ma'am, I believe."

They whirled around the floor once, twice; he held her tighter than convention permitted, for he was young, and terribly in love, and fearful of losing her. The power of his wanting was in his arm, and his almost fierce grip hurt her; but she loved the hurt. After all, he was a man, her Dwight. She lowered lace-veined lids and gave herself up wholly to the captivating rhythm of the music and the strength of his encircling arm.

Now they were by the ballroom vestibule and as he looked across his partner's creamy shoulder Fairchild saw a young man in zouave uniform who beckoned him imperatively. "Excuse me, darling," he whispered, then, as he reached the young enlisted man:

"Yes, Corporal?"

"Colonel Dutcher's compliments, sor. All officers are ordered to report at once to the armory."

"I'm called for instant duty, dear," Fairchild murmured. "Don't know what it is, but it's important, or they'd not have sent for me."

"Oh, Dwight, can't we even finish this?"

"No, dear; every minute counts. This is a war we're having. But"—as her eyes darkened with rebellion—"I'll be back to claim the dance, my dearest, never fear. Say you'll save it for me."

Her eyes were wide, moist, starry, and her lips trembled like a little child's. "Always and forever, dear heart. Come what may, this dance is yours, and yours alone. I'll never dance the *Blue Danube* with any other man. Claim it when you will. I'll hold it open for you—always."

Then, to the scandal of the chaperoning dowagers who were lined in straight-backed chairs along the wall, he bent and kissed her quickly. "I'll remember, dearest love. When you hear me say, 'My waltz, Ma'am, I believe,' you'll know that I've come back to claim the *Blue Danube* from you."

It had stopped snowing and grown colder since the ball began. A wind that seemed to scream with gleeful malice whipped down Broadway, snatching at their hats and clutching at their greatcoats as Lieutenant Fairchild and Corporal Gilroy climbed into a hansom-cab and set out for the armory.

Two hours later they marched to the Jersey City ferries and entrained for the South.

Drusilla sat before the cherry writing desk in her boudoir. Two candles in tall silver standards shed their light across the pad of correspondence paper which lay bare and blank before her, their flickering luminance struck flashes from the little diamond setting of the ring that lay beside the opened pad of paper, and from the larger stone that graced the circlet on the third finger of her left hand. "Dear Dwight," she wrote, then paused and nibbled at her penholder. This was going to be harder than she'd thought. She crumpled the sheet to a ball and threw it on the floor, then began again, "Dwight dearest." That was better, less formal, but—one couldn't be too affectionate when— She threw the second sheet of wadded paper down beside the first and started afresh.

The small ormolu clock on the dresser ticked away the minutes, and her pen scratched with a gently scraping sound across the linen paper. Sheet after sheet was torn or crumpled as she finished it; but finally the note was done. The writing was bold, ill-formed, altogether fashionable; its message was plain as any epitaph upon a tombstone.

Dear Dwight:

I loathe writing this, but Papa thinks I should tell you right away. After thinking matters over I know that our engagement was a mistake. You were young and so was I; you were fascinated by my pretty face (for I *am* pretty—my mirror tells the truth, even if the young men lie), I loved your pretty uniform and the pretty things you said, and we were both much more in love with love than with each other. After all, Dwight, what have we in common? You are devoted to your military career, "seeking the bubble reputation at the cannon's mouth," as the poet says, while I want a home, and a husband who can be with me and think as I do.

Papa says Mr. Lincoln's war may last another five years, and by that time I should be an old maid, even if you came back and still wanted me. You see, I'm twenty-one next April.

So, I think we'd better let by-gones be by-gones. Harold Martense wants me to marry him, and I'm sure that I've found love this time.

I'd send your ring back through the mail, but I'm sure some horrid Yankee soldier would steal it, so I'll just hold it here for you, and if you come back from the war, or when you're home on leave, if you'll call at the house Papa will give it to you.

Drusilla.

There, it was done, and a clever piece of composition, too. Not too flippant, not too serious; just the proper balance of gravity and frivolity. But final. Oh, definitely final. She picked up the small ring and looked into its tiny diamond, like a seeress gazing into a crystal. "You *were* a sweet old thing, Dwight," she murmured impulsively as she brushed her lips across the gleaming stone.

The evening had been hot and oppressive, but now a light breeze blew in from the river, fluttering the primly starched scrim curtains, making the straight candleflames sway dancingly. And with the breeze there came the distance-muted music of the orchestra of an excursion boat steaming home late from Block Island.

For a moment she heard without recognition, then suddenly her senses fitted the notes into the pattern of her memory. The *Blue Danube!* Against her will her heart echoed and re-echoed the music.

"Oh, Dwight—Dwight dearest, Dwight belovèd!" Her sob-choked exclamation was half moan, half scream,

117

pitched shrilly, but controlled. Papa must not hear her. She'd promised him—

She threw herself across the bed and pressed her face into the lavender-spiced pillow, weeping helplessly, noiselessly, till sheer exhaustion gave her a degree of peace.

Dr. Bogardus splashed the soapsuds from his hands and wiped them on the fresh huck towel which the orderly had just brought to the lavatory. "Dum it, Frisby," he said as his colleague took possession of the washbasin, "I can't understand that young Fairchild in B-2. The feller should 'a' died two weeks ago, with the apex of his left lung almost shot away, but—dum it all!—he hangs on like a pointer pup to a root. Seems as if he's waitin' for something before he finally decides to kick the bucket."

"H'm?" Dr. Frisby laved his hands and dried them methodically. "Funny thing about these tough young 'uns. Half the time they get well when we've given up all hope, and spoil our reputations—"

"This one won't," Bogardus denied. "He can't. Hasn't got an earthly chance; just livin' on his nerve. When that breaks—" He shrugged into his blouse and bent his head back as he hooked the collar fastenings. "Come on, let's eat. I've done ten amputations today, an' I'm hungry as a wolf."

"Any mail, Sister?" Dwight looked up hopefully as the young woman in the blue habit bustled past his bed, the points of her starched *cornette* flapping like a bird's wing with the motion of her walk.

The young sister of charity looked down pityingly. She had not withdrawn from the world long enough to regard men impersonally, and this pale-faced boy with the great eyes who asked so plaintively for mail each day wrung her heart. "No mail today, Lieutenant," she responded gently. "The trains from the North are all delayed by troop movements. Maybe you'll get your letter tomorrow."

She met Dr. Frisby as she left the ward. "Dr. Bogardus seems so sure that young man's going to die," she volunteered, "but I'm not certain. He has a dreadful wound, it's true; but I never saw a man who clung to life so fiercely—"

"Yep, Bogardus said he seemed to be waitin' for something before he finally makes up his mind to die—"

118

The sister smiled. A knowing, woman's smile. "He's waiting for a letter from his sweetheart, Doctor. The hope of it's sustaining him. When it comes—unless it comes too late—I shouldn't be surprised if he got well and fooled us all."

"Lieutenant Fairchild, here's your letter!" Sister Mary Agnes almost stumbled in her haste to reach Dwight's cot. "Now everything will be all right, and you'll get well—shall I read it to you?"

The big, unnaturally bright eyes in his pale face shone with an ethereal light. "Yes, please, if you will. I'm afraid I can't quite—"

"Never mind. Just rest quietly; I'll read it—" She had broken the seal and drawn out the sheet of folded paper. With a quick glance she scanned the irregular, fashionable writing, and for a moment all expression left her face. Then she smiled at him, not only with her lips, but with her eyes; eyes that were warm and understanding and kind. "It's a beautiful, sweet letter," she assured him. "Listen":

Dwight, my belovèd:

They tell me that you have been wounded, and when I heard the news it seemed the bullet tore through my flesh, too, for we are so soon to be one, my darling, that whatever hurts you hurts me, just as everything that gives you happiness makes me happy.

Do you know they say the war will soon be over, dearest one? And you'll be coming back to me with all your honors thick upon you. But I'll not see the hero with his medals or the victor who returns in triumph from the battle; I'll only see my own true love, for whose return I've hoped and waited so long. How happy we shall be, my dear! All the happy times we've had together were but the prelude to the happiness we have in store for us.

Good night, my dearest, and know that every day I miss you, and every night I pray for your return.

Always and forever yours,

Drusilla.

She glanced down at him as she finished. He was looking straight before him, eyes wide, as if he saw a glory he had never dreamed of limned against the whitewashed wall of the hospital ward. She heard his quick, light breathing, she saw the sweat that started to his forehead just below the hair-line. She knew the signs. Hastily she rose to summon Dr. Bogardus, then returned to kneel beside the cot and recite prayers for the dying. And for herself. It was a sin to lie, but she was not repentant. Even as she asked forgiveness for the lie she knew that she would do the same thing many times again if by such sinning she could guard a dying boy from heart-hurt.

Presently she heard the doctor grunt. "All right, Sister. Call the orderlies. Get 'im out o' here. We're short o' beds."

Outside in the warm sunshine an almost convalescent trooper from the Fifth Michigan Cavalry baked himself luxuriously against a wall and played his accordion. The notes came wheezily, and plainly the musician played by ear, but the tune was easily distinguishable. The *Blue Danube*.

Three hundred guests had passed the bride and bridegroom, showering congratulations and good wishes on them; now the wedding supper was completed, the last champagne toast drunk, and the company repaired to the ballroom where the orchestra was playing a soft prelude to the dance. The older people found seats by the wall, the youngsters looked expectantly toward Martense and his bride, for till they led off none might dance, and their feet were tingling to begin.

It had been one of those intolerable late-August days that sometimes afflict the west tip of Long Island, a day of humid heat that stopped the nostrils and clogged the throat, with neither life nor freshness in such air as moved, only more heat. But now a breeze was rising, whimpering through the pear trees in the garden, bringing a promise of rain. Thunder rolled and grumbled in the east out by Jamaica Bay, the horizon was brightened intermittently with the white glow of lightning.

"Shall we dance, my dear?" Young Mr. Martense bowed, reached out a white-gloved hand and clasped her small, sweet waist. The violin and clarinets struck up the *Blue Danube*, and in a moment they were whirling round the brightly lighted, mirrored room, the center of a hundred other whirling couples.

"You're cold?" he asked as she shuddered slightly in the circle of his arm. "Shall I have them close the windows?"

"Oh, no, please," she denied. "It isn't that I'm cold; it's just that—"

The storm burst on them with a screaming war-whoop. The building fairly staggered with the impact of the wind, the rain dashed with an angry hiss against the walls, and through the opened French windows lashed a spate of water almost solid as a rising wave.

The flaring gas flames in the chandeliers were fluttering like tattered banners in the gale. One after another they wavered, flattened, and went out. The room was dark as Erebus, the shrouding blackness echoed with the startled screams of women and the men's ejaculations.

"Excuse me, dear, I'll have things right in no time," Martense murmured, and in his excitement forgot to escort her from the floor.

She looked about her in bewilderment. Accustoming themselves to the darkness, her eyes could descry figures, but not features.

The orchestra was still playing and a few of the more daring couples danced, but she stood in a little zone of vacant space clutching her bouquet of bridal roses in the bend of one arm, her trailing veil of Valenciennes lace looped across the other.

Clear and piercing-sweet, the second movement of the waltz tune eddied through the darkness. She turned to make her way from the floor, but stopped in mid-step as a shadow, a bare shade darker than the darkness of the lightless room, loomed directly in her path.

"My waltz, Ma'am, I believe."

She felt her waist encircled by a strong arm. Not the formal embrace of conventional dancing, not the precise, stiff hold of her husband, but a tightening, almost stifling clasp that drew her to a broadcloth coat set with a double row of buttons. As she raised her hand involuntarily her fingers touched the gold lace of an epaulet. No one at the reception had been uniformed, a soldier would have seemed incongruous in that company. But this man—

"My waltz, Ma'am, I believe."

She drew back from the clutching, fierce embrace as she recalled his last words—her promise—but the arm about her tightened, and a laugh that had no hint of happiness or humor in it sounded softly in her ear.

"My waltz, Ma'am, I believe."

The words were taken up by the wind shrieking through the windows. They fell into a rhythm matching the cadences of the music.

She dropped her bouquet, and her stiffening fingers crawled up to her lips to stifle back a shrill cry of sheer terror.

Her heart was jerking like a thing in its death-throes. Her throat closed with compelling panic, and into every vein and artery an icy fluid seemed to pour in place of blood.

Her nerves were fraying out like slowly breaking threads. Her knees were weak as water, and she faltered, stumbled, all but fell; but the hungry-clasping arm about her held her up.

"My waltz, Ma'am, I believe."

Something burst like a bomb in her head. She was no longer fearful. This was glorious! The arm about her held her so close that it hurt; and she loved the pain of it.

Closer, tighter; hold me closer, dear, dear lover! Drag me down to hell or up to heaven with you. Anywhere—anywhere, as long as we're together!

She was sobbing; hard, dry, ugly sobs of heart-break, and laughing as she sobbed.

"My waltz, Ma'am, I believe."

"Yes—yes; your waltz! This and all my waltzes, belovèd. Never will I dance again with any other man; never shall another man so much as touch my hand."

The hurrying waiters forced the windows shut. They brought lights for the blown-out gas jets. Once more the room shone with the gleam of blazing chandeliers. The orchestra stopped playing, the dancers stood in a wide, frightened circle, watching the wild, whirling, pirouetting, spinning figure in the center of the floor.

Her bride's bouquet was thrown away and trampled underfoot, her veil was rent to tattered streamers, across her white shoulders the dark hair floated unbound, like the tresses of a drowned girl floating on the tide.

"Drusilla!" Harold Martense strode to her, laid a hand upon her arm. "Control yourself!"

She turned strange, empty eyes on him. Cold eyes, lifeless as the windows of a vacant house with all the curtains drawn—but with something peeping furtively underneath the lowered blinds.

She was humming an accompaniment to her dance. The *Blue Danube.* Her voice rose higher; rose and mounted like a quickening flame. It rose and shrilled and sharpened till it seemed no human throat could stand the piping strain of it.

Then, like a snapping violin string, its sound stopped suddenly, abruptly; utterly.

Her husband took her by the shoulders and shook her. "Stop this nonsense!" he commanded sharply. "Everything's all right, now—"

She looked at him as if she'd never seen him before; then, in a small, cold voice:

"He came back to me; back from the grave to claim the waltz I'd promised him the night he went away, and"—the racing, breathless words came in a tittering whisper—"*he took me with him!*"

Three days later she was sent to Blackwell's Island, pronounced incurably insane.

An Occurrence at Owl Creek Bridge

AMBROSE BIERCE

I

A man stood upon a railroad bridge in northern Alabama, looking down into the swift water twenty feet below. The man's hands were behind his back, the wrists bound with a cord. A rope closely encircled his neck. It was attached to a stout cross-timber above his head and the slack fell to the level of his knees. Some loose boards laid upon the sleepers supporting the metals of the railway supplied a footing for him and his executioners—two private soldiers of the Federal army, directed by a sergeant who in civil life may have been a deputy sheriff. At a short remove upon the same temporary platform was an officer in the uniform of his rank, armed. He was a captain. A sentinel at each end of the bridge stood with his rifle in the position known as "support," that is to say, vertical in front of the left shoulder, the hammer resting on the forearm thrown straight across the chest—a formal and unnatural position, enforcing an erect carriage of the body. It did not appear to be the duty of these two men to know what was occurring at the centre of the bridge; they merely blockaded the two ends of the foot planking that traversed it.

Beyond one of the sentinels nobody was in sight; the railroad ran straight away into a forest for a hundred yards, then, curving, was lost to view. Doubtless there was an outpost farther along. The other bank of the stream was open ground—a gentle acclivity topped with a stockade of vertical tree trunks, loopholed for rifles, with a single embrasure through which protruded the muzzle of a brass cannon commanding the bridge. Midway of the slope between bridge and fort were the spectators—a single company of infantry in line, at "parade rest," the butts of the rifles on the ground, the barrels inclining slightly backward against the right shoulder, the hands crossed upon the stock. A lieutenant stood at the right of the line, the point of his sword upon the ground, his left hand resting upon his right. Excepting the group of four at the centre of the bridge, not a man moved. The company faced the bridge, staring stonily, motionless. The sentinels, facing the banks of the stream, might have been statues to adorn the bridge. The captain stood with folded arms, silent, observing the work of his subordinates, but making no sign. Death is a dignitary who when he comes announced is to be received with formal manifestations of respect, even by those most familiar with him. In the code of military etiquette silence and fixity are forms of deference.

The man who was engaged in being hanged was apparently about thirty-five years of age. He was a civilian, if one might judge from his habit, which was that of a planter. His features were good—a straight nose, firm mouth, broad forehead, from which his long, dark hair was combed straight back, falling behind his ears to the collar of his well-fitting frock coat. He wore a mustache and pointed beard, but no whiskers; his eyes were large and dark gray, and had a kindly expression which one would hardly have expected in one whose neck was in the hemp. Evidently this was no vulgar assassin. The liberal military code makes provision for hanging many kinds of persons, and gentlemen are not excluded.

The preparations being complete, the two private soldiers stepped aside and each drew away the plank upon which he had been standing. The sergeant turned to the captain, saluted and placed himself immediately behind that officer, who in turn moved apart one pace. These movements left the condemned man and the sergeant standing on the two ends of the same plank, which spanned three of the cross-ties of the bridge. The end upon which the civilian stood almost, but not quite, reached a fourth. This plank had been held in place by the weight of the captain; it was now held by that of the sergeant. At a signal from the former the latter would step aside, the plank would tilt and the condemned man go down between two ties. The arrangement commended itself to his judgment as simple and effective. His face had not been covered nor his eyes bandaged. He looked a moment at his "unsteadfast footing," then let his gaze wander to the swirling water of the stream racing madly beneath his feet. A piece of dancing driftwood caught his attention and his eyes followed it down the current. How slowly it appeared to move! What a sluggish stream!

He closed his eyes in order to fix his last thoughts upon his wife and children. The water, touched to gold by the early sun, the brooding mists under the banks at some distance down the stream, the fort, the soldiers, the piece of drift—all had distracted him. And now he became conscious of a new disturbance. Striking through the thought of his dear ones was a sound which he could neither ignore nor understand, a sharp, distinct, metallic percussion like the stroke of a blacksmith's hammer upon the anvil; it had the same ringing quality. He wondered what it was, and whether immeasurably distant or nearby—it seemed both. Its recurrence was regular, but as slow as the tolling of a death knell. He awaited each stroke with impatience and—he knew not why—apprehension. The intervals of silence grew progressively longer; the delays became maddening. With their greater infrequency the sounds increased in strength and sharpness. They hurt his ear like the thrust of a knife; he feared he would shriek. What he heard was the ticking of his watch.

He unclosed his eyes and saw again the water below him. "If I could free my hands," he thought, "I might throw off the noose and spring into the stream. By diving I could evade the bullets and, swimming vigorously, reach the bank, take to the woods and get away home. My home, thank God, is as yet outside their lines; my wife and little ones are still beyond the invader's farthest advance."

As these thoughts, which have here to be set down in words, were flashed into the doomed man's brain rather than evolved from it the captain nodded to the sergeant. The sergeant stepped aside.

II

Peyton Farquhar was a well-to-do planter, of an old and highly respected Alabama family. Being a slave owner, and like other slave owners, a politician, he was naturally an original secessionist and ardently devoted to the Southern cause. Circumstances of an imperious nature, which it is unnecessary to relate here, had prevented him from taking service with the gallant army that had fought the disastrous campaigns ending with the fall of Corinth, and he chafed under the inglorious restraint, longing for the release of his energies, the larger life of the soldier, the opportunity for distinction. That opportunity, he felt, would come, as it comes to all in war time. Meanwhile he did what he could. No service was too humble for him to perform in aid of the South, no adventure too perilous for him to undertake if consistent with the character of a civilian who was at heart a soldier, and who in good faith and without too much qualification assented to at least a part of the frankly villainous dictum that all is fair in love and war.

One evening while Farquhar and his wife were sitting on a rustic bench near the entrance to his grounds, a gray-clad soldier rode up to the gate and asked for a drink of water. Mrs. Farquhar was only too happy to serve him with her own white hands. While she was fetching the water her husband approached the dusty horseman and inquired eagerly for news from the front.

"The Yanks are repairing the railroads," said the man, "and are getting ready for another advance. They have reached the Owl Creek bridge, put it in order and built a stockade on the north bank. The commandant has issued an order, which is posted everywhere, declaring that any civilian caught interfering with the railroad, its bridges, tunnels or trains will be summarily hanged. I saw the order."

"How far is it to the Owl Creek bridge?" Farquhar asked.

"About thirty miles."

"Is there no force on this side the creek?"

"Only a picket post half a mile out, on the railroad, and a single sentinel at this end of the bridge."

"Suppose a man—a civilian and student of hanging—should elude the picket post and perhaps get the better of the sentinel," said Farquhar, smiling, "what could he accomplish?"

The soldier reflected. "I was there a month ago," he replied. "I observed that the flood of last winter had lodged a great quantity of driftwood against the wooden pier at this end of the bridge. It is now dry and would burn like tow."

The lady had now brought the water, which the soldier drank. He thanked her ceremoniously, bowed to her husband and rode away. An hour later, after nightfall, he repassed the plantation, going northward in the direction from which he had come. He was a Federal scout.

III

As Peyton Farquhar fell straight downward through the bridge he lost consciousness and was as one already dead. From this state he was awakened—ages later, it seemed to him—by the pain of a sharp pressure upon his throat, followed by a sense of suffocation. Keen, poignant agonies seemed to shoot from his neck downward through every fibre of his body and limbs. These pains appeared to flash along well-defined lines of ramification and to beat with an inconceivably rapid periodicity. They seemed like streams of pulsating fire heating him to an intolerable temperature. As to his head, he was conscious of nothing but a feeling of fulness—of congestion. These sensations were unaccompanied by thought. The intellectual part of his nature was already effaced; he had power only to feel, and feeling was torment. He was conscious of motion. Encompassed in a luminous cloud, of which he was now merely the fiery heart, without material substance, he swung through unthinkable arcs of oscillation, like a vast pendulum. Then all at once, with terrible suddenness, the light about him shot upward with the noise of a loud plash; a frightful roaring was in his ears, and all was cold and dark. The power of thought was restored; he knew that the rope had broken and he had fallen into the stream. There was no additional strangulation; the noose about his neck was already suffocating him and kept the water from his lungs. To die of hanging at the bottom of a river!—the idea seemed to him ludicrous. He opened his eyes in the darkness and saw above him a gleam of light, but how distant, how inaccessible! He was still sinking, for the light became fainter and fainter until it was a mere glimmer. Then it began to grow and brighten, and he knew that he was rising toward the surface—knew it with reluctance, for he was now very comfortable. "To be hanged and drowned," he thought, "that is not so bad; but I do not wish to be shot. No; I will not be shot; that is not fair."

He was not conscious of an effort, but a sharp pain in his wrist apprised him that he was trying to free his hands. He gave the struggle his attention, as an idler might observe the feat of a juggler, without interest in the outcome. What splendid effort!—what magnificent, what superhuman strength! Ah, that was a fine endeavor! Bravo! The cord fell away; his arms parted and floated upward, the hands dimly seen on each side in the growing light. He watched them with a new interest as first one and then the other pounced upon the noose at his neck. They tore it away and thrust it fiercely aside, its undulations resembling those of a water-snake. "Put it back, put it back!" He thought he shouted these words to his hands, for the undoing of the noose had been succeeded by the direst pang that he had yet experienced. His neck ached horribly; his brain was on fire; his heart, which had been fluttering faintly, gave a great leap, trying to force itself out at his mouth. His whole body was racked and wrenched with an insupportable anguish! But his disobedient hands gave no heed to the command. They beat the water vigorously with quick, downward strokes, forcing him to the surface. He felt his head emerge; his eyes were blinded by the sunlight; his chest expanded convulsively, and with a supreme and crowning agony his lungs engulfed a great draught of air, which instantly he expelled in a shriek!

He was now in full possession of his physical senses. They were, indeed, preternaturally keen and alert. Something in the awful disturbance of his organic system had so exalted and refined them that they made record of things never before perceived. He felt the ripples upon his face and heard their separate sounds as they struck. He looked at the forest on the bank of the stream, saw the individual trees, the leaves and the veining of each leaf—saw the very insects upon them: the locusts, the brilliant-bodied flies, the gray spiders stretching their webs from twig to twig. He noted the prismatic colors in all the dewdrops upon a million blades of grass. The humming of the gnats that danced above the eddies of the stream, the beating of the dragon-flies' wings, the strokes of the water-spiders' legs, like oars which had lifted their boat—all these made audible music. A fish slid along beneath his eyes and he heard the rush of its body parting the water.

He had come to the surface facing down the stream; in a moment the visible world seemed to wheel slowly round, himself the pivotal point, and he saw the bridge, the fort, the soldiers upon the bridge, the captain, the sergeant, the two privates, his executioners. They were in silhouette against the blue sky. They shouted and gesticulated, pointing at him. The captain had drawn his pistol, but did not fire; the others were unarmed. Their movements were grotesque and horrible, their forms gigantic.

Suddenly he heard a sharp report and something struck the water smartly within a few inches of his head, spattering his face with spray. He heard a second report, and saw one of the sentinels with his rifle at his shoulder, a light cloud of blue smoke rising from the muzzle. The man in the water saw the eye of the man on the bridge gazing into his own through the sights of the rifle. He observed that it was a gray eye and remembered having read that gray eyes were keenest, and that all famous marksmen had them. Nevertheless, this one had missed.

A counter-swirl had caught Farquhar and turned him half round; he was again looking into the forest on the bank opposite the fort. The sound of a clear, high voice in a monotonous singsong now rang out behind him and came across the water with a distinctness that pierced and subdued all other sounds, even the beating of the ripples in his ears. Although no soldier, he had frequented camps enough to know the dread significance of that deliberate, drawling, aspirated chant; the lieutenant on shore was taking a part in the morning's work. How coldly and pitilessly—with what an even, calm intonation, presaging, and enforcing tranquillity in the men—with what accurately measured intervals fell those cruel words:

"Attention, company!...Shoulder arms!...Ready!...
Aim!...Fire!"

Farquhar dived—dived as deeply as he could. The water
roared in his ears like the voice of Niagara, yet he heard the
dulled thunder of the volley and, rising again toward the
surface, met shining bits of metal, singularly flattened, oscillating slowly downward. Some of them touched him on
the face and hands, then fell away, continuing their descent.
One lodged between his collar and neck; it was uncomfortably warm and he snatched it out.

As he rose to the surface, gasping for breath, he saw that
he had been a long time under water; he was perceptibly
farther down stream—nearer to safety. The soldiers had
almost finished reloading; the metal ramrods flashed all at
once in the sunshine as they were drawn from the barrels,
turned in the air, and thrust into their sockets. The two
sentinels fired again, independently and ineffectually.

The hunted man saw all this over his shoulder; he was
now swimming vigorously with the current. His brain was
as energetic as his arms and legs; he thought with the
rapidity of lightning.

"The officer," he reasoned, "will not make that
martinet's error a second time. It is as easy to dodge a volley
as a single shot. He has probably already given the command
to fire at will. God help me, I cannot dodge them all!"

An appalling plash within two yards of him was followed by a loud, rushing sound, *diminuendo,* which seemed
to travel back through the air to the fort and died in an
explosion which stirred the very river to its deeps! A rising
sheet of water curved over him, fell down upon him, blinded
him, strangled him! The cannon had taken a hand in the
game. As he shook his head free from the commotion of the
smitten water he heard the deflected shot humming through
the air ahead, and in an instant it was cracking and smashing
the branches in the forest beyond.

"They will not do that again," he thought; "the next
time they will use a charge of grape. I must keep my eye upon
the gun; the smoke will apprise me—the report arrives too
late; it lags behind the missile. That is a good gun."

Suddenly he felt himself whirled round and round—
spinning like a top. The water, the banks, the forests, the
now distant bridge, fort and men—all were commingled and

blurred. Objects were represented by their colors only; circular horizontal streaks of color—that was all he saw. He had been caught in a vortex and was being whirled on with a velocity of advance and gyration that made him giddy and sick. In a few moments he was flung upon the gravel at the foot of the left bank of the stream—the southern bank—and behind a projecting point which concealed him from his enemies. The sudden arrest of his motion, the abrasion of one of his hands on the gravel, restored him, and he wept with delight. He dug his fingers into the sand, threw it over himself in handfuls and audibly blessed it. It looked like diamonds, rubies, emeralds; he could think of nothing beautiful which it did not resemble. The trees upon the bank were giant garden plants; he noted a definite order in their arrangement, inhaled the fragrance of their blooms. A strange, roseate light shone through the spaces among their trunks and the wind made in their branches the music of æolian harps. He had no wish to perfect his escape—was content to remain in that enchanting spot until retaken.

A whiz and rattle of grapeshot among the branches high above his head roused him from his dream. The baffled cannoneer had fired him a random farewell. He sprang to his feet, rushed up the sloping bank, and plunged into the forest.

All that day he traveled, laying his course by the rounding sun. The forest seemed interminable; nowhere did he discover a break in it, not even a woodman's road. He had not known that he lived in so wild a region. There was something uncanny in the revelation.

By nightfall he was fatigued, footsore, famishing. The thought of his wife and children urged him on. At last he found a road which led him in what he knew to be the right direction. It was as wide and straight as a city street, yet it seemed untraveled. No fields bordered it, no dwelling anywhere. Not so much as the barking of a dog suggested human habitation. The black bodies of the trees formed a straight wall on both sides, terminating on the horizon in a point, like a diagram in a lesson in perspective. Overhead, as he looked up through this rift in the wood, shone great golden stars looking unfamiliar and grouped in strange constellations. He was sure they were arranged in some order which had a secret and malign significance. The wood on either side was full of singular noises, among which—once, twice, and again—he distinctly heard whispers in an unknown tongue.

His neck was in pain and lifting his hand to it he found it horribly swollen. He knew that it had a circle of black where the rope had bruised it. His eyes felt congested; he could no longer close them. His tongue was swollen with thirst; he relieved its fever by thrusting it forward from between his teeth into the cold air. How softly the turf had carpeted the untraveled avenue—he could no longer feel the roadway beneath his feet!

Doubtless, despite his suffering, he had fallen asleep while walking, for now he sees another scene—perhaps he has merely recovered from a delirium. He stands at the gate of his own home. All is as he left it, and all bright and beautiful in the morning sunshine. He must have traveled the entire night. As he pushes open the gate and passes up the wide white walk, he sees a flutter of female garments; his wife, looking fresh and cool and sweet, steps down from the veranda to meet him. At the bottom of the steps she stands waiting, with a smile of ineffable joy, an attitude of matchless grace and dignity. Ah, how beautiful she is! He springs forward with extended arms. As he is about to clasp her he feels a stunning blow upon the back of the neck; a blinding white light blazes all about him with a sound like the shock of a cannon—then all is darkness and silence!

Peyton Farquhar was dead; his body, with a broken neck, swung gently from side to side beneath the timbers of the Owl Creek bridge.

Fearful Rock

MANLY WADE WELLMAN

1
The Sacrifice

Enid Mandifer tried to stand up under what she had just heard. She managed it, but her ears rang, her eyes misted. She felt as if she were drowning.

The voice of Persil Mandifer came through the fog, level and slow, with the hint of that foreign accent which nobody could identify:

"Now that you know that you are not really my daughter, perhaps you are curious as to why I adopted you."

Curious...was that the word to use? But this man who was not her father after all, he delighted in understatements. Enid's eyes had grown clearer now. She was able to move, to obey Persil Mandifer's invitation to seat herself. She saw him, half sprawling in his rocking chair against the plastered wall of the parlor, under the painting of his ancient friend Aaron Burr. Was the rumor true, she mused, that Burr had not really died, that he still lived and planned ambitiously to make himself a throne in America? But Aaron Burr would have to be an old, old man—a hundred years old, or more than a hundred.

Persil Mandifer's own age might have been anything, but probably he was nearer seventy than fifty. Physically he was the narrowest of men, in shoulders, hips, temples and legs alike, so that he appeared distorted and compressed. White hair, like combed thistledown, fitted itself in ordered streaks to his high skull. His eyes, dull and dark as musket balls, peered expressionlessly above the nose like a stiletto, the chin like the pointed toe of a fancy boot. The fleshlessness of his legs was accentuated by tight trousers, strapped under the insteps. At his throat sprouted a frill of lace, after a fashion twenty-five years old.

At his left, on a stool, crouched his enormous son Larue. Larue's body was a collection of soft-looking globes and bladders—a tremendous belly, round-kneed short legs, puffy hands, a gross bald head between fat shoulders. His white linen suit was only a shade paler than his skin, and his loose, faded-pink lips moved incessantly. Once Enid had heard him talking to himself, had been close enough to distinguish the words. Over and over he had said: "I'll kill you. I'll kill you. I'll kill you."

These two men had reared her from babyhood, here in this low, spacious manor of brick and timber in the Ozark country. Sixteen or eighteen years ago there had been Indians hereabouts, but they were gone, and the few settlers were on remote farms. The Mandifers dwelt alone with their slaves, who were unusually solemn and taciturn for Negroes.

Persil Mandifer was continuing: "I have brought you up as a gentleman would bring up his real daughter—for the sole and simple end of making her a good wife. That explains, my dear, the governess, the finishing-school at St. Louis, the books, the journeys we have undertaken to New Orleans and elsewhere. I regret that this distressing war between the states," and he paused to draw from his pocket his enameled snuff-box, "should have made recent junkets impracticable. However, the time has come, and you are not to be despised. Your marriage is now to befall you."

"Marriage," mumbled Larue, in a voice that Enid was barely able to hear. His fingers interlaced, like fat white worms in a jumble. His eyes were for Enid, his ears for his father.

Enid saw that she must respond. She did so: "You have—chosen a husband for me?"

Persil Mandifer's lips crawled into a smile, very wide on his narrow blade of a face, and he took a pinch of snuff.

"Your husband, my dear, was chosen before ever you came into this world," he replied. The smile grew broader, but Enid did not think it cheerful. "Does your mirror do you justice?" he teased her. "Enid, my foster-daughter, does it tell you truly that you are a beauty, with a face all lustrous and oval, eyes full of tender fire, a cascade of golden-brown curls to frame the whole?" His gaze wandered upon her body, and his eyelids drooped. "Does it convince you, Enid, that your figure combines rarely those traits of fragility and rondure that are never so desirable as when they occur together? Ah, Enid, had I myself met you, or one like you, thirty years ago—"

"Father!" growled Larue, as though at sacrilege. Persil Mandifer chuckled. His left hand, white and slender with a dark cameo upon the forefinger, extended and patted Larue's repellent bald pate, in superior affection.

"Never fear, son," crooned Persil Mandifer. "Enid shall go a pure bride to him who waits her." His other hand crept into the breast of his coat and drew forth something on a chain. It looked like a crucifix.

"Tell me," pleaded the girl, "tell me, Fa—" She broke off, for she could not call him father. "What is the name of the one I am to marry?"

"His name?" said Larue, as though aghast at her ignorance.

"His name?" repeated the lean man in the rocking chair. The crucifix-like object in his hands began to swing idly and rhythmically, while he paid out chain to make its pendulum motion wider and slower. "He has no name."

Enid felt her lips grow cold and dry. "He has no—"

"He is the Nameless One," said Persil Mandifer, and she could discern the capital letters in the last two words he spoke.

"Look," said Larue, out of the corner of his weak mouth that was nearest his father. "She thinks that she is getting ready to run."

"She will not run," assured Persil Mandifer. "She will sit and listen, and watch what I have here in my hand." The object of the chain seemed to be growing in size and clarity of outline. Enid felt that it might not be a crucifix, after all.

"The Nameless One is also ageless," continued Persil Mandifer. "My dear, I dislike telling you all about him, and

137

it is not really necessary. All you need know is that we—my fathers and I—have served him here, and in Europe, since the days when France was Gaul. Yes, and before that."

The swinging object really was increasing in her sight. And the basic cross was no cross, but a three-armed thing like a capital T. Nor was the body-like figure spiked to it; it seemed to twine and clamber upon that T-shape, like a monkey on a bracket. Like a monkey, it was grotesque, disproportionate, a mockery. That climbing creature was made of gold, or of something gilded over. The T-shaped support was as black and bright as jet.

Enid thought that the golden creature was dull, as if tarnished, and that it appeared to move, an effect created, perhaps, by the rhythmic swinging on the chain.

"Our profits from the association have been great," Persil Mandifer droned. "Yet we have given greatly. Four times in each hundred years must a bride be offered."

Mist was gathering once more, in Enid's eyes and brain, a thicker mist than the one that had come from the shock of hearing that she was an adopted orphan. Yet through it all she saw the swinging device, the monkey-like climber upon the T. And through it all she heard Mandifer's voice:

"When my real daughter, the last female of my race, went to the Nameless One, I wondered where our next bride would come from. And so, twenty years ago, I took you from a foundling asylum at Nashville."

It was becoming plausible to her now. There was a power to be worshipped, to be feared, to be fed with young women. She must go—no, this sort of belief was wrong. It had no element of decency in it, it was only beaten into her by the spell of the pendulum-swinging charm. Yet she had heard certain directions, orders as to what to do.

"You will act in the manner I have described, and say the things I have repeated, tonight at sundown," Mandifer informed her, as though from a great distance. "You will surrender yourself to the Nameless One, as it was ordained when first you came into my possession."

"No," she tried to say, but her lips would not even stir. Something had crept into her, a will not her own, which was forcing her to accept defeat. She knew she must go—where?

"To Fearful Rock," said the voice of Mandifer, as though he had heard and answered the question she had not spoken.

138

"Go there, to that house where once my father lived and worshipped, that house which, upon the occasion of his rather mysterious death, I left. It is now our place of devotion and sacrifice. Go there, Enid, tonight at sundown, in the manner I have prescribed...."

2
The Cavalry Patrol

Lieutenant Kane Lanark was one of those strange and vicious heritage-anomalies of one of the most paradoxical of wars—a war where a great Virginian was high in Northern command, and a great Pennsylvanian stubbornly defended one of the South's principal strongholds; where the two presidents were both born in Kentucky, indeed within scant miles of each other; where father strove against son, and brother against brother, even more frequently and tragically than in all the jangly verses and fustian dramas of the day.

Lanark's birthplace was a Maryland farm, moderately prosperous. His education had been completed at the Virginia Military Institute, where he was one of a very few who were inspired by a quiet, bearded professor of mathematics who later became the Stonewall of the Confederacy, perhaps the continent's greatest tactician. The older Lanark was strongly for state's rights and mildly for slavery, though he possessed no Negro chattels. Kane, the younger of two sons, had carried those same attitudes with him as much as seven miles past the Kansas border, whither he had gone in 1861 to look for employment and adventure.

At that lonely point he met with Southern guerrillas, certain loose-shirted, weapon-laden gentry whose leader, a gaunt man with large, worried eyes, bore the craggy name of Quantrill and was to be called by a later historian the bloodiest man in American history. Young Kane Lanark, surrounded by sudden leveled guns, protested his sympathy with the South by birth, education and personal preference. Quantrill replied, rather sententiously, that while this might be true, Lanark's horse and money-belt had a Yankee look to them, and would be taken as prisoners of war.

After the guerrillas had galloped away, with a derisive laugh hanging in the air behind them, Lanark trudged back to the border and a little settlement, where he begged a ride by freight wagon to St. Joseph, Missouri. There he enlisted with a Union cavalry regiment just then in the forming, and his starkness of manner, with evidences about him of military education and good sense, caused his fellow recruits to elect him a sergeant.

Late that year, Lanark rode with a patrol through southern Missouri, where fortune brought him and his comrades face to face with Quantrill's guerrillas, the same that had plundered Lanark. The lieutenant in charge of the Federal cavalry set a most hysterical example for flight, and died of six Southern bullets placed accurately between his shoulder blades; but Lanark, as ranking non-commissioned officer, rallied the others, succeeded in withdrawing them in order before the superior force. As he rode last of the retreat, he had the fierce pleasure of engaging and sabering an overzealous guerrilla, who had caught up with him. The patrol rejoined its regiment with only two lost, the colonel was pleased to voice congratulations and Sergeant Lanark became Lieutenant Lanark, vice the slain officer.

In April of 1862, General Curtis, recently the victor in the desperately fought battle of Pea Ridge, showed trust and understanding when he gave Lieutenant Lanark a scouting party of twenty picked riders, with orders to seek yet another encounter with the marauding Quantrill. Few Union officers wanted anything to do with Quantrill, but Lanark, remembering his harsh treatment at those avaricious hands, yearned to kill the guerrilla chieftain with his own proper sword. On the afternoon of April fifth, beneath a sun bright but none too warm, the scouting patrol rode down a trail at the bottom of a great, trough-like valley just south of the Missouri-Arkansas border. Two pairs of men, those with the surest-footed mounts, acted as flanking parties high on the opposite slopes, and a watchful corporal by the name of Googan walked his horse well in advance of the main body. The others rode two and two, with Lanark at the head and Sergeant Jaeger, heavy-set and morosely keen of eye, at the rear.

A photograph survives of Lieutenant Kane Lanark as he appeared that very spring—his breadth of shoulder and slimness of waist accentuated by the snug blue cavalry jacket that terminated at his sword-belt, his ruddy, beak-nosed face shaded by a wide black hat with a gold cord. He wore a mustache, trim but not gay, and his long chin alone of all his command went smooth-shaven. To these details be it added that he rode his bay gelding easily, with a light, sure hand on the reins, and that he had the air of one who knew his present business.

The valley opened at length upon a wide level platter of land among high, pine-tufted hills. The flat expanse was no more than half timbered, though clever enemies might advance unseen across it if they exercised caution and foresight enough to slip from one belt or clump of trees to the next. Almost at the center of the level, a good five miles from where Lanark now halted his command, stood a single great chimney or finger of rock, its lean tip more than twice the height of the tallest tree within view.

To this geologic curiosity the eyes of Lieutenant Lanark snapped at once.

"Sergeant!" he called, and Jaeger sidled his horse close.

"We'll head for that rock, and stop there," Lanark announced. "It's a natural watch-tower, and from the top of it we can see everything, even better than we could if we rode clear across flat ground to those hills. And if Quantrill is west of us, which I'm sure he is, I'd like to see him coming a long way off, so as to know whether to fight or run."

"I agree with you, sir," said Jaeger. He peered through narrow, puffy lids at the pinnacle, and gnawed his shaggy lower lip. "I shall lift up mine eyes unto the rocks, from whence cometh my help," he misquoted reverently. The sergeant was full of garbled Scripture, and the men called him "Bible" Jaeger behind that wide back of his. This did not mean that he was soft, dreamy or easily fooled; Curtis had chosen him as sagely as he had chosen Lanark.

Staying in the open as much as possible, the party advanced upon the rock. They found it standing above a soft, grassy hollow, which in turn ran eastward from the base of the rock to a considerable ravine, dark and full of timber. As they spread out to the approach, they found something else: a house stood in the hollow, shadowed by the great pinnacle.

"It looks deserted, sir," volunteered Jaeger, at Lanark's bridle-elbow. "No sign of life."

"Perhaps," said Lanark. "Deploy the men, and we'll close in from all sides. Then you, with one man, enter the back door. I'll take another and enter the front."

141

"Good, sir." The sergeant kneed his horse into a faster walk, passing from one to another of the three corporals with muttered orders. Within sixty seconds the patrol closed upon the house like a twenty-fingered hand. Lanark saw that the building had once been pretentious—two stories, stoutly made of good lumber that must have been carted from a distance, with shuttered windows and a high peaked roof. Now it was a paint-starved gray, with deep veins and traceries of dirty black upon its clapboards. He dismounted before the piazza with its four pillar-like posts, and threw his reins to a trooper.

"Suggs!" he called, and obediently his own personal orderly, a plump blond youth, dropped out of the saddle. Together they walked up on the resounding planks of the piazza. Lanark, his ungloved right hand swinging free beside his holster, knocked at the heavy front door with his left fist. There was no answer. He tried the knob, and after a moment of shoving, the hinges creaked and the door went open.

They walked into a dark front hall, then into a parlor with dust upon the rug and the fine furniture, and rectangles of pallor upon the walls where pictures had once hung for years. They could hear echoes of their every movement, as anyone will hear in a house to which he is not accustomed. Beyond the parlor, they came to an ornate chandelier with crystal pendants, and at the rear stood a sideboard of dark, hard wood. Its drawers all hung half open, as if the silver and linen had been hastily removed. Above it hung plate-racks, also empty.

Feet sounded in a room to the rear, and then Jaeger's voice, asking if his lieutenant were inside. Lanark met him in the kitchen, conferred; then together they mounted the stairs in the front hall.

Several musty bedrooms, darkened by closed shutters, occupied the second floor. The beds had dirty mattresses, but no sheets or blankets.

"All clear in the house," pronounced Lanark. "Jaeger, go and detail a squad to reconnoiter in that little ravine east of here—we want no rebel sharpshooters sneaking up on us from that point. Then leave a picket there, put a man on top of the rock, and guards at the front and rear of this house. And have some of the others police up the house itself. We may stay here for two days, even longer."

The sergeant saluted, then went to bellow his orders, and troopers dashed hither and thither to obey. In a moment the sound of sweeping arose from the parlor. Lanark, to whom it suggested spring cleaning, sneezed at thought of the dust, then gave Suggs directions about the care of his bay. Unbuckling his saber, he hung it upon the saddle, but his revolver he retained. "You're in charge, Jaeger," he called, and sauntered away toward the wooded cleft.

His legs needed the exercise; he could feel them straightening by degrees after their long clamping to his saddle-flaps. He was uncomfortably dusty, too, and there must be water at the bottom of the ravine. Walking into the shade of the trees, he heard, or fancied he heard, a trickling sound. The slope was steep here, and he walked fast to maintain an easy balance upon it, for a minute and then two. There was water ahead, all right, for it gleamed through the leafage. And something else gleamed, something pink.

That pinkness was certainly flesh. His right hand dropped quickly to his revolver-butt, and he moved forward carefully. Stooping, he took advantage of the bushy cover, at the same time avoiding a touch that might snap or rustle the foliage. He could hear a voice now, soft and rhythmic. Lanark frowned. A woman's voice? His right hand still at his weapon, his left caught and carefully drew down a spray of willow. He gazed into an open space beyond.

It was a woman, all right, within twenty yards of him. She stood ankle-deep in a swift, narrow rush of brook-water, and her fine body was nude, every graceful curve of it, with a cascade of golden-brown hair falling and floating about her shoulders. She seemed to be praying, but her eyes were not lifted. They stared at a hand-mirror, that she held up to catch the last flash of the setting sun.

3
The Image in the Cellar

Lanark, a young, serious-minded bachelor in an era when women swaddled themselves inches deep in fabric, had never seen such a sight before; and to his credit be it said that his first and strongest emotion was proper embarrassment for the girl in the stream. He had a momentary impulse to slip back and away. Then he remembered that he had ordered a patrol to explore this place; it would be here within moments.

Therefore he stepped into the open, wondering at the time, as well as later, if he did well.

"Miss," he said gently. "Miss, you'd better put on your things. My men—"

She stared, squeaked in fear, dropped the mirror and stood motionless. Then she seemed to gather herself for flight. Lanark realized that the trees beyond her were thick and might hide enemies, that she was probably a resident of this rebel-inclined region and might be a decoy for such as himself. He whipped out his revolver, holding it at the ready but not pointing it.

"Don't run," he warned her sharply. "Are those your clothes beside you? Put them on at once."

She caught up a dress of flowered calico and fairly flung it on over her head. His embarrassment subsided a little, and he came another pace or two into the open. She was pushing her feet—very small feet they were—into heelless shoes. Her hands quickly gathered up some underthings and wadded them into a bundle. She gazed at him apprehensively, questioningly. Her hastily donned dress remained unfastened at the throat, and he could see the panicky stir of her heart in her half-bared bosom.

"I'm sorry," he went on, "but I think you'd better come up to the house with me."

"House?" she repeated fearfully, and her dark, wide eyes turned to look beyond him. Plainly she knew which house he meant. "You—live there?"

"I'm staying there at this time."

"You—came for me?" Apparently she had expected someone to come.

But instead of answering, he put a question of his own. "To whom were you talking just now? I could hear you."

"I—I said the words. The words my fath—" She broke off, wretchedly, and Lanark was forced to think how pretty she was in her confusion. "The words that Persil Mandifer told me to say." Her eyes on his, she continued softly: "I came to meet the Nameless One. Are you the—Nameless One?"

"I am certainly not nameless," he replied. "I am Lieutenant Lanark, of the Federal Army of the Frontier, at your service." He bowed slightly, which made it more formal. "Now, come along with me."

He took her by the wrist, which shook in his big left hand. Together they went back eastward through the ravine, in the direction of the house.

Before they reached it, she told him her name, and that the big natural pillar was called Fearful Rock. She also assured him that she knew nothing of Quantrill and his guerrillas; and a fourth item of news shook Lanark to his spurred heels, the first non-military matter that had impressed him in more than a year.

An hour later, Lanark and Jaeger finished an interview with her in the parlor. They called Suggs, who conducted the young woman up to one of the bedrooms. Then lieutenant and sergeant faced each other. The light was dim, but each saw bafflement and uneasiness in the face of the other.

"Well?" challenged Lanark.

Jaeger produced a clasp-knife, opened it, and pared thoughtfully at a thumbnail. "I'll take my oath," he ventured, "that this Miss Enid Mandifer is telling the gospel truth."

"Truth!" exploded Lanark scornfully. "Mountain-folk ignorance, I call it. Nobody believes in those devil-things these days."

"Oh, yes, somebody does," said Jaeger, mildly but definitely. "I do." He put away his knife and fumbled within his blue army shirt. "Look here, Lieutenant."

It was a small book he held out, little more than a pamphlet in size and thickness. On its cover of gray paper appeared the smudged woodcut of an owl against a full moon, and the title:

John George Hohman's
POW-WOWS
or
LONG LOST FRIEND

"I got it when I was a young lad in Pennsylvania," explained Jaeger, almost reverently. "Lots of Pennsylvania people carry this book, as I do." He opened the little volume, and read from the back of the title page:

"'Whosoever carries this book with him is safe from all his enemies, visible or invisible; and whoever has this book with him cannot die without the holy corpse of Jesus Christ, nor drown in any water nor burn up in any fire, nor can any unjust sentence be passed upon him.'"

Lanark put out his hand for the book, and Jaeger surrendered it, somewhat hesitantly. "I've heard of supposed witches in Pennsylvania," said the officer. "Hexes, I believe they're called. Is this a witch book?"

"No, sir. Nothing about black magic. See the cross on that page? It's a protection against witches."

"I thought that only Catholics used the cross," said Lanark.

"No. Not only Catholics."

"Hmm." Lanark passed the thing back. "Superstition, I call it. Nevertheless, you speak this much truth: that girl is in earnest, she believes what she told us. Her father, or stepfather, or whoever he is, sent her up here on some ridiculous errand—perhaps a dangerous one." He paused. "Or I may be misjudging her. It may be a clever scheme, Jaeger—a scheme to get a spy in among us."

The sergeant's big bearded head wagged negation. "No, sir. If she was telling a lie, it'd be a more believable one, wouldn't it?" He opened his talisman book again. "If the lieutenant please, there's a charm in here, against being shot or stabbed. It might be a good thing, seeing there's a war going on—perhaps the lieutenant would like me to copy it out?"

"No, thanks." Lanark drew forth his own charm against evil and nervousness, a leather case that contained cheroots. Jaeger, who had convictions against the use of tobacco, turned away disapprovingly as his superior bit off the end of a fragrant brown cylinder and kindled a match.

"Let me look at that what-do-you-call-it book again," he requested, and for a second time Jaeger passed the little volume over, then saluted and retired.

Darkness was gathering early, what with the position of the house in the grassy hollow, and the pinnacle of Fearful Rock standing between it and the sinking sun to westward. Lanark called for Suggs to bring a candle, and, when the orderly obeyed, directed him to take some kind of supper upstairs to Enid Mandifer. Left alone, the young officer seated himself in a newly dusted armchair of massive dark wood, emitted a cloud of blue tobacco smoke, and opened the *Long Lost Friend*.

It had no publication date, but John George Hohman, the author, dated his preface from Berks County, Pennsylvania, on July 31, 1819. In the secondary preface, filled with testimonials as to the success of Hohman's miraculous cures, was included the pious ejaculation: "The Lord bless the beginning and the end of this little work, and be with us, that we may not misuse it, and thus commit a heavy sin!"

"Amen to that!" said Lanark to himself, quite soberly. Despite his assured remarks to Jaeger, he was somewhat repelled and nervous because of the things Enid Mandifer had told him.

Was there, then, potentiality for such supernatural evil in this enlightened Nineteenth Century, even in the pages of the book he held? He read further, and came upon a charm to be recited against violence and danger, perhaps the very one Jaeger had offered to copy for him. It began rather sonorously: "The peace of our Lord Jesus Christ be with me. Oh shot, stand still! In the name of the mighty prophets Agtion and Elias, and do not kill me...."

Lanark remembered the name of Elias from his boyhood Sunday schooling, but Agtion's identity, as a prophet or otherwise, escaped him. He resolved to ask Jaeger; and, as though the thought had acted as a summons, Jaeger came almost running into the room.

"Lieutenant, sir! Lieutenant!" he said hoarsely.

"Yes, Sergeant Jaeger?" Lanark rose, stared questioningly, and held out the book. Jaeger took it automatically, and as automatically stowed it inside his shirt.

"I can prove, sir, that there's a real devil here," he mouthed unsteadily.

"What?" demanded Lanark. "Do you realize what you're saying, man? Explain yourself."

"Come, sir," Jaeger almost pleaded, and led the way into the kitchen. "It's down in the cellar."

From a little heap on a table he picked up a candle, and then opened a door full of darkness.

The stairs to the cellar were shaky to Lanark's feet, and beneath him was solid black shadow, smelling strongly of damp earth. Jaeger, stamping heavily ahead, looked back and upward. That broad, bearded face, that had not lost its full-blooded flush in the hottest fighting at Pea Ridge, had grown so pallid as almost to give off sickly light. Lanark began to wonder if all this theatrical approach would not make the promised devil seem ridiculous, anticlimactic—the flutter of an owl, the scamper of a rat, or something of that sort.

"You have the candle, sergeant," he reminded, and the echo of his voice momentarily startled him. "Strike a match, will you?"

"Yes, sir." Jaeger had raised a knee to tighten his stripe-sided trousers. A snapping scrape, a burst of flame, and the candle glow illuminated them both. It revealed, too, the cellar, walled with stones but floored with clay. As they finished the descent, Lanark could feel the soft grittiness of that clay under his bootsoles. All around them lay rubbish— boxes, casks, stacks of broken pots and dishes, bundles of kindling.

"Here," Jaeger was saying, "here is what I found."

He walked around the foot of the stairs. Beneath the slope of the flight lay a long, narrow case, made of plain, heavy boards. It was unpainted and appeared ancient. As Jaeger lowered the light in his hand, Lanark saw that the joinings were secured with huge nails, apparently forged by hand. Such nails had been used in building the older sheds on his father's Maryland estate. Now there was a creak of wooden protest as Jaeger pried up the loosened lid of the coffin-like box.

Inside lay something long and ruddy. Lanark saw a head and shoulders, and started violently. Jaeger spoke again:

"An image, sir. A heathen image." The light made grotesque the sergeant's face, one heavy half fully illumined, the other secret and lost in the black shadow. "Look at it."

Lanark, too, stooped for a closer examination. The form was of human length, or rather more; but it was not finished, was neither divided into legs below nor extended into arms at the roughly shaped shoulders. The head, too, had been molded without features, though from either side, where the ears should have been, it sprouted up-curved horns like a bison's. Lanark felt a chill creep upon him, whence he knew not.

"It's Satan's own image," Jaeger was mouthing deeply. "'Thou shalt not make unto thee any graven image—'"

With one foot he turned the coffin-box upon its side. Lanark took a quick stride backward, just in time to prevent the ruddy form from dropping out upon his toes. A moment later, Jaeger had spurned the thing. It broke, with a crashing sound like crockery, and two more trampling kicks of the sergeant's heavy boots smashed it to bits.

"Stop!" cried Lanark, too late. "Why did you break it? I wanted to have a good look at the thing."

"But it is not good for men to look upon the devil's works," responded Jaeger, almost pontifically.

"Don't advise me, sergeant," said Lanark bleakly. "Remember that I am your officer, and that I don't need instruction as to what I may look at." He looked down at the fragments. "Hmm, the thing was hollow, and quite brittle. It seems to have been stuffed with straw—no, excelsior. Wood shavings, anyway." He investigated the fluffy inner mass with a toe. "Hullo, there's something inside of the stuff."

"I wouldn't touch it, sir," warned Jaeger, but this time it was he who spoke too late. Lanark's boot-toe had nudged the object into plain sight, and Lanark had put down his gauntleted left hand and picked it up.

"What is this?" he asked himself aloud. "Looks like some sort of strongbox—foreign, I'd say, and quite old. Jaeger, we'll go upstairs."

In the kitchen, with a strong light from several candles, they examined the find quite closely. It was a dark oblong, like a small dispatch-case or, as Lanark had commented, a strongbox. Though as hard as iron, it was not iron, nor any metal either of them had ever known.

"How does it open?" was Lanark's next question, turning the case over in his hands. "It doesn't seem to have hinges on it. Is this the lid—or this?"

"I couldn't say." Jaeger peered, his eyes growing narrow with perplexity. "No hinges, as the lieutenant just said."

"None visible, nor yet a lock." Lanark thumped the box experimentally, and proved it hollow. Then he lifted it close to his ear and shook it. There was a faint rustle, as of papers loosely rolled or folded. "Perhaps," the officer went on, "this separate slice isn't a lid at all. There may be a spring to press, or something that slides back and lets another plate come loose."

But Suggs was entering from the front of the house. "Lieutenant, sir! Something's happened to Newton—he was watching on the rock. Will the lieutenant come? And Sergeant Jaeger, too."

The suggestion of duty brought back the color and self-control that Jaeger had lost. "What's happened to Newton?" he demanded at once, and hurried away with Suggs.

Lanark waited in the kitchen for only a moment. He wanted to leave the box, but did not want his troopers meddling with it. He spied, beside the heavy iron stove, a fireplace, and in its side the metal door to an old brick oven. He pulled that door open, thrust the box in, closed the door again, and followed Suggs and Jaeger.

They had gone out upon the front porch. There, with Corporal Gray and a blank-faced trooper on guard, lay the silent form of Newton, its face covered with a newspaper.

Almost every man of the gathered patrol knew a corpse when he saw one, and it took no second glance to know that Newton was quite dead.

4
The Mandifers

Jaeger, bending, lifted the newspaper and then dropped it back. He said something that, for all his religiosity, might have been an oath.

"What's the matter, sergeant?" demanded Lanark.

Jaeger's brows were clamped in a tense frown, and his beard was actually trembling. "His face, sir. It's terrible."

"A wound?" asked Lanark, and lifted the paper in turn. He, too, let it fall back, and his exclamation of horror and amazement was unquestionably profane.

"There ain't no wound on him, Lieutenant Lanark," offered Suggs, pushing his wan, plump face to the forefront of the troopers. "We heard Newton yell—heard him from the top of the rock yonder."

All eyes turned gingerly toward the promontory.

"That's right, sir," added Corporal Gray. "I'd just sent Newton up, to relieve Josserand."

"You heard him yell," prompted Lanark. "Go on, what happened?"

"I hailed him back," said the corporal, "but he said nothing. So I climbed up—that north side's the easiest to climb. Newton was standing at the top, standing straight up with his carbine at the ready. He must have been dead right then."

"You mean, he was struck somehow as you watched?"

Gray shook his head. "No, sir. I think he was dead as he stood up. He didn't move or speak, and when I touched him he sort of coiled down—like an empty coat falling off a clothesline." Gray's hand made a downward-floating gesture in illustration. "When I turned him over I saw his face, all twisted and scared-looking, like—like what the lieutenant has seen. And I sung out for Suggs and McSween to come up and help me bring him down."

Lanark gazed at Newton's body. "He was looking which way?"

"Over yonder, eastward." Gray pointed unsteadily. "Like it might have been beyond the draw and them trees in it."

Lanark and Jaeger peered into the waning light, that was now dusk. Jaeger mumbled what Lanark had already been thinking—that Newton had died without wounds, at or near the moment when the horned image had been shattered upon the cellar floor.

Lanark nodded, and dismissed several vague but disturbing inspirations. "You say he died standing up, Gray. Was he leaning on his gun?"

"No, sir. He stood on his two feet, and held his carbine at the ready. Sounds impossible, a dead man standing up like that, but that's how it was."

"Bring his blanket and cover him up," said Lanark. "Put a guard over him, and we'll bury him tomorrow. Don't let any of the men look at his face. We've got to give him some kind of funeral." He turned to Jaeger. "Have you a prayer book, sergeant?"

Jaeger had fished out the *Long Lost Friend* volume. He was reading something aloud, as though it were a prayer: "'...and be and remain with us on the water and upon the land,'" he pattered out. "'May the Eternal Godhead also—'"

"Stop that heathen nonsense," Lanark almost roared. "You're supposed to be an example to the men, sergeant. Put that book away."

Jaeger obeyed, his big face reproachful. "It was a spell against evil spirits," he explained, and for a moment Lanark wished that he had waited for the end. He shrugged and issued further orders.

"I want all the lamps lighted in the house, and perhaps a fire out here in the yard," he told the men. "We'll keep guard both here and in that gully to the east. If there is a mystery, we'll solve it."

"Pardon me, sir," volunteered a well-bred voice, in which one felt rather than heard the tiny touch of foreign accent. "I can solve the mystery for you, though you may not thank me."

Two men had come into view, were drawing up beside the little knot of troopers. How had they approached? Through the patrolled brush of the ravine? Around the corner of the house? Nobody had seen them coming, and Lanark, at least, started violently. He glowered at this new enigma.

The man who had spoken paused at the foot of the porch steps, so that lamplight shone upon him through the open front door. He was skeleton-gaunt, in face and body, and even his bones were small. His eyes burned forth from deep pits in his narrow, high skull, and his clothing was that of a dandy of the forties. In his twig-like fingers he clasped bunches of herbs.

His companion stood to one side in the shadow, and could be seen only as a huge coarse lump of a man.

"I am Persil Mandifer," the thin creature introduced himself. "I came here to gather from the gardens," and he held out his handfuls of leaves and stalks. "You, sir, you are in command of these soldiers, are you not? Then know that you are trespassing."

"The expediencies of war," replied Lanark easily, for he had seen Suggs and Corporal Gray bring their carbines forward in their hands. "You'll have to forgive our intrusion."

A scornful mouth opened in the emaciated face, and a soft, superior chuckle made itself heard. "Oh, but this is not my estate. I am allowed here, yes—but it is not mine. The real Master—" The gaunt figure shrugged, and the voice paused for a moment. The bright eyes sought Newton's body. "From what I see and what I heard as I came up to you, there has been trouble. You have transgressed somehow, and have begun to suffer."

"To you Southerners, all Union soldiers are trespassers and transgressors," suggested Lanark, but the other laughed and shook his fleshless white head.

"You misunderstand, I fear. I care nothing about this war, except that I am amused to see so many people killed. I bear no part in it. Of course, when I came to pluck herbs, and saw your sentry at the top of Fearful Rock—" Persil Mandifer eyed again the corpse of Newton. "There he lies, eh? It was my privilege and power to project a vision up to him in his loneliness that, I think, put an end to his part of this puerile strife."

Lanark's own face grew hard. "Mr. Mandifer," he said bleakly, "you seem to be enjoying a quiet laugh at our expense. But I should point out that we greatly outnumber you, and are armed. I'm greatly tempted to place you under arrest."

"Then resist temptation," advised Mandifer urbanely. "It might be disastrous to you if we became enemies."

"Then be kind enough to explain what you're talking about," commanded Lanark. Something swam into the forefront of his consciousness. "You say that your name is Mandifer. We found a girl named Enid Mandifer in the gully yonder. She told us a very strange story. Are you her step-father? The one who mesmerized her and—"

"She talked to you?" Mandifer's soft voice suddenly shifted to a windy roar that broke Lanark's questioning abruptly in two. "She came, and did not make the sacrifice of herself? She shall expiate, sir, and you with her!"

Lanark had had enough of this high-handed civilian's airs. He made a motion with his left hand to Corporal Gray, whose carbine-barrel glinted in the light from the house as it leveled itself at Mandifer's skull-head.

"You're under arrest," Lanark informed the two men.

The bigger one growled, the first sound he had made. He threw his enormous body forward in a sudden leaping stride, his gross hands extended as though to clutch Lanark. Jaeger, at the lieutenant's side, quickly drew his revolver and fired from the hip. The enormous body fell, rolled over and subsided.

"You have killed my son!" shrieked Mandifer.

"Take hold of him, you two," ordered Lanark, and Suggs and Josserand obeyed.

The gaunt form of Mandifer achieved one explosive struggle, then fell tautly motionless with the big hands of the troopers upon his elbows.

"Thanks, Jaeger," continued Lanark. "That was done quickly and well. Some of you drag this body up on the porch and cover it. Gray, tumble upstairs and bring down that girl we found."

While waiting for the corporal to return, Lanark ordered further that a bonfire be built to banish a patch of the deepening darkness. It was beginning to shoot up its bright tongues as the corporal ushered Enid Mandifer out upon the porch.

She had arranged her disordered clothing, and even contrived to put up her hair somehow, loosely but attractively. The firelight brought out a certain strength of line and angle in her face, and made her eyes shine darkly. She was manifestly frightened at the sight of her stepfather and the blanket-covered corpses to one side; but she faced determinedly a flood of half-understandable invectives from the emaciated man. She answered him, too; Lanark did not know what she meant by most of the things she said, but gathered correctly that she was refusing, finally and completely, to do something.

"Then I shall say no more," gritted out the spidery Mandifer, and his bared teeth were of the flat, chalky white of long-dead bone. "I place this matter in the hands of the Nameless One. He will not forgive, will not forget."

Enid moved a step toward Lanark, who put out a hand and touched her arm reassuringly. The mounting flame of the bonfire lighted up all who watched and listened—the withered, glaring mummy that was Persil Mandifer, the frightened but defiant shapeliness of Enid in her flower-patterned gown, Lanark in his sudden attitude of protection, the ring of troopers in their dusty blue blouses. With the half-lighted front of the weathered old house like a stage set behind them, and alternate red lights and sooty shadows

154

playing over all, they might have been a tableau in some highly melodramatic opera.

"Silence," Lanark was grating. "For the last time, Mr. Mandifer, let me remind you that I have placed you under arrest. If you don't calm down immediately and speak only when you're spoken to, I'll have my men tie you flat to four stakes and put a gag in your mouth."

Mandifer subsided at once, just as he was on the point of hurling another harsh threat at Enid.

"That's much better," said Lanark. "Sergeant Jaeger, it strikes me that we'd better get our pickets out to guard this position."

Mandifer cleared his throat with actual diffidence. "Lieutenant Lanark—that is your name, I gather," he said in the soft voice which he had employed when he had first appeared. "Permit me, sir, to say but two words." He peered as though to be sure of consent. "I have it in my mind that it is too late, useless, to place any kind of guard against surprise."

"What do you mean?" asked Lanark.

"It is all of a piece with your offending of him who owns this house and the land which encompasses it," continued Mandifer. "I believe that a body of your enemies, mounted men of the Southern forces, are upon you. That man who died upon the brow of Fearful Rock might have seen them coming, but he was brought down sightless and voiceless, and nobody was assigned in his place."

He spoke truth. Gray, in his agitation, had not posted a fresh sentry. Lanark drew his lips tight beneath his mustache.

"Once more you feel that it is a time to joke with us, Mr. Mandifer," he growled. "I have already suggested gagging you and staking you out."

"But listen," Mandifer urged him.

Suddenly hoofs thundered, men yelled a double-noted defiance, high and savage—*"Yee-hee!"*

It was the rebel yell.

Quantrill's guerrillas rode out of the dark and upon them.

5
Blood in the Night

Neither Lanark nor the others remembered that they began to fight for their lives; they only knew all at once that they were doing it. There was a prolonged harsh rattle of gunshots like a blast of hail upon hard wood; Lanark, by chance or unconscious choice, snatched at and drew his sword instead of his revolver.

A horse's flying shoulder struck him, throwing him backward but not down. As he reeled to save his footing, he saved also his own life; for the rider, a form all cascading black beard and slouch hat, thrust a pistol almost into the lieutenant's face and fired. The flash was blinding, the ball ripped Lanark's cheek like a whiplash, and then the saber in his hand swung, like a scythe reaping wheat. By luck rather than design, the edge bit the guerrilla's gun-wrist. Lanark saw the hand fly away as though on wings, its fingers still clutching the pistol, all agleam in the firelight. Blood gushed from the stump of the rider's right arm, like water from a fountain, and Lanark felt upon himself a spatter as of hot rain. He threw himself in, clutched the man's legs with his free arm and, as the body sagged heavily from above upon his head and shoulder, he heaved it clear out of the saddle.

The horse was plunging and whinnying, but Lanark clutched its reins and got his foot into the stirrup. The bonfire seemed to be growing strangely brighter, and the mounted guerrillas were plainly discernible, raging and trampling among his disorganized men. Corporal Gray went down, dying almost under Lanark's feet. Amid the deafening drum roll of shots, Sergeant Jaeger's bull-like voice could be heard: "Stop, thieves and horsemen, in the name of God!" It sounded like an exorcism, as though the Confederate raiders were devils.

Lanark had managed to climb into the saddle of his captured mount. He dropped the bridle upon his pommel, reached across his belly with his left hand, and dragged free his revolver. At a little distance, beyond the tossing heads of several horses, he thought he saw the visage of Quantrill, clean-shaven and fierce. He fired at it, but he had no faith in his own left-handed snap-shooting. He felt the horse frantic and unguided, shoving and striving against another horse. Quarters were too close for a saber-stroke, and he fired again with his revolver. The guerrilla spun out of the saddle. Lanark had a glimpse he would never forget, of great bulging eyes and a sharp-pointed mustache.

Again the rebel yell, flying from mouth to bearded mouth, and then an answering shout, deeper and more sustained; some troopers had run out of the house and, standing on the porch, were firing with their carbines. It was growing lighter, with a blue light. Lanark did not understand that.

Quantrill did not understand it, either. He and Lanark had come almost within striking distance of each other, but the guerrilla chief was gazing past his enemy, in the direction of the house. His mouth was open, with strain-lines around it. His eyes glowed. He feared what he saw.

"Remember me, you thieving swine!" yelled Lanark, and tried to thrust with his saber. But Quantrill had reined back and away, not from the sword but from the light that was growing stronger and bluer. He thundered an order, something that Lanark could not catch but which the guerrillas understood and obeyed. Then Quantrill was fleeing. Some guerrillas dashed between him and Lanark. They, too, were in flight. All the guerrillas were in flight. Somebody roared in triumph and fired with a carbine—it sounded like Sergeant Jaeger. The battle was over, within moments of its beginning.

Lanark managed to catch his reins, in the tips of the fingers that held his revolver, and brought the horse to a standstill before it followed Quantrill's men into the dark. One of his own party caught and held the bits, and Lanark dismounted. At last he had time to look at the house.

It was afire, every wall and sill and timber of it, burning all at once, and completely. And it burnt deep blue, as though seen through the glass of an old-fashioned bitters bottle. It was falling to pieces with the consuming heat, and they had to draw back from it. Lanark stared around to reckon his losses.

Nearest the piazza lay three bodies, trampled and broken-looking. Some men ran in and dragged them out of danger; they were Persil Mandifer, badly battered by horses' feet, and the two who had held him, Josserand and Lanark's

157

orderly, Suggs. Both the troopers had been shot through the head, probably at the first volley from the guerrillas.

Corporal Gray was stone-dead, with five or six bullets in him, and three more troopers had been killed, while four were wounded, but not critically. Jaeger, examining them, pronounced that they could all ride if the lieutenant wished it.

"I wish it, all right," said Lanark ruefully. "We leave first thing in the morning. Hmm, six dead and four hurt, not counting poor Newton, who's there in the fire. Half my command—and, the way I forgot the first principles of military vigilance, I don't deserve as much luck as that. I think the burning house is what frightened the guerrillas. What began it?"

Nobody knew. They had all been fighting too desperately to have any idea. The three men who had been picketing the gully, and who had dashed back to assault the guerrillas on the flank, had seen the blue flames burst out, as it were from a hundred places; that was the best view anybody had.

"All the killing wasn't done by Quantrill," Jaeger comforted his lieutenant. "Five dead guerrillas, sir—no, six. One was picked up a little way off, where he'd been dragged by his foot in the stirrup. Others got wounded, I'll be bound. Pretty even thing, all in all."

"And we still have one prisoner," supplemented Corporal Googan.

He jerked his head toward Enid Mandifer, who stood unhurt, unruffled almost, gazing raptly at the great geyser of blue flame that had been the house and temple of her stepfather's nameless deity.

It was a gray morning, and from the first streaks of it Sergeant Jaeger had kept the unwounded troopers busy, making a trench-like grave halfway between the spot where the house had stood and the gully to the east. When the bodies were counted again, there were only twelve; Persil Mandifer's was missing, and the only explanation was that it had been caught somehow in the flames. The ruins of the house, that still smoked with a choking vapor as of sulfur gas, gave up a few crisped bones that apparently had been Newton, the sentry who had died from unknown causes; but no giant skeleton was found to remind one of the passing of Persil Mandifer's son.

"No matter," said Lanark to Jaeger. "We know that they were both dead, and past our worrying about. Put the other bodies in—our men at this end, the guerrillas at the other."

The order was carried out. Once again Lanark asked about a prayer book. A lad by the name of Duckin said that he had owned one, but that it had been burned with the rest of his kit in the blue flame that destroyed the house.

"Then I'll have to do it from memory," decided Lanark.

He drew up the surviving ten men at the side of the trench. Jaeger took a position beside him, and, just behind the sergeant, Enid Mandifer stood.

Lanark self-consciously turned over his clutter of thoughts, searching for odds and ends of his youthful religious teachings. "'Man that is born of woman hath but short time to live, and is full of misery,'" he managed to repeat. "'He cometh up, and is cut down, like a flower.'" As he said the words "cut down," he remembered his saber-stroke of the night before, and how he had shorn away a man's hand. That man, with his heavy black beard, lay in this trench before them, with the severed hand under him. Lanark was barely able to beat down a shudder. "'In the midst of life,'" he went on, "'we are in death.'"

There he was obliged to pause. Sergeant Jaeger, on inspiration, took one pace forward and threw into the trench a handful of gritty earth.

"'Ashes to ashes, dust to dust,'" remembered Lanark. "'Unto Almighty God we commit these bodies'"—he was sure that that was a misquotation worthy of Jaeger himself, and made shift to finish with one more tag from his memory: "'...in sure and certain hope of the Resurrection unto eternal life.'"

He faced toward the file of men. Four of them had been told to fall in under arms, and at his order they raised their carbines and fired a volley into the air. After that, the trench was filled in.

Jaeger then cleared his throat and began to give orders concerning horses, saddles and what possessions had been spared by the fire. Lanark walked aside, and found Enid Mandifer keeping pace with him.

"You are going back to your army?" she asked.

159

"Yes, at once. I was sent here to see if I could find and damage Quantrill's band. I found him, and gave at least as good as I got."

"Thank you," she said, "for everything you've done for me."

He smiled deprecatingly, and it hurt his bullet-burnt cheek.

"I did nothing," he protested, and both of them realized that it was the truth. "All that has happened—it just happened."

He drew his eyes into narrow gashes, as if brooding over the past twelve hours.

"I'm halfway inclined to believe what your stepfather said about a supernatural influence here. But what about you, Miss Mandifer?"

She tried to smile in turn, not very successfully.

"I can go back to my home. I'll be alone there."

"Alone?"

"I have a few servants."

"You'll be safe?"

"As safe as anywhere."

He clasped his hands behind him. "I don't know how to say it, but I have begun to feel responsible for you. I want to know that all will be well."

"Thank you," she said a second time. "You owe me nothing."

"Perhaps not. We do not know each other. We have spoken together only three or four times. Yet you will be in my mind. I want to make a promise."

"Yes?"

They had paused in their little stroll, almost beside the newly filled grave trench. Lanark was frowning, Enid Mandifer nervous and expectant.

"This war," he said weightily, "is going to last much longer than people thought at first. We—the Union—have done pretty well in the West here, but Lee is making fools of our generals back East. We may have to fight for years, and even then we may not win."

"I hope, Mr.—I mean, Lieutenant Lanark," stammered the girl, "I hope that you will live safely through it."

"I hope so, too. And if I am spared, if I am alive and well when peace comes, I swear that I shall return to this place. I shall make sure that you, too, are alive and well."

He finished, very certain that he could not have used stiffer, more stupid words; but Enid Mandifer smiled now, radiantly and gratefully.

"I shall pray for you, Lieutenant Lanark. Now, your men are ready to leave. Go, and I shall watch."

"No," he demurred. "Go yourself, get away from this dreadful place."

She bowed her head in assent, and walked quickly away. At some distance she paused, turned, and waved her hand above her head.

Lanark took off his broad, black hat and waved in answer. Then he faced about, strode smartly back into the yard beside the charred ruins. Mounting his bay gelding, he gave the order to depart.

6
Return

It was spring again, the warm, bright spring of the year 1866, when Kane Lanark rode again into Fearful Rock country.

His horse was a roan gray this time; the bay gelding had been shot under him, along with two other horses, during the hard-fought three days at Westport, the "Gettysburg of the West," when a few regulars and the Kansas militia turned back General Sterling Price's raid through Missouri. Lanark had been a captain then, and a major thereafter, leading a cavalry expedition into Kentucky. He narrowly missed being in at the finish of Quantrill, whose death by the hand of another he bitterly resented. Early in 1865 he was badly wounded in a skirmish with Confederate horsemen under General Basil Duke. Thereafter he could ride as well as ever, but when he walked he limped.

Lanark's uniform had been replaced by a soft hat and black frock coat, his face was browner and his mustache thicker, and his cheek bore the jaggedly healed scar of the guerrilla pistol-bullet. He was richer, too; the death of his older brother, Captain Douglas Lanark of the Confederate artillery, at Chancellorsville, had left him his father's only heir. Yet he was recognizable as the young lieutenant who had ridden into this district four years gone.

Approaching from the east instead of the north, he came upon the plain with its grass levels, its clumps of bushes and trees, from another and lower point. Far away on the northward horizon rose a sharp little finger; that would be Fearful Rock, on top of which Trooper Newton had once died, horrified and unwounded. Now, then, which way would lie the house he sought for? He idled his roan along the trail, and encountered at last an aged, ragged Negro on a mule.

"Hello, uncle," Lanark greeted him, and they both reined up. "Which way is the Mandifer place?"

"Mandifuh?" repeated the slow, high voice of the old man. "Mandifuh, suh, cap'n? Ah doan know no Mandifuh."

"Nonsense, uncle," said Lanark, but without sharpness, for he liked Negroes. "The Mandifer family has lived around here for years. Didn't you ever know Mr. Persil Mandifer and his stepdaughter, Miss Enid?"

"Puhsil Mandifuh?" It was plain that the old fellow had heard and spoken the name before, else he would have stumbled over its unfamiliarities. "No, suh, cap'n. Ah doan nevah heah tella such gemman."

Lanark gazed past the mule and its tattered rider. "Isn't that a little house among those willows?"

The kinky head turned and peered. "Yes, suh, cap'n. Dat place b'long to Pahson Jaguh."

"Who?" demanded Lanark, almost standing up in his stirrups in his sudden interest. "Did you say Jaeger? What kind of man is he?"

"He jes a pahson—Yankee pahson," replied the Negro, a trifle nervous at this display of excitement. "Big man, suh, got red face. He Yankee. You ain' no Yankee, cap'n, suh. Whaffo you want Pahson Jaguh?"

"Never mind," said Lanark, and thrust a silver quarter into the withered brown palm. He also handed over one of his long, fragrant cheroots. "Thanks, uncle," he added briskly, then spurred his horse and rode on past.

Reaching the patch of willows, he found that the trees formed an open curve that faced the road, and that within this curve stood a rough but snug-looking cabin, built of sawn, unpainted planks and home-split shingles. Among the brush to the rear stood a smaller shed, apparently a stable, and a pen for chickens or a pig. Lanark reined up in front, swung out of his saddle, and tethered his horse to a thorny shrub at the trailside. As he drew tight the knot of the halter-rope, the door of heavy boards opened with a creak. His old sergeant stepped into view.

Jaeger was a few pounds heavier, if anything, than when Lanark had last seen him. His hair was longer, and his beard had grown to the center of his broad chest. He wore blue jeans tucked into worn old cavalry boots, a collarless checked shirt fastened with big brass studs, and leather suspenders. He stared somewhat blankly as Lanark called him by name and walked up to the doorstep, favoring his injured leg.

"It's Captain Lanark, isn't it?" Jaeger hazarded. "My eyes—" He paused, fished in a hip pocket and produced steel-rimmed spectacles. When he donned them, they appeared to aid his vision. "Indeed it is Captain Lanark! Or Major Lanark—yes, you were promoted—"

"I'm Mr. Lanark now," smiled back the visitor. "The war's over, Jaeger. Only this minute did I hear of you in the country. How does it happen that you settled in this place?"

"Come in, sir." Jaeger pushed the door wide open, and ushered Lanark into an unfinished front room, well lighted by windows on three sides. "It's not a strange story," he went on as he brought forward a well-mended wooden chair for the guest, and himself sat on a small keg. "You will remember, sir, that the land hereabouts is under a most unhallowed influence. When the war came to an end, I felt strong upon me the call to another conflict—a crusade against evil." He turned up his eyes, as though to subpoena the powers of heaven as witnesses to his devotion. "I preach here, the gospels and the true godly life."

"What is your denomination?" asked Lanark.

Jaeger coughed, as though abashed. "To my sorrow, I am ordained of no church; yet might this not be part of heaven's plan? I may be here to lead a strong new movement against hell's legions."

Lanark nodded as though to agree with this surmise, and studied Jaeger anew. There was nothing left in manner or speech to suggest that here had been a fierce fighter and model soldier, but the old rude power was not gone. Lanark then asked about the community, and learned that there were but seven white families within a twenty-mile radius. To these Jaeger habitually preached of a Sunday morning, at one farm home or another, and in the afternoon he was wont to exhort the more numerous Negroes.

Lanark had by now the opening for his important question. "What about the Mandifer place? Remember the girl we met, and her stepfather?"

"Enid Mandifer!" breathed Jaeger huskily, and his right hand fluttered up. Lanark remembered that Jaeger had once assured him that not only Catholics warded off evil with the sign of the cross.

"Yes, Enid Mandifer." Lanark leaned forward. "Long ago, Jaeger, I made a promise that I would come and make sure that she prospered. Just now I met an old Negro who swore that he had never heard the name."

Jaeger began to talk, steadily but with a sort of breathless awe, about what went on in the Fearful Rock country. It was not merely that men died—the death of men was not sufficient to horrify folk around whom a war had raged. But corpses, when found, held grimaces that nobody cared to look upon, and no blood remained in their bodies. Cattle, too, had been slain, mangled dreadfully—perhaps by the strange, unidentifiable creatures that prowled by moonlight and chattered in voices that sounded human. One farmer of the vicinity, who had ridden with Quantrill, had twice met strollers after dusk, and had recognized them for comrades whom he knew to be dead.

"And the center of this devil's business," concluded Jaeger, "is the farm that belonged to Persil Mandifer." He drew a deep, tired-sounding breath. "As the desert and the habitation of dragons, so is it with that farm. No trees live, and no grass. From a distance, one can see a woman. It is Enid Mandifer."

"Where is the place?" asked Lanark directly.

Jaeger looked at him for long moments without answering. When he did speak, it was an effort to change the subject. "You will eat here with me at noon," he said. "I have a Negro servant, and he is a good cook."

"I ate a very late breakfast at a farmhouse east of here," Lanark put him off. Then he repeated, "Where is the Mandifer place?"

"Let me speak this once," Jaeger temporized. "As you have said, we are no longer at war—no longer officer and man. We are equals, and I am able to refuse to guide you."

Lanark got up from his chair. "That is true, but you will not be acting the part of a friend."

"I will tell you the way, on one condition." Jaeger's eyes and voice pleaded. "Say that you will return to this house for supper and a bed, and that you will be within my door by sundown."

"All right," said Lanark. "I agree. Now, which way does that farm lie?"

Jaeger led him to the door. He pointed. "This trail joins a road beyond, an old road that is seldom used. Turn north upon it, and you will come to a part which is grown up in weeds. Nobody passes that way. Follow on until you find an old house, built low, with the earth dry and bare around it. That is the dwelling-place of Enid Mandifer."

Lanark found himself biting his lip. He started to step across the threshold, but Jaeger put a detaining hand on his arm. "Carry this as you go."

He was holding out a little book with a gray paper cover. It had seen usage and trouble since last Lanark had noticed it in Jaeger's hands; its back was mended with a pasted strip of dark cloth, and its edges were frayed and gnawed-looking, as though rats had been at it. But the front cover still said plainly:

John George Hohman's
POW-WOWS
or
LONG LOST FRIEND

"Carry this," said Jaeger again, and then quoted glibly: "'Whoever carries this book with him is safe from all his enemies, visible or invisible; and whoever has this book with him cannot die without the holy corpse of Jesus Christ, nor drown in any water, nor burn up in any fire, nor can any unjust sentence be passed upon him.'"

Lanark grinned in spite of himself and his new concern. "Is this the kind of protection that a minister of God should offer me?" he inquired, half jokingly.

165

"I have told you long ago that the *Long Lost Friend* is a good book, and a blessed one." Jaeger thrust it into Lanark's right-hand coat pocket. His guest let it remain, and held out his own hand in friendly termination of the visit.

"Good-bye," said Lanark. "I'll come back before sundown, if that will please you."

He limped out to his horse, untied it and mounted. Then, following Jaeger's instructions, he rode forward until he reached the old road, turned north and proceeded past the point where weeds had covered the unused surface. Before the sun had fallen far in the sky, he was come to his destination.

It was a squat, specious house, the bricks of its trimming weathered and the dark brown paint of its timbers beginning to crack. Behind it stood unrepaired stables, seemingly empty. In the yard stood what had been wide-branched trees, now leafless and lean as skeleton paws held up to a relentless heaven. And there was no grass. The earth was utterly sterile and hard, as though rain had not fallen since the beginning of time.

Enid Mandifer had been watching him from the open door. When she saw that his eyes had found her, she called him by name.

7
The Rock Again

Then there was silence. Lanark sat his tired roan and gazed at Enid, rather hungrily, but only a segment of his attention was for her. The silence crowded in upon him. His unconscious awareness grew conscious—conscious of that blunt, pure absence of sound. There was no twitter of birds, no hum of insects. Not a breath of wind stirred in the leafless branches of the trees. Not even echoes came from afar. The air was dead, as water is dead in a still, stale pond.

He dismounted then, and the creak of his saddle and the scrape of his bootsole upon the bald earth came sharp and shocking to his quiet-filled ears. A hitching-rail stood there, old-seeming to be in so new a country as this. Lanark tethered his horse, pausing to touch its nose reassuringly—it, too, felt uneasy in the thick silence. Then he limped up a gravel-faced path and stepped upon a porch that rang to his feet like a great drum.

Enid Mandifer came through the door and closed it behind her. Plainly she did not want him to come inside. She was dressed in brown alpaca, high-necked, long-sleeved, tight above the waist and voluminous below. Otherwise she looked exactly as she had looked when she bade him good-bye beside the ravine, even to the strained, sleepless look that made sorrowful her fine oval face.

"Here I am," said Lanark. "I promised that I'd come, you remember."

She was gazing into his eyes, as though she hoped to discover something there. "You came," she replied, "because you could not rest in another part of the country."

"That's right," he nodded, and smiled, but she did not smile back.

"We are doomed, all of us," she went on, in a low voice. "Mr. Jaeger—the big man who was one of your soldiers—"

"I know. He lives not far from here."

"Yes. He, too, had to return. And I live—here." She lifted her hands a trifle, in hopeless inclusion of the dreary scene. "I wonder why I do not run away, or why, remaining, I do not go mad. But I do neither."

"Tell me," he urged, and touched her elbow. She let him take her arm and lead her from the porch into the yard that was like a surface of tile. The spring sun comforted them, and he knew that it had been cold, so near to the closed front door of Persil Mandifer's old house.

She moved with him to a little rustic bench under one of the dead trees. Still holding her by the arm, he could feel at the tips of his fingers the shock of her footfalls, as though she trod stiffly. She, in turn, quite evidently was aware of his limp, and felt distress; but, tactfully, she did not inquire about it. When they sat down together, she spoke.

"When I came home that day," she began, "I made a hunt through all of my stepfather's desks and cupboards. I found many papers, but nothing that told me of the things that so shocked us both. I did find money, a small chest filled with French and American gold coins. In the evening I called the slaves together and told them that their master and his son were dead.

"Next morning, when I wakened, I found that every slave had run off, except one old woman. She, nearly a hundred years old and very feeble, told me that fear had come to them in the night, and that they had run like rabbits. With them had gone the horses, and all but one cow."

"They deserted you!" cried Lanark hotly.

"If they truly felt the fear that came here to make its dwelling-place!" Enid Mandifer smiled sadly, as if in forgiveness of the fugitives. "But to resume; the old aunty and I made out here somehow. The war went on, but it seemed far away. We watched the grass die before June, the leaves fall, the beauty of this place vanish."

"I am wondering about that death of grass and leaves," put in Lanark. "You connect it, somehow, with the unholiness at Fearful Rock; yet things grow there."

"Nobody is being punished there," she reminded succinctly. "Well, we had the chickens and the cow, but no crops would grow. If they had, we needed hands to farm them. Last winter aunty died, too. I buried her myself, in the back yard."

"With nobody to help you?"

"I found out that nobody cared or dared to help." Enid said that very slowly, and did not elaborate upon it. "One Negro, who lives down the road a mile, has had some mercy. When I need anything, I carry one of my gold pieces to him. He buys for me, and in a day or so I seek him out and get whatever it is. He keeps the change for his trouble."

Lanark, who had thought it cold upon the porch of the house, now mopped his brow as though it were a day in August. "You must leave here," he said.

"I have no place to go," she replied, "and if I had I would not dare."

"You would not dare?" he echoed uncomprehendingly.

"I must tell you something else. It is that my stepfather and Larue—his son—are still here."

"What do you mean? They were killed," Lanark protested. "I saw them fall. I myself examined their bodies."

"They were killed, yes. But they are here, perhaps within earshot."

It was his turn to gaze searchingly into her eyes. He looked for madness, but he found none. She was apparently sane and truthful.

"I do not see them," she was saying, "or, at most, I see only their sliding shadows in the evening. But I know of them, just around a corner or behind a chair. Have you never known and recognized someone just behind you, before you looked? Sometimes they sneer or smile. Have you," she asked, "ever felt someone smiling at you, even though you could not see him?"

Lanark knew what she meant. "But stop and think," he urged, trying to hearten her, "that nothing has happened to you—nothing too dreadful—although so much was promised when you failed to go through with that ceremony."

She smiled, very thinly. "You think that nothing has happened to me? You do not know the curse of living here, alone and haunted. You do not understand the sense I have of something tightening and thickening about me; tightening and thickening inside of me, too." Her hand touched her breast, and trembled. "I have said that I have not gone mad. That does not mean that I shall never go mad."

"Do not be resigned to any such idea," said Lanark, almost roughly, so earnest was he in trying to win her from the thought.

"Madness may come—in the good time of those who may wish it. My mind will die. And things will feed upon it, as buzzards would feed upon my dead body."

Her thin smile faded away. Lanark felt his throat growing as dry as lime, and cleared it noisily. Silence was still dense around them. He asked her, quite formally, what she found to do.

"My stepfather had many books, most of them old," was her answer. "At night I light one lamp—I must husband my oil—and sit well within its circle of light. Nothing ever comes into that circle. And I read books. Every night I read also a chapter from a Bible that belonged to my old aunty. When I sleep, I hold that Bible against my heart."

He rose nervously, and she rose with him. "Must you go so soon?" she asked, like a courteous hostess.

Lanark bit his mustache. "Enid Mandifer, come out of here with me."

"I can't."

"You can. You shall. My horse will carry both of us."

She shook her head, and the smile was back, sad and tender this time. "Perhaps you cannot understand, and I know that I cannot tell you. But if I stay here, the evil stays here with me. If I go, it will follow and infect the world. Go away alone."

She meant it, and he did not know what to say or do.

"I shall go," he agreed finally, with an air of bafflement, "but I shall be back."

Suddenly he kissed her. Then he turned and limped rapidly away, raging at the feeling of defeat that had him by the back of the neck. Then, as he reached his horse he found himself glad to be leaving the spot, even though Enid Mandifer remained behind, alone. He cursed with a vehemence that made the roan flinch, untied the halter and mounted. Away he rode, to the magnified clatter of hoofs. He looked back, not once but several times. Each time he saw Enid Mandifer, smaller and smaller, standing beside the bench under the naked tree. She was gazing, not along the road after him, but at the spot where he had mounted his horse. It was as though he had vanished from her sight at that point.

Lanark damned himself as one who retreated before an enemy, but he felt that it was not as simple as that. Helplessness, not fear, had routed him. He was leaving Enid Mandifer, but again he promised in his heart to return.

Somewhere along the weed-teemed road, the silence fell from him like a heavy garment slipping away, and the world hummed and sighed again.

After some time he drew rein and fumbled in his saddlebag. He had lied to Jaeger about his late breakfast, and now he was grown hungry. His fingers touched and drew out two hardtacks—they were plentiful and cheap, so recently was the war finished and the army demobilized—and a bit of raw bacon. He sandwiched the streaky smoked flesh between the big square crackers and ate without dismounting. Often, he considered, he had been content with worse fare. Then his thoughts went to the place he had quitted, the girl he had left there. Finally he skimmed the horizon with his eye.

To north and east he saw the spire of Fearful Rock, like a dark threatening finger lifted against him. The challenge of it was too much to ignore.

He turned his horse off the road and headed in that direction. It was a longer journey than he had thought, perhaps because he had to ride slowly through some dark swampground with a smell of rotten grass about it. When he came near enough, he slanted his course to the east, and so came to the point from which he first approached the rock and the house that had then stood in its shadow.

A crow flapped overhead, cawing lonesomely. Lanark's horse seemed to falter in its stride, as though it had seen a snake on the path, and he had to spur it along toward its destination. He could make out the inequalities of the rock, as clearly as though they had been sketched in with a pen, and the new spring greenery of the brush and trees in the gully beyond to the westward; but the tumbledown ruins of the house were somehow blurred, as though a gray mist or cloud hung there.

Lanark wished that his old command rode with him, at least that he had coaxed Jaeger along; but he was close to the spot now, and would go in, however uneasily, for a closer look.

The roan stopped suddenly, and Lanark's spur made it sidle without advancing. He scolded it in an undertone, slid out of the saddle and threaded his left arm through the reins. Pulling the beast along, he limped toward the spot where the house had once stood.

The sun seemed to be going down.

8
The Grapple by the Grave

Lanark stumped for a furlong or more, to the yard of the old house, and the horse followed unwillingly—so unwillingly that had there been a tree or a stump at hand, Lanark would have tethered and left it. When he paused at last, under the lee of the great natural obelisk that was Fearful Rock, the twilight was upon him. Yet he could see pretty plainly the collapsed, blackened ruins of the dwelling that four years gone had burned before his eyes in devil-blue flame.

He came close to the brink of the foundation-hollow, and gazed narrowly into it. Part of the chimney still stood, broken off at about a level with the surface of the ground, the rubbish that had been its upper part lying in jagged heaps about its base. Chill seemed to rise from that littered depression, something like the chill he had guessed at rather than felt when he had faced Enid Mandifer upon her porch. The chill came slowly, almost stealthily, about his legs and thighs, creeping snake-like under his clothing to tingle the skin upon his belly. He shuddered despite himself, and the roan nuzzled his shoulder in sympathy. Lanark lifted a hand and stroked the beast's cheek, then moved back from where the house had stood.

He gazed westward, in the direction of the gully. There, midway between the foundation-hollow and the natural one, was a much smaller opening in the earth, a pit filled with shadow. He remembered ordering a grave dug there, a grave for twelve men. Well, it seemed to be open now, or partially open.

He plodded toward it, reached it and gazed down in the fading light. He judged that the dead of his own command still lay where their comrades had put them, in a close row of six toward the east. It was the westward end of the trench that had been dug up, the place where the guerrillas had been laid. Perhaps the burial had been spied upon, and the Southerners had returned to recover their fallen friends.

Yet there was something below there, something pallid and flabby-looking. Lanark had come to make sure of things, and he stooped, then climbed down, favoring his old wound. It was darker in the ditch than above; yet he judged by the looseness of earth under his feet that in one spot, at least, there had been fresh digging—or, perhaps, some other person walking and examining. And the pallid patch was in reality two pallid patches, like discarded cloaks or jackets. Still holding the end of his horse's bridle, he put down his free hand to investigate.

Human hair tickled his fingers, and he snatched them back with an exclamation. Then he dug in his pocket, brought out a match, and snapped it aglow on the edge of his thumbnail.

He gazed downward for a full second before he dropped the light. It went out before it touched the bottom of the hole. But Lanark had seen enough.

Two human skins lay there—white, empty human skins. The legs of them sprawled like discarded court stockings, the hands of them like forgotten gauntlets. And tousled hair covered the collapsed heads of them....

He felt light-headed and sick. Frantically he struggled up out of that grave, and barely had he come to his knees on the ground above, when his horse snorted and jerked its bridle free from his grasp. Lanark sprang up, tingling all over. Across the trench, black and broad, stood a human—or semi-human—figure.

Lanark felt a certain draining cold at cheek and brow. Yet his voice was steady as he spoke, challengingly:

"What do you want?"

The creature opposite stooped, then bent its thick legs. It was going to jump across the ditch. Lanark took a quick backward step toward his horse—an old Colt's revolver was tucked into his right saddlebag.

But the sudden move on his part was too much for the jangled nerves of the beast. It whickered, squealed, and jerked around. A moment later it bolted away toward the east.

At the same time, the form on the other side of the open grave lunged forward, cleared the space, and came at Lanark.

But it was attacking one who had been in close fights before, and emerged the victor. Lanark, though partially a cripple, had lost nothing of a cavalryman's toughness and resolution. He sprang backward, let his assailant's charge slow before it reached him, then lashed out with his left fist. His gloved knuckles touched soft flesh at what seemed to be the side of the face, flesh that gave under them. Lanark brought over his right, missed with it, and fell violently against the body of the other. For a moment he smelled corruption, and then found his feet and retreated again.

The black shape drew itself stoopingly down, as though to muster and concentrate its volume of vigor. It launched itself at Lanark's legs, with two arms extended. The veteran tried to dodge again, this time sidewise, but his lameness made him slow. Hands reached and fastened upon him, one

clutching his thigh, the other clawing at the left-hand pocket of his coat.

But in the moment of capture, the foul-smelling thing
seemed to shudder and snatch itself away, as though the
touch of Lanark had burned it. A moan came from somewhere in its direction. The crouched body straightened, the
arms lifted in cringing protection of the face. Lanark, mys-
tified but desperately glad, himself advanced to the attack.
As he came close he threw his weight. It bowled the other
backward and over, and he fell hard upon it. His own hands,
sinewy and sure, groped quickly upon dank, sticky-seeming
garments, found a rumpled collar and then a throat.

That throat appeared to be muddy, or at any rate slippery and foul. With an effort Lanark sank his fingertips into
it, throttling grimly and with honest intention to kill. There
was no resistance, only a quivering of the body under his
knee. The arms that screened the face fell quivering away to
either side. At that moment a bright moon shimmered from
behind a passing veil of cloud. Lanark gazed down into the
face of his enemy.

A puffy, livid, filth-clotted face—but he knew it. Those
spiked mustaches, those bulging eyes, the shape, contour
and complexion....

"You're one of Quantrill's—" accused Lanark between
clenched teeth. Then his voice blocked itself, and his hands
jerked away from their stranglehold. His mouth gaped open.

"I killed you once!" he cried.

Between him and the body he had pinned down there
drifted a wild whirl of vision. He saw again the fight in the
blue fireglow, the assailant who spurred against him, the
flash of his own revolver, the limp collapse of the other. He
saw, too, the burial next morning—blue-coated troopers
shoveling loam down upon a silent row of figures; and, ere
clods hid it, a face peeping through a disarranged blanket, a
face with staring eyes and mustaches like twin knife-points.

Then his eyes were clear again, and he was on his feet
and running. His stiff leg gave him pain, but he slackened
speed no whit. Once he looked back. A strange blueness, like
a dim reflection of the fire long ago, hung around the base
of Fearful Rock. In the midst of it, he saw not one but several
figures. They were not moving—not walking, anyway—but
he could swear that they gazed after him.

Something tripped him, a root or a fallen branch. He rose, neither quickly nor confidently, aching in all his limbs. The moon had come up, he took time to realize. Then he suddenly turned dizzy and faint all over, as never in any battle he had seen, not even Pea Ridge and Westport; for something bulky and dark was moving toward and against him.

Then it whinnied softly, and his heart stole down from his throat—it was his runaway horse.

Lanark was fain to stand for long seconds, with his arm across the saddle, before he mounted. Then he turned the animal's head southward and shook the bridle to make it walk. At least he was able to examine himself for injuries.

Though winded, he was not bruised or hurt, but he was covered with earth and mold, and his side pocket had been almost ripped from his coat. That had happened when the—the creature yonder had tried to grapple him. He wondered how it had been forced to retreat so suddenly. He put his hand in the pocket.

He touched a little book there, and drew it forth.

It was Jaeger's *Long Lost Friend*.

A good hour later, Lanark rode into the yard of his ex-sergeant. The moon was high, and Jaeger was sitting upon the front stoop.

Silently the owner of the little house rose, took Lanark's bridle rein and held the horse while Lanark dismounted. Then he led the beast around to the rear yard, where the little shed stood. In front of this he helped Lanark unbridle and unsaddle the roan.

A Negro boy appeared, diffident in his mute offer of help, and Jaeger directed him to rub the beast down with a wisp of hay before giving it water or grain. Then he led Lanark to the front of the house.

Jaeger spoke at the threshold: "I thank God you are come back safely."

9
Debate and Decision

Jaeger's Negro servant was quite as good a cook as promised. Lanark, eating chicken stew and biscuits, reflected that only twice before had he been so ravenous—upon receiving the news of Lee's surrender at Appomattox, and after the funeral of his mother. When he had finished, he drew forth a cheroot. His hand shook as he lighted it. Jaeger gave him one of the old looks of respectful disapproval, but did not comment. Instead he led Lanark to the most comfortable chair in the parlor and seated himself upon the keg. Then he said: "Tell me."

Lanark told him, rather less coherently than here set down, the adventures of the evening. Again and again he groped in his mind for explanations, but not once found any to offer.

"It is fit for the devil," pronounced Jaeger when his old commander had finished. "Did I not say that you should have stayed away from that woman? You're well out of the business."

"I'm well into it you mean," Lanark fairly snapped back. "What can you think of me, Jaeger, when you suggest that I might let things stand as they are?"

The frontier preacher massaged his shaggy jowl with thoughtful knuckles. "You have been a man of war and an officer of death," he said heavily. "God taught your hands to fight. Yet your enemies are not those who perish by the sword." He held out his hand. "You say you still have the book I lent you?"

From his torn pocket Lanark drew Hohman's *Long Lost Friend*. Jaeger took it and stared at the cover. "The marks of fingers," he muttered, in something like awe. He examined the smudges closely, putting on his spectacles to do so, then lifted the book to his nose. His nostrils wrinkled, as if in distaste, and he passed the thing back. "Smell it," he directed.

Lanark did so. About the slimy-looking prints on the cover hung a sickening odor of decayed flesh.

"The demon that attacked you, that touched this book, died long ago," went on Jaeger. "You know as much—you killed him with your own hand. Yet he fights you this very night."

"Maybe you have a suggestion," Lanark flung out, impatient at the assured and almost snobbish air of mystery that colored the manner of his old comrade in arms. "If this is a piece of hell broke loose, perhaps you did the breaking. Remember that image—that idol-thing with horns—that you smashed in the cellar? You probably freed all the evil upon the world when you did that."

Jaeger frowned, but pursued his lecture. "This very book, this *Long Lost Friend,* saved you from the demon's clutch," he said. "It is a notable talisman and shield. But with the shield one must have a sword, with which to attack in turn."

"All right," challenged Lanark. "Where is your sword?"

"It is a product of a mighty pen," Jaeger informed him sententiously. He turned in his seat and drew from a box against the wall a book. Like the *Long Lost Friend,* it was bound in paper, but of a cream color. Its title stood forth in bold black letters:

THE SECRETS
OF
ALBERTUS MAGNUS

"A translation from the German and the Latin," explained Jaeger. "Printed, I think, in New York. This book is full of wisdom, although I wonder if it is evil, unlawful wisdom."

"I don't care if it is." Lanark almost snatched the book. "Any weapon must be used. And I doubt if Albertus Magnus was evil. Wasn't he a churchman, and didn't he teach Saint Thomas Aquinas?" He leafed through the beginning of the book. "Here's a charm, Jaeger, to be spoken in the name of God. That doesn't sound unholy."

"Satan can recite scripture to his own ends," misquoted Jaeger. "I don't remember who said that, but—"

"Shakespeare said it, or something very like it," Lanark informed him. "Look here, Jaeger, farther on. Here's a spell against witchcraft and evil spirits."

"I have counted at least thirty such in that book," responded the other. "Are you coming to believe in them, sir?"

Lanark looked up from the page. His face was earnest and, in a way, humble.

"I'm constrained to believe in many unbelievable things. If my experience tonight truly befell me, then I must believe in charms of safety. Supernatural evil like that must have its contrary supernatural good."

Jaeger pushed his spectacles up on his forehead and smiled in his beard. "I have heard it told," he said, "that charms and spells work only when one believes in them."

"You sound confident of that, at least," Lanark smiled back. "Maybe you will help me, after all."

"Maybe I will."

The two gazed into each other's eyes, and then their hands came out, at the same moment. Lanark's lean fingers crushed Jaeger's coarser ones.

"Let's be gone," urged Lanark at once, but the preacher shook his head emphatically.

"Slowly, slowly," he temporized. "Cool your spirit, and take council. He that ruleth his temper is greater than he that taketh a city." Once more he put out his hand for the cream-colored volume of Albertus Magnus, and began to search through it.

"Do you think to comfort me from that book?" asked Lanark.

"It has more than comfort," Jaeger assured him. "It has guidance." He found what he was looking for, pulled down his spectacles again, and read aloud:

"'Two wicked eyes have overshadowed me, but three other eyes are overshadowing me—the one of God the Father, the second of God the Son, the third of God the Holy Spirit; they watch my body and soul, my blood and bone; I shall be protected in the name of God.'"

His voice was that of a prayerful man reading Scripture, and Lanark felt moved despite himself. Jaeger closed the book gently and kept it in his hand.

"Albertus Magnus has many such charms and assurances," he volunteered. "In this small book, less than two hundred pages, I find a score and more of ways for punishing and thwarting evil spirits, or those who summon evil spirits." He shook his head, as if in sudden wrath, and turned up his spectacled eyes. "O Lord!" he muttered. "How long must devils plague us for our sins?"

Growing calmer once more, he read again from the book of Albertus Magnus. There was a recipe for invisibility, which involved the making of a thumb-stall from the ear of a black cat boiled in the milk of a black cow; an invocation to "Bedgoblin and all ye evil spirits"; several strange rituals, similar to those Lanark remembered from the *Long Lost*

Friend, to render one immune to wounds received in battle; and a rime to speak while cutting and preparing a forked stick of hazel to use in hunting for water or treasure. As a boy, Lanark had once seen water "witched," and now he wondered if the rod-bearer had gained his knowledge from Albertus Magnus.

"'Take an earthen pot, not glazed,'" Jaeger was reading on, "'and yarn spun by a girl not seven years old'—"

He broke off abruptly, with a little inarticulate gasp. The book slammed shut between his hands. His eyes were bright and hot, and his face pale to the roots of his beard. When he spoke, it was in a hoarse whisper:

"That was a spell to control witches, in the name of Lucifer, king of hell. Didn't I say that this book was evil?"

"You must forget that," Lanark counseled him soberly. "I will admit that the book might cause sorrow and wickedness, if it were in wicked hands; but I do not think that you are anything but a good man."

"Thank you," said Jaeger simply. He rose and went to his table, then returned with an iron inkpot and a stump of a pen. "Let me have your right hand."

Lanark held out his palm, as though to a fortune-teller. Upon the skin Jaeger traced slowly, in heavy capital letters, a square of five words:

S A T O R

A R E P O

T E N E T

O P E R A

R O T A S

Under this, very boldly, three crosses:

X X X

"A charm," the preacher told Lanark as he labored with the pen. "These mystic words and the crosses will defend you in your slumber, from all wicked spirits. So says Albertus Magnus, and Hohman as well."

"What do they mean?"

"I do not know that." Jaeger blew hotly upon Lanark's palm to dry the ink. "Will you now write the same thing for me, in my right hand?"

"If you wish." Lanark, in turn, dipped in the inkpot and began to copy the diagram. *"Opera* is a word I know," he observed, "and *tenet* is another. *Sator* may be some form of the old pagan word, *satyr*—a kind of horned human monster—"

He finished the work in silence. Then he lighted another cigar. His hand was as steady as a gun-rest this time, and the match did not even flicker in his fingertips. He felt somehow stronger, better, more confident.

"You'll give me a place to sleep for the night?" he suggested.

"Yes. I have only pallets, but you and I have slept on harder couches before this."

Within half an hour both men were sound asleep.

10
Enid Mandifer Again

The silence was not so deadly the following noon as Lanark and Jaeger dismounted at the hitching-rack in front of Enid Mandifer's; perhaps this was because there were two horses to stamp and snort, two bridles to jingle, two saddles to creak, two pairs of boots to spurn the pathway toward the door.

Enid Mandifer, with a home-sewn sunbonnet of calico upon her head, came around the side of the house just as the two men were about to step upon the porch. She called out to them, anxiously polite, and stood with one hand clutched upon her wide skirt of brown alpaca.

"Mr. Lanark," she ventured, "I hoped that you would come again. I have something to show you."

It was Jaeger who spoke in reply: "Miss Mandifer, perhaps you may remember me. I'm Parson Jaeger, I live south of here. Look." He held out something—the *Long Lost Friend* book. "Did you ever see anything of this sort?"

She took it without hesitation, gazing interestedly at the cover. Lanark saw her soft pink lips move, silently framing the odd words of the title. Then she opened it and studied the first page. After a moment she turned several leaves, and a little frown of perplexity touched her bonnet-shaded brow. "These are receipts—recipes—of some kind," she said slowly. "Why do you show them to me, Mr. Jaeger?"

The ex-sergeant had been watching her closely, his hands upon his heavy hips, his beard thrust forward and his head tilted back. He put forth his hand and received back the *Long Lost Friend*.

"Excuse me, Miss Mandifer, if I have suspected you unjustly," he said handsomely if cryptically. Then he glanced sidewise at Lanark, as though to refresh a memory that needed no refreshing—a memory of a living-dead horror that had recoiled at very touch of the little volume.

Enid Mandifer was speaking once more: "Mr. Lanark, I had a dreadful night after you left. Dreams...or maybe not dreams. I felt things come and stand by my bed. This morning, on a bit of paper that lay on the floor—"

From a pocket in the folds of her skirt, she produced a white scrap. Lanark accepted it from her. Jaeger came closer to look.

"Writing," growled Jaeger. "In what language is that?"

"It's English," pronounced Lanark, "but set down backward—from right to left, as Leonardo da Vinci wrote."

The young woman nodded eagerly at this, as though to say that she had already seen as much.

"Have you a mirror?" Jaeger asked her, then came to a simpler solution. He took the paper and held it up to the light, written side away from him. "Now it shows through," he announced. "Will one of you try to read? I haven't my glasses with me."

Lanark squinted and made shift to read:

"'Any man may look lightly into heaven, to the highest star; but who dares require of the bowels of Earth their abysmal secrets?'"

"That is my stepfather's handwriting," whispered Enid, her head close to Lanark's shoulder.

He read on: "'The rewards of Good are unproven; but the revenges of Evil are great, and manifest on all sides. Fear will always vanquish love.'"

He grinned slightly, harshly. Jaeger remembered having seen that grin in the old army days, before a battle.

"I think we're being warned," Lanark said to his old sergeant. "It's a challenge, meant to frighten us. But challenges have always drawn me."

"I can't believe," said Enid, "that fear will vanquish love." She blushed suddenly and rosily, as if embarrassed by

181

her own words. "That is probably beside the point," she resumed. "What I began to say was that the sight of my stepfather's writing—why is it reversed like that?—the sight, anyway, has brought things back into my mind."

"What things?" Jaeger demanded eagerly. "Come into the house, Miss Mandifer, and tell us."

"Oh, not into the house," she demurred at once. "It's dark in there—damp and cold. Let's go out here, to the seat under the tree."

She conducted them to the bench whither Lanark had accompanied her the day before.

"Now," Jaeger prompted her, and she began:

"I remember of hearing him, when I was a child, as he talked to his son Larue and they thought I did not listen or did not comprehend. He told of these very things, these views he has written. He said, as if teaching Larue, 'Fear is stronger than love; where love can but plead, fear can command.'"

"A devil's doctrine!" grunted Jaeger, and Lanark nodded agreement.

"He said more," went on Enid. "He spoke of 'Those Below,' and of how they 'rule by fear, and therefore are stronger than Those on High, who rule by weak love.'"

"Blasphemy," commented Jaeger, in his beard.

"Those statements fit what I remember of his talk," Lanark put in. "He spoke, just before we fought the guerrillas, of some great evil to come from flouting Those Below."

"I remember," nodded Jaeger. "Go on, young woman."

"Then there was the box."

"The box?" repeated both men quickly.

"Yes. It was a small case, of dark gray metal, or stone—or something. This, too, was when I was little. He offered it to Larue, and laughed when Larue could not open it."

Jaeger and Lanark darted looks at each other. They were remembering such a box.

"My stepfather then took it back," Enid related, "and said that it held his fate and fortune; that he would live and prosper until the secret writing within it should be taken forth and destroyed."

"I remember where that box is," Lanark said breathlessly to Jaeger. "In the old oven, at—"

182

"We could not open it, either," interrupted the preacher.

"He spoke of that, too," Enid told them. "It would never open, he told Larue, save in the 'place of the Nameless One'—that must be where the house burned—and at midnight under a full moon."

"A full moon!" exclaimed Lanark.

"There is a full moon tonight," said Jaeger.

11
Return of the Sacrifice

Through the cross-hatching of new-leafed branches the full moon shone down from its zenith. Lanark and Enid Mandifer walked gingerly through the night-filled timber in the gully beyond which, they knew, lay the ruins of the house where so much repellent mystery had been born.

"It's just eleven o'clock," whispered Lanark, looking at his big silver watch. He was dressed in white shirt and dark trousers, without coat, hat or gloves. His revolver rode in the front of his waistband, and as he limped along, the sheath of Jaeger's old cavalry saber thumped and rasped his left boot-top. "We must be almost there."

"We are there," replied Enid. "Here's the clearing, and the little brook of water."

She was right. They had come to the open space where first they had met. The moonlight made the ground and its new grass pallid, and struck frosty-gold lights from the runlet in the very center of the clearing. Beyond, to the west, lay menacing shadows.

Enid stooped and laid upon the ground the hand-mirror she carried. "Stand to one side," she said, "and please don't look."

Lanark obeyed, and the girl began to undress.

The young man felt dew at his mustache, and a chill in his heart that was not from dew. He stared into the trees beyond the clearing, trying to have faith in Jaeger's plan. "We must make the devils come forth and face us," the sergeant-preacher had argued. "Miss Mandifer shall be our decoy, to draw them out where we can get at them. All is very strange, but this much we know—the unholy worship did go on; Miss Mandifer was to be sacrificed as part of it;

and, when the sacrifice was not completed, all these evil things happened. We have the hauntings, the blue fire of the house, the creature that attacked Mr. Lanark, and a host of other mysteries to credit to these causes. Let us profit by what little we have found out, and put an end to the Devil's rule in this country."

It had all sounded logical, but Lanark, listening, had been hesitant until Enid herself agreed. Then it was that Jaeger, strengthening his self-assumed position of leadership, had made the assignments. Enid would make the journey, as before, from her house to the gully, there strip and say the words with which her stepfather had charged her four springs ago. Lanark, armed, would accompany her as guard. Jaeger himself would circle far to the east and approach the ruins from the opposite direction, observing, and, if need be, attacking.

These preparations Lanark reviewed mentally, while he heard Enid's bare feet splashing timidly in the water. It came to him, a bit too late, that the arms he bore might not avail against supernatural enemies. Yet Jaeger had seemed confident.... Enid was speaking, apparently repeating the ritual that was supposed to summon the unnamed god-demon of Persil Mandifer:

"A maid, alone and pure, I stand, not upon water nor on land; I hold a mirror in my hand, in which to see what Fate may send...." She broke off and screamed.

Lanark whipped around. The girl stood, misty-pale in the wash of moonlight, all crouched and curved together like a bow.

"It was coming!" she quavered. "I saw it in the mirror—over yonder, among those trees—"

Lanark glared across the little strip of water and the moonlit grass beyond. Ten paces away, between two trunks, something shone in the shadows—shone darkly, like tar, though the filtered moon-rays did not touch it. He saw nothing of the shape, save that it moved and lived—and watched.

He drew his revolver and fired, twice. There was a crash of twigs, as though something had flinched backward at the reports.

Lanark splashed through the water and, despite his limp, charged at the place where the presence lurked.

12
Jaeger

It had been some minutes before eleven o'clock when Jaeger reined in his old black horse at a distance of two miles from Fearful Rock.

Most of those now alive who knew Jaeger personally are apt to describe him as he was when they were young and he was old—a burly graybeard, a notable preacher and exhorter, particularly at funerals. He preferred the New Testament to the Old, though he was apt to misquote his texts from either; and he loved children, and once preached a telling sermon against the proposition of infant damnation. His tombstone, at Fort Smith, Arkansas, bears as epitaph a verse from the third chapter of the first book of Samuel: *Here am I, for thou didst call me.*

Jaeger when young is harder to study and to visualize. However, the diary of a long-dead farmer's wife of Pennsylvania records that the "Jaeger boy" was dull but serious at school, and that his appetite for mince pie amounted to a passion. In Topeka, Kansas, lives a retired railroad conductor whose father, on the pre-Rebellion frontier, once heard Jaeger defy Southern hoodlums to shoot him for voting Free-state in a territorial election. Ex-Major Kane Lanark mentioned Jaeger frequently and with admiration in the remarkable pen-and-ink memoir on which the present narrative is based.

How he approached Fearful Rock, and what he encountered there, he himself often described verbally to such of his friends as pretended that they believed him.

The moonlight showed him a stunted tree, with one gnarled root looping up out of the earth, and to that root he tethered his animal. Then, like Lanark, he threw off his coat, strapping it to the cantle of his saddle, and unfastened his "hickory" blue shirt at the throat. From a saddlebag he drew a trusty-looking revolver, its barrel sawed off. Turning its butt toward the moon, he spun the cylinder to make sure that it was loaded. Then he thrust it into his belt without benefit of holster, and started on foot toward the rock and its remains of a house.

Approaching, he sought by instinct the cover of trees and bush clumps, moving smoothly and noiselessly; Jaeger had been noted during his service in the Army of the Frontier for his ability to scout at night, an ability which he credited to the fact that he had been born in the darkest hours. He made almost as good progress as though he had been moving in broad daylight. At eleven o'clock sharp, as he guessed—like many men who never carry watches, he had become good at judging the time—he was within two hundred yards of the rock itself, and cover had run out. There he paused, chin-deep in a clump of early weeds.

Lanark and the girl as he surmised, must be well into the gully by this time. He, Jaeger, smiled as he remembered with what alacrity Lanark had accepted the assignment of bodyguard to Enid Mandifer. Those two young people acted as if they were on the brink of falling in love, and no mistake....

His eyes were making out details of the scene ahead. Was even the full moon so bright as all this? He could not see very clearly the ruined foundations, for they sat in a depression of the earth. Yet there seemed to be a clinging blue light at about that point, a feeble but undeniable blue. Mentally he compared it to deep, still water, then to the poorest of skimmed milk. Jaeger remembered the flames that once had burned there, blue as amethyst.

But the blue light was not solid, and it had no heat. Within it, dimmed as though by mist, stood and moved— figures. They were human, at least they were upright; and they stood in a row, like soldiers, all but two. That pair was dark-seeming, and one was grossly thick, the other thin as an exclamation point. The line moved, bent, formed a weaving circle which spread as its units opened their order. Jaeger had never seen such a maneuver in four years of army service.

Now the circle was moving, rolling around; the figures were tramping counterclockwise—"withershins" was the old-fashioned word for that kind of motion, as Jaeger remembered from his boyhood in Pennsylvania. The two darker figures, the ones that had stood separate, were nowhere to be seen; perhaps they were inclosed in the center of the turning circle, the moving shapes of which numbered six. There had been six of Quantrill's guerrillas that died in almost that spot.

The ground was bare except for spring grass, but Jaeger made shift to crawl forward on hands and knees, his eyes fixed on the group ahead, his beard bristling nervously upon his set chin. He crept ten yards, twenty yards, forty. Some high stalks of grass, killed but not leveled by winter, afforded him a bit of cover, and he paused again, taking care not to rustle the dry stems. He could see the maneuvering creatures more plainly.

They were men, all right, standing each upon two legs, waving each two arms. No, one of them had only an arm and a stump. Had not one of Quantrill's men—yes! It came to the back of Jaeger's mind that Lanark himself had cut away an enemy's pistol hand with a stroke of his saber. Again he reflected that there had been six dead guerrillas, and that six were the forms treading so strange a measure yonder. He began to crawl forward again. Sweat made a slow, cold trickle along his spine.

But the two that had stood separate from the six were not to be seen anywhere, inside the circle or out. And Jaeger began to fancy that his first far glimpse had shown him something strange about that pair of dark forms, something inhuman or sub-human.

Then a shot rang out, clear and sharp. It came from beyond the circle of creatures and the blue-misted ruins. A second shot followed it.

Jaeger almost rose into plain view in the moonlight, but fell flat a moment later. Indeed, he might well have been seen by those he spied upon, had they not all turned in the direction whence the shots had sounded. Jaeger heard voices, a murmur of them with nothing that sounded like articulate words. He made bold to rise on his hands for a closer look. The six figures were moving eastward, as though to investigate.

Jaeger lifted himself to hands and knees, then rose to a crouch. He ran forward, drawing his gun as he did so. The great uneven shaft that was Fearful Rock gave him a bar of shadow into which he plunged gratefully, and a moment later he was at the edge of the ruin-filled foundation hole, perhaps at the same point where Lanark had stood the night before.

From that pit rose the diluted blue radiance that seemed to involve this quarter. Staring thus closely, Jaeger found the light similar to that given off by rotten wood, or fungi, or certain brands of lucifer matches. It was like an echo of light, he pondered rather absently, and almost grinned at his own malapropism. But he was not here to make jokes with himself.

He listened, peered about, then began moving cautiously along the lip of the foundation hole. Another shot he heard, and a loud, defiant yell that sounded like Lanark; then an answering burst of laughter, throaty and muffled, that seemed to come from several mouths at once. Jaeger felt a new and fiercer chill. He, an earnest Protestant from birth, signed himself with the cross—signed himself with the right hand that clutched his revolver.

Yet there was no doubt as to which way lay his duty. He skirted the open foundation of the ruined house, moved eastward over the trampled earth where the six things had formed their open-order circle. Like Lanark, he saw the opened grave-trench. He paused and gazed down.

Two sack-like blotches of pallor lay there—Lanark had described them correctly: they were empty human skins. Jaeger paused. There was no sound from ahead; he peered and saw the ravine to eastward, filled with trees and gloom. He hesitated at plunging in, the place was so ideal an ambush. Even as he paused, his toes at the brink of the opened grave, he heard a smashing, rustling noise. Bodies were returning through the twigs and leafage of the ravine, returning swiftly.

Had they met Lanark and vanquished him? Had they spied or sensed Jaeger in their rear?

He was beside the grave, and since the first year of the war he had known what to do, with enemy approaching and a deep hole at hand. He dived in, head first like a chipmunk into its burrow, and landed on the bottom on all fours.

His first act was to shake his revolver, lest sand had stopped the muzzle.

A charm from the *Long Lost Friend* book whispered itself through his brain, a marksman's charm to bring accuracy with the gun. He repeated it, half audibly, without knowing what the words might mean:

"Ut nemo in sense tentant, descendre nemo; at precendenti spectatur mantica tergo."

At that instant his eyes fell upon the nearest of the two pallid, empty skins, which lay full in the moonlight. He forgot everything else. For he knew that collapsed face, even without the sharp stiletto-like bone of the nose to jut forth in its center. He knew that narrowness through the jowls and temples, that height of brow, that hair white as thistledown.

Persil Mandifer's skull had been inside. It must have been there, and living, recently. Jaeger's left hand crept out, and drew quickly back as though it had touched a snake. The texture of the skin was soft, clammy, moist...*fresh!*

And the other pallidity like a great empty bladder—that could have fitted no other body than the gross one of Larue Mandifer.

Thus, Jaeger realized, had Lanark entered the grave on the night before, and found these same two skins. Looking up, Lanark had found a horrid enemy waiting to grapple him.

Jaeger, too, looked up.

A towering silhouette shut out half the starry sky overhead.

13
Lanark

The combination of pluck and common sense is something of a rarity, and men who possess that combination are apt to go far. Kane Lanark was such a man, and though he charged unhesitatingly across the little strip of water and at the unknown thing in the trees, he was not outrunning his discretion.

He had seen men die in his time, many of them in abject flight, with bullets overtaking them in the spine or the back of the head. It was nothing pleasant to watch, but it crystallized within his mind the realization that dread of death is no armor against danger, and that an enemy attacked is far less formidable than an enemy attacking. That brace of maxims comforted him and bore him up in more tight places than one.

And General Blunt of the Army of the Frontier, an officer who was all that his name implies and who was never given to overstatement, once so unbent as to say in official writing that Captain Kane Lanark was an ornament to any combat force.

And so his rush was nothing frantic. All that faltered was his lame leg. He meant to destroy the thing that had showed itself, but fully as definitely he meant not to be destroyed by it. As he ran, he flung his revolver across to his left hand and dragged free the saber that danced at his side.

But the creature he wanted to meet did not bide his coming. He heard another crash and rattle—it had backed into some shrubs or bushes farther in among the trees. He paused under the branches of the first belt of timber, well aware that he was probably a fair mark for a bullet. Yet he did not expect a gun in the hands of whatever lurked ahead; he was not sure at all that it even had hands.

Of a sudden he felt, rather than saw, motion upon his left flank. He pivoted upon the heel of his sound right foot and, lifting the saber, spat professionally between hilt and palm. He meant killing, did Lanark, but nothing presented itself. A chuckle drifted to him, a contemptuous burble of sound; he thought of what Enid had said about divining her stepfather's mockery. Again the cackle, dying away toward the left.

But up ahead came more noise of motion, and this was identifiable as feet—heavy, measured tramping of feet. New and stupid recruits walked like that, in their first drills. So did tired soldiers on the march. And the feet were coming his way.

Lanark's first reaction to this realization was of relief. Marching men, even enemies, would be welcome because he knew how to deal with them. Then he thought of Enid behind him, probably in retreat out of the gully. He must give her time to get away. He moved westward, toward the approaching party, but with caution and silence.

The moonlight came patchily down through the lattice-like mass of branches and twigs, and again Lanark saw motion. This time it was directly ahead. He counted five, then six figures, quite human. The moonlight, when they moved in it, gave him glimpses of butternut shirts, white faces. One had a great waterfall of beard.

Lanark drew a deep breath. "Stand!" he shouted, and with his left hand leveled his pistol.

They stood, but only for a moment. Each figure's attitude shifted ever so slightly as Lanark moved a pace forward. The trees were sparse around him, and the moon shone stronger through their branches. He recognized the man with the great beard—he did not need to see that one arm was hewed away halfway between wrist and elbow. Another face was equally familiar, with its sharp mustaches and wide eyes; he had stared into it no longer ago than last night.

The six guerrillas stirred into motion again, approaching and closing in. Lanark had them before him in a semi-circle.

"Stand!" he said again, and when they did not he fired, full for the center of that black beard in the forefront. The body of the guerrillas started and staggered—no more. It had been hit, but it was not going to fall. Lanark knew a sudden damp closeness about him, as though he stood in a small room full of sweaty garments. The six figures were converging, like beasts seeking a common trough or manger.

He did not shoot again. The man he had shot was not bleeding. Six pairs of eyes fixed themselves upon him, with a steadiness that was more than unwinking. He wondered, inconsequentially, if those eyes had lids.... Now they were within reach.

He fell quickly on guard with his saber, whirling it to left and then to right, the old moulinets he had learned in the fencing-room at the Virginia Military Institute. Again the half-dozen approachers came to an abrupt stop, one or two flinching back from the twinkling tongue of steel. Lanark extended his arm, made a wider horizontal sweep with his point, and the space before him widened. The two forms at the horns of the semi-circle began to slip forward and outward, as though to pass him and take him in the rear.

"That won't do," Lanark said aloud, and hopped quickly forward, then lunged at the blackbeard. His point met flesh, or at least a soft substance. No bones impeded it. A moment later his basket-hilt thudded against the butternut shirt front, the figure reeled backward from the force of the blow. With a practiced wrench, Lanark cleared his weapon, cutting fiercely at another who was moving upon him with an unnerving lightness. His edge came home, and he drew it vigorously toward himself—a bread-slicing maneuver that would surely lay flesh open to the bone, disable one assailant. But the creature only tottered and came in again, and Lanark saw that the face he had hacked almost in two was the one with bulge eyes and spike mustaches.

All he could do was side-step and then retreat—retreat eastward in the direction of Fearful Rock. The black-bearded thing was down, stumbled or swooning, and he sprang across it. As he did so the body writhed just beneath him, clutching with one hand upward. Hooked by an ankle, Lanark fell sprawling at full length, losing his revolver but not his sword. He twisted over at his left side, hacking murderously in the direction of his feet. As once before, he cut away a hand and wrist and was free. He surged to his feet, and found the blackbeard also up, thrusting its hairy, fishy-white face at him. With dark rage swelling his every muscle, Lanark carried his right arm back across his chest, his right hand with the hilt going over his left shoulder. Then he struck at the hairy head with all the power of arm and shoulder and, turning his body, thrust in its weight behind the blow. The head flew from the shoulders, as though it had been stuck there ever so lightly.

Then the others were pushing around and upon him. Lanark smelled blood, rot, dampness, filth. He heard, for the first time, soft snickering voices, that spoke no words but seemed to be sneering at him for the entertainment of one another. The work was too close to thrust; he hacked and hewed, and struck with the curved guard as with brass knuckles. And they fell back from him, all but one form that could not see.

It tottered heavily and gropingly toward him, hunching its headless shoulders and holding out its handless arms, as though it played with him a game of blind-man's buff. And from that horrid truncated enemy Lanark fled, fled like a deer for all his lameness.

They followed, but they made slow, stupid work of it. Lanark's sword, which could not kill, had wounded them all. He was well ahead, coming to rising ground, toiling upward out of the gully, into the open country shadowed by Fearful Rock.

He paused there, clear of the trees, wiped his clammy brow with the sleeve of his left arm. The moon was so bright overhead that it almost blinded him. He became aware of a kneading, clasping sensation at his right ankle, and looked down to see what caused it.

A hand clung there, a hand without arm or body. It was a pale hand that moved and crawled, as if trying to mount his boot-leg and get at his belly—his heart—his throat. The bright moon showed him the strained tendons of it, and the scant coarse hair upon its wide back.

Lanark opened his lips to scream like any woman, but no sound came. With his other foot he scraped the thing loose and away. Its fingers quitted their hold grudgingly, and under the sole of his boot they curled and writhed upward, like the legs of an overturned crab. They fastened upon his instep.

When, with the point of his saber, he forced the thing free again, still he saw that it lived and groped for a hold upon him. With his lip clenched bloodily between his teeth, he chopped and minced at the horrid little thing, and even then its severed fingers humped and inched upon the ground, like worms.

"It won't die," Lanark murmured hoarsely, aloud; often in the past he had thought that speaking thus, when one was alone, presaged insanity. "It won't die—not though I chop it into atoms until the evil is driven away."

Then he wondered, for the first time since he had left Enid, where Jaeger was. He turned in the direction of the rock and the ruined house, and walked wearily for perhaps twenty paces. He was swimming in sweat, and blood throbbed in his ears.

Then he found himself looking into the open grave where the guerrillas had lain, whence they had issued to fight once more. At the bottom he saw the two palenesses that were empty skins.

He saw something else—a dark form that was trying to scramble out. Once again he tightened his grip upon the hilt of his saber.

At the same instant he knew that still another creature was hurrying out of the gully and at him from behind.

14
Enid

Lanark's guess was wrong; Enid Mandifer had not retreated westward up the gully.

She had stared, all in a heart-stopping chill, as Lanark made for the thing that terrified her. As though of themselves, her hands reached down to the earth, found her dress, and pulled it over her head. She thrust her feet into her shoes. Then she moved, at only a fast walk, after Lanark.

There was really nothing else she could have done, and Lanark might have known that, had he been able to take thought in the moments that followed. Had she fled, she would have had no place to go save to the house where once her stepfather had lived; and it would be no refuge, but a place of whispering horror. Too, she would be alone, dreadfully alone. It took no meditation on her part to settle the fact that Lanark was her one hope of protection. As a matter of simple fact, he would have done well to remain with her, on the defensive; but then, he could not have foreseen what was waiting in the shadowed woods beyond.

She did carry something that might serve as a weapon—the hand-mirror. And in a pocket of her dress lay the Bible, of which she had once told Lanark. She had read much in it, driven by terror, and I daresay it was as much a talisman to her as was the *Long Lost Friend* to Jaeger. Her lips pattered a verse from it: "Deliver me from mine enemies, O my God...for lo, they lie in wait for my soul."

It was hard for her to decide what she had expected to find within the rim of trees beyond the clearing. Lanark was not in sight, but a commotion had risen some little distance ahead. Enid moved onward, because she must.

She heard Lanark's pistol shot, and then what sounded like several men struggling. She tried to peer and see, but there was only a swirl of violent motion, and through it the flash of steel—that would be Lanark's saber. She crouched behind a wide trunk.

"That is useless," said an accented voice she knew, close at her elbow.

She spun around, stared and sprang away. It was not her stepfather that stood there. The form was human to some degree—it had arms and legs, and a featureless head; but its nakedness was slimy wet and dark, and about it clung a smell of blood.

"That is useless," muttered once more the voice of Persil Mandifer. "You do not hide from the power that rules this place."

Behind the first dark slimness came a second shape, a gross immensity, equally black and foul and shiny. Larue?

"You have offered yourself," said Persil Mandifer, though Enid could see no lips move in the filthy-seeming shadow that should have been a face. "I think you will be accepted this time. Of course, it cannot profit me—what I am now, I shall be always. Perhaps you, too—"

Larue's voice chuckled, and Enid ran, toward where Lanark had been fighting. That would be more endurable than this mad dream forced upon her. Anything would be more endurable. Twigs and thorns plucked at her skirt like spiteful fingers, but she ripped away from them and ran. She came into another clearing, a small one. The moon, striking between the boughs, made here a pool of light and touched up something of metal.

It was Lanark's revolver. Enid bent and seized it. A few feet away rested something else, something rather like a strangely shaggy cabbage. As Enid touched the gun, she saw what that fringed rondure was. A head, but living, as though its owner had been buried to his bearded chin.

"What—" she began to ask aloud. It was surely living, its eyebrows arched and scowled and its gleaming eyes moved. Its tongue crawled out and licked grinning, hairy lips. She saw its smile, hard and brief as a knife flashed for a moment from its scabbard.

Enid Mandifer almost dropped the revolver. She had become sickeningly aware that the head possessed no body.

"There is the rest of him," spoke Persil Mandifer, again behind her shoulder. And she saw a heart-shaking terror, staggering and groping between the trees, a body without a head or hands.

She ran again, but slowly and painfully, as though this were in truth a nightmare. The headless hulk seemed to divine her effort at retreat, for it dragged itself clumsily across, as though to cut her off. It held out its handless stumps of arms.

"No use to shoot," came Persil Mandifer's mocking comment—he was following swiftly. "That poor creature cannot be killed again."

Other shapes were approaching from all sides, shapes dressed in filthy, ragged clothes. The face of one was divided by a dark cleft, as though Lanark's saber had split it, but no blood showed. Another seemed to have no lower jaw; the remaining top of his face jutted forward, like the short visage of a snake lifted to strike. These things had eyes, turned unblinkingly upon her; they could see and approach.

The headless torso blundered at her again, went past by inches. It recovered itself and turned. It knew, somehow, that she was there; it was trying to capture her. She shrank away, staring around for an avenue of escape.

"Be thankful," droned Persil Mandifer from somewhere. "These are no more than dead men, whipped into a mockery of life. They will prepare you a little for the wonders to come."

But Enid had commanded her shuddering muscles. She ran. One of the things caught her sleeve, but the cloth tore and she won free. She heard sounds that could hardly be called voices, from the mouths of such as had mouths. And Persil Mandifer laughed quietly, and said something in a language Enid had never heard before. The thick voice of his son Larue answered him in the same tongue, then called out in English:

"Enid, you only run in the direction we want you to run!"

It was true, and there was nothing that she could do about it. The entities behind her were following, not very fast, like herdsmen leisurely driving a sheep in the way it should go. And she knew that the sides of the gully, to north and south, could never be climbed. There was only the slope ahead to the eastward, up which Lanark must have gone. The thought of him strengthened her. If the two of them found the king-horror, the Nameless One, at the base of Fearful Rock, they could face it together.

She was aware that she had come out of the timber of the ravine.

All was moonlight here, painted by the soft pallor in grays and silvers and shadow-blacks. There was the rock lifted among the stars, there the stretch of clump-dotted plain—and here, almost before her, Lanark.

He stood poised above a hole in the ground, his saber lifted above his head as though to begin a downward sweep. Something burly was climbing up out of that hole. But, even as he tightened his sinews to strike, Lanark whirled around, and his eyes glared murderously at Enid.

15
Evil's End

"Don't!" Enid screamed. "Don't, it's only I—"

Lanark growled, and spun back to face what was now hoisting itself above ground level.

"And be careful of me, too," said the object. "It's Jaeger, Mr. Lanark."

The point of the saber lowered. The three of them were standing close together on the edge of the opened grave. Lanark looked down. He saw at the bottom the two areas of loose white.

"Are those the—"

"Yes," Jaeger replied without waiting for him to finish. "Two human skins. They are fresh; soft and damp." Enid was listening, but she was past shuddering. "One of them," continued Jaeger, "was taken from Persil Mandifer. I know his face."

He made a scuffing kick-motion with one boot. Clods flew into the grave, falling with a dull plop, as upon wet blankets. He kicked more earth down, swiftly and savagely.

"Help me," he said to the others. "Salt should be thrown on those skins—that's what the old legends say—but we have no salt. Dirt will have to do. Don't you see?" he almost shrieked. "Somewhere near here, two bodies are hiding, or moving about, without these skins to cover them."

Both Lanark and Enid knew they had seen those bodies. In a moment three pairs of feet were thrusting earth down into the grave.

"Don't!" It was a wail from the trees in the ravine, a wail in the voice of Persil Mandifer. "We must return to those skins before dawn!"

Two black silhouettes, wetly shiny in the moonlight, had come into the open. Behind them straggled six more, the guerrillas.

"Don't!" came the cry again, this time a command. "You cannot destroy us now. It is midnight, the hour of the Nameless One."

At the word "midnight" an idea fairly exploded itself in Lanark's brain. He thrust his sword into the hands of his old sergeant.

"Guard against them," he said in the old tone of command. "That book of yours may serve as shield, and Enid's Bible. I have something else to do."

He turned and ran around the edge of the grave, then toward the hole that was filled with the ruins of the old house; the hole that emitted a glow of weak blue light.

Into it he flung himself, wondering if this diluted gleam of the old unearthly blaze would burn him. It did not; his booted legs felt warmth like that of a hot stove, no more. From above he heard the voice of Jaeger, shouting, tensely and masterfully, a formula from the *Long Lost Friend:*

"Ye evil things, stand and look upon me for a moment, while I charm three drops of blood from you, which you have forfeited. The first from your teeth, the second from your lungs, the third from your heart's own main." Louder went his voice, and higher, as though he had to fight to keep down his hysteria: "God bid me vanquish you all!"

Lanark had reached the upward column of the broken chimney. All about his feet lay fragments, glowing blue. He shoved at them with his toe. There was an oblong of metal. He touched it—yes, that had been a door to an old brick oven. He lifted it. Underneath lay what he had hidden four years ago—a case of unknown construction.

But as he picked it up, he saw that it had a lid. What had Enid overheard from her stepfather, so long ago? "...that he would live and prosper until the secret writing should be taken forth and destroyed...it would never open, save at the place of the Nameless One, at midnight under a full moon."

With his thumbnail he pried at the lid, and it came open easily. The box seemed full of darkness, and when he thrust in his hands he felt something crumble, like paper burned to ashes. That was what it was—ashes. He turned the case over, and let the flakes fall out, like strange black snow.

From somewhere resounded a shriek, or chorus of shrieks. Then a woman weeping—that would be Enid—and a cry of "God be thanked!" unmistakably from Jaeger. The blue light died away all around Lanark, and his legs were cool. The old basement had fallen strangely dark. Then he was aware of great fatigue, the trembling of his hands, the ropy weakness of his lamed leg. And he could not climb out again, until Jaeger came and put down a hand.

At rosy dawn the three sat on the front stoop of Jaeger's cabin. Enid was pouring coffee from a serviceable old black pot.

"We shall never know all that happened and portended," said Jaeger, taking a mouthful of home-made bread, "but what we have seen will tell us all that we should know."

"This much is plain," added Lanark. "Persil Mandifer worshipped an evil spirit, and that evil spirit had life and power."

"Perhaps we would know everything, if the paper in the box had not burned in the fire," went on Jaeger. "That is probably as well—that it burned, I mean. Some secrets are just as well never told." He fell thoughtful, pulled his beard, and went on. "Even burned, the power of that document worked; but when the ashes fell from their case, all was over. The bodies of the guerrillas were dry bones on the instant, and as for the skinless things that moved and spoke as Mandifer and his son—"

He broke off, for Enid had turned deathly pale at memory of that part of the business.

"We shall go back when the sun is well up," said Lanark, "and put those things back to rest in their grave."

He sat for a moment, coffee cup in hand, and gazed into the brightening sky.

To the two items he had spoken of as plainly indicated, he mentally added a third; the worship carried on by Persil Mandifer—was that name French, perhaps Main-de-Fer?—was tremendously old. He, Persil, must have received teachings in it from a former votary, his father perhaps, and must have conducted a complex and secret ritual for decades.

The attempted sacrifice rite for which Enid had been destined was something the world would never know, not as regards the climax. For a little band of Yankee horsemen, with himself at their head, had blundered into the situation, throwing it completely out of order and spelling for it the beginning of the end.

The end had come. Lanark was sure of that. How much of the power and motivity of the worship had been exerted by the Nameless One that now must continue nameless, how much of it was Persil Mandifer's doing, how much was accident of nature and horror-hallucination of witnesses, nobody could now decide. As Jaeger had suggested, it was probably as well that part of the mystery would remain. Things being as they were, one might pick up the threads of his normal human existence, and be happy and fearless.

But he could not forget what he had seen. The two Mandifers, able to live or to counterfeit life by creeping from their skins at night, had perished as inexplicably as they had been resurrected. The guerrillas, too, whose corpses had challenged him, must be finding a grateful rest now that the awful semblance of life had quitted their slack, butchered limbs. And the blue fire that had burst forth in the midst of the old battle, to linger ghostwise for years; the horned image that Jaeger had broken; the seeming powers of the *Long Lost Friend,* as an amulet and a storehouse of charms— these were items in the strange fabric. He would remember them forever, without rationalizing them.

He drank coffee, into which someone, probably Enid, had dropped sugar while he mused. Rationalization, he decided, was not enough, had never been enough. To judge a large and dark mystery by what vestigial portions touched one, was to err like the blind men in the old doggerel who, groping at an elephant here and there, called it in turn a snake, a spear, a tree, a fan, a wall. Better not to brood or ponder upon what had happened. Try to be thankful, and forget.

"I shall build my church under Fearful Rock," Jaeger was saying, "and it shall be called Fearful Rock no more, but Welcome Rock."

Lanark looked up. Enid had come and seated herself beside him. He studied her profile. Suddenly he could read her thoughts, as plainly as though they were written upon her cheek.

She was thinking that grass would grow anew in her front yard, and that she would marry Kane Lanark as soon as he asked her.

Author Notes

JOHN JAKES was born in Illinois in 1932 and educated at DePauw University (A.B., 1953) and Ohio State University (M.A., 1954). An advertising copywriter for twenty years, he turned to freelance writing in 1971, producing mysteries, westerns, and science fiction. In 1974 he hit best-seller lists with the Kent Family Chronicles, eight large volumes depicting the history of America through the adventures of one family. His Civil War novel, *North and South* (1982), has been made into a television miniseries. Jakes hopes his books have brought an appreciation of American history to many people who may never read formal history.

JOHN BENNETT, best known for his children's book *Master Skylark*, was born in 1865 and educated at the University of South Carolina. He had a series of careers as successful illustrator, mapmaker, guitarist, and advertising producer, as well as writer. Along with Harvey Allan and Dubose Heyward, Bennett co-founded the Poetry Society of South Carolina. His 1946 book *Doctor to the Dead* is based on legends of old Charleston, some of them from Civil War days. He died in 1956.

MARY ELIZABETH COUNSELMAN, born on a Georgia plantation in 1911, grew up hearing stories of Civil War adventures from participants. After attending the University of Alabama and Montevallo University, she became a professional writer, her fiction and poetry appearing in such magazines as *The Saturday Evening Post* and *Jungle Stories*. She is best known for her supernatural fiction, collected in *Half in Shadow* (1978), which includes "The Three Marked Pennies," the most popular story in the history of the long-running *Weird Tales*.

DAN SIMMONS, educated at Wabash College in Indiana and Washington University in St. Louis, had been teaching elementary school in his home state of Colorado for eleven years when his first accepted short story tied for first place and won a thousand-dollar prize in a contest sponsored by *The Twilight Zone*. His first novel, *Song of Kali*, was inspired by his travels, particularly in India; it won the World Fantasy Award in 1986. Subsequent works have included a vampire novel, *Carrion Crypt* (1988), and a science fiction novel, *Hyperion* (1989), both highly praised.

JOHN WILLIAM DeFORREST was born in Connecticut, the son of a rich cotton merchant who died when DeForrest was thirteen. Brought up in Europe, he began writing histories and travel books that won him an honorary M.A. from Yale University in 1859. He served as a captain in the Union Army during the Civil War and is best known as the author of the Civil War novel *Miss Ravenel's Conversion from Secession to Loyalty* (1867). DeForrest died in Connecticut in 1905.

SEABURY QUINN, born in Washington, D.C., in 1889, received a law degree from National University in 1910, served in the U.S. Army during World War I, and taught medical jurisprudence. He is best known as the creator of the occult detective Dr. Jules de Grandin. Quinn's books include *Roads* (1948), *Is the Devil a Gentleman?* (1970), and seven volumes of de Grandin stories, such as *The Phantom-Fighter* (1966). In addition he published some five hundred short stories, 148 of them in *Weird Tales*. He died on Christmas Eve 1969.

AMBROSE BIERCE was born in Ohio in 1842 and joined the 9th Indiana Infantry as a drummer boy. Twice wounded, he was a brevet major at war's end. In San Francisco he became one of the nation's most famous journalists, noted for his bitter wit (one of his book reviews said simply, "The covers of this book are too far apart"). He also wrote mordant, often cruel and shocking stories of the Civil War, collected in *Tales of Soldiers and Civilians* (1891), and stories of horror and the supernatural, such as "The Damned Thing." He disappeared in Mexico in 1913 under circumstances as mysterious as any in his fiction.

MANLY WADE WELLMAN, the son of a medical mission-ary, was born in Portuguese West Africa in 1903. He came to the United States in 1909 and was educated at Wichita State University and Columbia University. In 1930 he quit a reporter's job to become a full-time writer. He has published mysteries—winning first prize in the 1946 contest of *Ellery Queen's Mystery Magazine*—and biographies—such as that of Confederate General Wade Hampton, *Giant in Gray* (1949)—but is best known for his supernatural and horror fiction. The latter was a mainstay of magazines like *Weird Tales* and has been collected in two massive volumes, *Worse Things Waiting* (1973) and *Lonesome Vigils* (1982). Wellman's best-known character is Silver John, who battles supernatural evil. The author died in 1986.

VANCE RANDOLPH was born in Kansas in 1892 and was educated at Kansas State University (A.B., 1914) and Clark University (M.A., 1915). A noted folklorist specializing in the lore of the Ozarks, he has been a teacher of psychology, a scriptwriter, a supervisor for the Federal Writers Project during the depression, and an infantry soldier during World War II. Randolph is best known for his recordings of Ozark legends and folk tales in such books as *Who Blowed Up the Church House?* (1947) and *We Always Lie to Strangers* (1951).